LOVE

A LOVE SERIES NOVEL

Also by Michelle Cuttino

Published by Big Body Publishing LLC

Me & Mrs. Jones – Part I
Me & Mrs. Jones 2
Me & Mrs. Jones 3
Love Is Blind (A Love Series Novel)

Published by Strebor/Simon & Schuster

Zane Presents…Cougar Cocktales

LOVE and Happiness

The hardest thing to do is watch the one you love, love another...

A LOVE SERIES NOVEL

Big Body Publishing...*Where Bigger Is Always Better!*

Big Body Publishing, LLC
P.O. Box 830
Bronx, NY 10473

ISBN-10: 0692219439
ISBN-13: 978-0-692-21943-0
First Big Body Publishing Printing: June 2014
Printed in the United States of America

The Big Body Publishing Press Room can bring its authors to your live event. For more information, or to book an event, contact the Big Body Publishing Press Room at press@bigbodypublishing.com.

10 9 8 7 6 5 4 3 2 1

Edited by: Sweet Georgia Press, LLC
Cover Design by: AMB Branding & Design

www.MichelleCuttino.com
www.BigBodyPublishing.com

A Note From
Michelle Cuttino

This book is dedicated to my Angel in Heaven,
my niece,

Simone Shaquilla Harper

(March 23, 2005 - April 11, 2012)
May you continue to Sleep In Peace
and serve as my inspiration.
Whenever I want to give up, you send me a rainbow.
I Love You Forever, My Monie
and
I Love You More!

Acknowledgments

To my Big Body Publishing Team, I want to say thanks for helping to bring my dreams into fruition. J'son M. Lee (Sweet Georgia Press, LLC), you are more than just my editor; you are also a great friend and confidante. I'm looking forward to continuing this fruitful and rewarding friendship and business relationship with you. Thank you for being you. I love you, Boo! To LaShawn Walls (iZiggy Promotions, LLC) and Leah Frieday (AleahDesign), your creativity and friendships are invaluable to me. Thank you for dealing with my crazy concepts, demanding deadlines and last minute and/or middle-of-the-night epiphanies. More importantly, thank you for bringing my visions to life.

To my extensive social media family and my "Big Body's Word of the Day" lovers, I want to say thank you for keeping me smiling. To those I follow and to my fans and followers, you are my motivation and I love each and every one of you. It's my pleasure to have you all in my circle.

To Tamika Newhouse, Vonda Howard, N'Tyse, Julia Press Simmons and Felisha Bradshaw—I want to say thank you my Sisters for helping me build a brand through your resources. I truly love and appreciate each of you.

To Jennifer Silberstein, Kelvin Cameron and Jakar Brown, Thank you for reading my first draft and giving me your candid feedback. The love I hold in my heart for each of you is everlasting and sincere. Thank you for your genuine friendship, unwavering love and support, and know that you will always have mine in return. I love you all so much.

To my Stone Source family, it's been thirteen crazy years and I couldn't ask for a better "family" to work with. I want to give a special Thank You to those closest to me, Brant Abrams, Gemma Harri, Lisa Castellucci, Ellen Fullan, Jorgen Engersgaard, Christina Campoverde, George

Morales, David Seltzer, Michael Ambrosio, Linda Bui, Mitchell Kalmar, Ron Silano, Michael Castro, Paul Caruso, Tom Harty, Travis Persad, Jennifer Mane, Rose Rodriguez, Erica Puccio, Jordana Jacobs, Karen Tierra, Barry Breitburg, Darcie Orr, Noemi Rovirosa and Kiara Perdomo.

To my L.I.P. (Lafayette Island Posse) Family, ONE LOVE! You know who you are. We lost some soldiers, but we're still united and stronger than ever. I Love You, FAM!

To Ernie Smith, Sr. and Christopher Collins, Sr. – you will always have a special place in my heart, because you gave me the best parts of you—my son and step-son, Ernie T. Smith, Jr. and Christopher "CJ" Collins, Jr.

To my extended family—The Smith Family (special shout out to my sister, Sylvia Smith), John Paul Morris (you already know how much I love and appreciate you), Byron Wade (I love you, my Fuzzy Wuzzy Teddy Bear), Stephanie "Big Sexy" & Samantha Adkins, Lisa Freeman, Chitunda Capers, Aubrey & Adrienne Holder, Jameel & Lataccia Mcleod, Arielle Small, Anthony Womble, Delroy Simmons, Stephen Carter, Tawanna Pierce (my sister/daughter forever), Rasheeda Petersen, Samarit Rivers, The Williams Family, James T. Dozier, Mark A. Walker, Dominique Linnen, The Pressley Family, Ronald Freeman, Tricia Salabarria and Marcella Green—this thing we have is forever. Never take my love for granted and I will return the favor.

To my Roots—the Cuttinos, Robinsons, Franklins, and Gambles, family is forever. To all my grandparents, aunts, uncles, nieces and nephews, I love you all from the bottom of my heart. To my immediate first and second cousins (special shout out to my heart, Pondrell Grimmage), we were raised as brothers and sisters. Don't ever think I take your role in my life lightly. I love each and every one of you.

To my siblings, Monica, Janell, Tonya, Germaine, Ashley, Celeste and Lauren, I wish we were all closer, but know that my love is unchanging. Paulette, our bond will never be broken. I love you, Girl!

To Stephanie Cuttino and my extended children—my stepson Christopher Collins, Jr., Tyesha Cuttino, Maurice Strickland, Jr., Monroe W. Smith III, Jeffrey Harper, Jr. and Cheyenne Cuttino—I love each of you in my own special way. Each of you mean something different to me, but the universal feeling I share for all of you is my undying love. Daughter/Ma/Mommie/Auntie loves you all so very, very much.

To my parents, Jimmy Cuttino & Alma Cuttino, words cannot describe how much I love the both of you. From day one, you taught me to be strong, independent and giving. You both pushed me to be the best me I can be and acknowledged every single stride I've made. Your pride and devotion shaped my every step and I wouldn't be the person I am without you. I'm Daddy's Girl and Mommy's Pearl and I wouldn't trade either of you for anything in this world.

Last but definitely not least, I want to say Thank You to the reason I breathe—my son, Ernie T. Smith, Jr. Ernie, you are my heart. I owe everything that I am to you, because I've lived for you since the day you were born. You are my son, my best friend, my biggest supporter and the love of my life. There is nothing in this world I wouldn't do for you. Thank you for being you. You are simply the best and I Love You MORE! Forever and For Always. Infinity times Infinity ☺!

If I forgot anyone, please charge it to my head and not my heart!

Love Always,
Michelle "Big Body" Cuttino

ROXANNE

Whenever Mark looked at me that way, I knew what was coming next. Fifteen minutes, which felt more like fifteen hours, of his sweaty body on top of mine—pounding at the nucleus of my thighs in search of some unfamiliar pleasure. And tonight, when he's on top of me with the mundane, I know my mind will lead me far away into the arms of the one person who showed me what lovemaking was really all about.

"What's on your mind?" Mark asked as he playfully ran his fingers from my knee to my inner thigh.

"You," I lied, praying that tonight would be the night he'd go down on me. I subconsciously began massaging the back of his head, running my fingers through his curly black hair. He positioned himself on top of me, looked deep into my eyes, and spoke softly.

"Honey, what can I do to make you happy tonight?"

"What do you mean by make me happy?"

"What does it sound like? Roxy, you've brought me so much pleasure in my life, and tonight I just want to return the favor. So, what will it be?"

I opened my mouth to speak, but he gently covered my lips with his fingers.

"Don't answer. Let me guess." With that, he jumped off the bed and disappeared into the bathroom.

"Mark, what are you doing?"

"You'll see," he screamed back from the other side of the open door. I heard running water, and I could see the steam in the air. *Great,* I thought. *Just what I need—a second shower.*

I lay back on the pillows and closed my eyes. I envisioned Mark standing in front of the bed—half-naked—with the red light pouring from the bathroom door, casting a mysterious glow around his tall, muscular frame. He walked over to the bed and kissed me deeply. Then smiled at me handsomely, showing off bright whites against his smooth-as-a-baby's-ass, blue-black complexion. He lowered himself in front of me, placing his head between my knees, kissing my legs seductively.

"Are you ready?" He asked, in a deep, husky voice that I used to find sexy, but not anymore.

"Yes," I replied throatily, anticipating the fervor he would send me into once his oral descent began. I spread my legs wider, hiked my teddy up around my waist and sucked in my stomach. I hoped to show off my flawless, wooly afro and my one-day-old bikini wax, but I knew full well that even with all the sucking in in the world my lower belly fat was still obstructing his view. I reached for him and kissed him deeply.

"Be patient," he whispered into my ear, as I felt myself being pulled off the bed by my hands. I opened my eyes, and saw that Mark was now pushing me towards the bathroom. I realized then that the kiss was real, but everything before that was a dream. My teddy was down around my thighs, and the black bikinis I put on earlier were still intact. Mark stood me before the tub, which was overflowing with suds from the expensive bath foam he bought me for Valentine's Day. Candles lined the edging, and the overwhelming smell of Vanilla attacked my senses.

"What's all this?"

"Ambiance," he whispered. "Now relax, and let nature take its course."

"Nature, huh?"

"Yes. Human nature."

He began undressing me. I smiled, not only at him, but at my own perverse fantasy as well. I followed his eyes, which marveled at my full figure. In spite of all my lumps, bumps and grooves, Mark always looked at me like my body was flawless—like I was flawless. His hungry eyes always made me melt. He carefully inched my panties down, nonchalantly casting them aside. He met my gaze as he rose slowly. His right hand moved up my inner thighs, stopping just short of my love box. His fingers lingered there for a moment, deliberately grazing my pubic hairs. I wanted to kiss him, but I didn't want to thwart the electricity running rampant between the two of us.

"Get in." He motioned towards the vat filled with bubbles.

I wanted to echo his command, and gesture towards my center, which was now fragrant with the aroma of my sexual desire, but I complied with his wishes instead. I allowed myself to surrender, as the warm liquid covered me completely. I dangled my legs over the edge suggestively, and invited him to join me. He declined.

"What the hell do you mean, no?" I wanted to shout at him, but I kept my composure and settled for something less biting. "Why not, baby? The water is very relaxing."

"I know, but this is your night, and I want you to enjoy it. Come on, sit up."

I felt like a child again as he lathered the body sponge and began scrubbing my back gently, moving around to my breasts, and down towards my legs. Not forgetting to give each toe just the right amount of attention. He slowly and inadvertently washed away my blues with every swipe of the sponge, which was now floating in the foamy water. He pulled me up and knelt before me, taking a bar of soap in his palms. He then placed his sudsy hands between my thick thighs, and gently fingered my core—purifying my body. I moaned and writhed with anticipation, not only because it felt sinfully good, but also because I could see him growing through his silk boxers. His manhood tensed, pulsated, and became longer and harder with each rotation of his finger.

"Are you okay?" he teased, as he eased up on his finger gyrations.

I didn't answer; euphoria had taken over. I shivered instinctively and succumbed as the warm water he poured from the pink basin ran down my body. It felt as if the water was cleansing my soul, and openly removing the dirt and residue of my sins. I leaned back and savored the intensity of the foaming milk bath. I tried hard to control my urge to floor Mark, rip off his shorts and ride his chocolate stallion until my inner walls were sore and chafe. It had been eons since our last can't-walk-straight sexual marathon, and I truly hoped tonight would terminate the drought.

Unfortunately, the lustful desire I felt in the bathroom almost immediately dissipated once we reached the bedroom. I was having difficulty getting myself back in the mood despite the fact Mark was now massaging my breasts, and making wet circles around my nipple with his tongue. It's probably due to the fact that Mark has a way of making the most passionate act seem mechanical. Plus, his inability to be nothing more than self-indulgent nowadays didn't help matters. In the beginning, I used to fake it—yelling and screaming like the powerful thrusting of his pelvis was causing me agonizing sexual pleasure. But I was young back then and inexperienced. Not that I'm one of those types that have been around the block and back, but I know what gets me off, and three minutes of monotonous jabbing isn't it. So I've learned to whimper instead, and save my powerful lungs for something more useful, like singing off key to Jazmine Sullivan while zipping down the expressway in my Escalade. The way things seemed to be going, I was no longer pressing for foreplay. Hell at this rate, I'd settle for any play.

Please let tonight be different, I thought, as Mark parted my legs and positioned himself between them once again. I feigned elation as his tongue explored every inch of my upper body. He stopped automatically at where my belly button should be, but my additional flesh kept it hidden. He kissed my rolls instead, not daring to venture any lower into uncharted territory. *Chicken shit.* I began to think about the many times my forbidden lover, Ayana, descended upon my essence like a baby crying for her bottle. I recollected how her lips consumed my love like it was a nipple, and she cooed and suckled until she absorbed every drop of moisture my soul possessed.

I was suddenly yanked from my secret world by the strength of Mark's lips, kissing my lower stomach, spiraling downwards to my outer thighs, leisurely spreading my legs wider. Using his thumb and forefinger to open my vaginal walls, he placed his stiff tongue deep inside my carnal region with the precision of a bee in search of the sweet nectar only derived from a flower. *Hallelujer!* It was like the heavens opened up, and Jesus himself was smiling down on me. I could feel myself beaming, and I heard my mother's voice say, *"You don't grin when you're thinking about salvation."* Well, if this was my downfall, let me go out with a bang.

As my gasps grew louder, his tongue got stronger, and even his fingers digging into my posterior felt less threatening—almost satisfying. My hips seemed to devour what was left of his head. My fingers violently dug into his hair, pressing him into me, blurring the distinction of my ending and his beginning. We became one, as my milky secretion cascaded down his lips and chin, and dampened the sheets. I reached for him, and he entered me forcefully. Tonight, instead of his usual hasty pounding, Mark's movements felt more like a rhythmic pulsation. Our bodies shifted with the same desire. We were like two synchronized swimmers executing their routine with precision. The way he maneuvered his body inside mine made me relinquish all my inhibitions. For the first time in a long time, the vocal shrieks and wails escaping my lips were genuine. I don't even think he knew the difference. Or did he? I opened my eyes to steal a look at his expression. To my dismay, he was returning my gaze with a sinister look in his eyes. At that moment, I felt myself tensing. By the look on his face, I could tell that his penis felt the transformation way before his brain did. He flinched and pulled himself out of my barren walls.

"What happened?" He asked angrily. "I thought you were enjoying yourself for once."

"I thought I was, too, but obviously I was wrong." I flung my body off the side of the bed and ran into the bathroom, slamming the door behind me. I stared at myself in the mirror. I could see the fire in my eyes and the smoke coming from my ears. I was boiling, and had to calm myself down.

I winced as the icy water ran down my body, washing away all signs of Mark's desecration. There I was, letting go, and that bastard was getting his rocks off staring at the ugly sex faces I was making. He was excited because he finally got me just where he wanted me—carefree, vulnerable, and one orgasm away from agreeing to that huge wedding he kept telling me about. How the hell was I supposed to face him now? I could kick myself for finally giving in. I mean, after two years of courting, three years of living together and five years of faking satisfaction, you would think I could humor the son of a bitch for another six months. Then what? Take the death walk down the aisle and sell my soul to the Devil? Ayana was right. That's mommy's dream, not mine. I looked down at my hand and watched as the large diamond sparkled under the force of the water. Regardless of whose dream it was, time was running out, and I had already pushed our wedding date back ten times. It was something I could no longer avoid. I had to make up my mind, and decide whether I was going to go through with it or not. Too bad the answer to that question escaped me five years ago, when Mark placed this gaudy ring on my finger. I stepped out the shower, and jumped as Mark handed me a towel.

"What the fuck are you doing in here?" I roared, "I thought I locked the door!"

"You did, but I have my ways. Besides, I wanted to make sure you were all right."

He watched me with that same self-assured cockiness he exhibited in bed twenty minutes earlier, and I couldn't stand it. I wanted to scratch his eyes out, then watch the blood pour down his face, and drip onto that ugly-ass lime green mat he held with such high regards. But I didn't. I regained my composure, and spoke sweetly.

"Why don't you give me a few minutes, and we can finish off where we started."

"What?" he choked out, eyeing me suspiciously. "I thought you were through."

"Can't a woman have a change of heart?"

"I guess, but..."

"Good," I interrupted. "Now go make yourself comfortable in the bedroom, and I'll be out soon."

I didn't wait for a response. I nudged him out the bathroom, and pushed the door shut behind him. I leaned against it, smiling to myself, happy to have caught his smug ass off guard. I dried off, pulled my tresses back into a bun, and checked out my body in the mirror. I was older and much wider now, but Mark still thought I was the sexiest bitch in the world. I had naturally kinky brown hair that fell below my shoulders, and big brown eyes I used to be ashamed of. My body was massive, and my curves would make a winding highway jealous. I stared at my muffin top, my pet name for the belly mass falling over my *girl*, and exhaled loudly to build up my strength.

I opened the door and stared at my prey. Mark sat up on the bed, grinning widely and waiting for another chance to tame the wild beast living within me. Two can play that game. This love slave just stole the whip from Master, and I was about to even the score.

The noise level in our bedroom last night was extreme. Wild jungle sounds. Heart-wrenching gasps. High-pitched shrieks. Throaty moans. A blasphemous exclamation of lust and desire—and that was only on Mark's part. My demeanor was more subdued—aloof even. I was more like a spectator to the sport instead of a participant. To add insult to injury, Mark awoke to my curvaceous derriere filling out his pajama bottoms. I passively insinuated I procured the dominant role, and was now the self-proclaimed Mandingo Warrior Princess. She, who wore the pants in the house. I must admit I loved the feeling of triumph. Nothing could compare to witnessing that tail-between-the-legs, humiliated stroll Mark displayed. Nothing. We didn't even speak to each other this morning. He simply brushed my cheek with his lips and muttered an unfeeling good-bye before fleeing to work, leaving me in an alleviated state in front of my computer. I smirked with victory as the cursor blinked at me, and I concluded I would master my speechwriting the same way I conquered Mark's ass.

Well, so much for wishful thinking. Two hours had

passed, and the only thing I'd come up with was, "Good Morning, Ladies and Gentlemen." And the crowd goes wild! *Uh, thank you... please, please be seated. You're too kind.* I slammed my fists on the desk and put my face in my hands. What the hell could I say to a room full of wealthy folks that would make them trust me with their marketing portfolios? I'm not affiliated with any of the big boys. My little S Corporation was barely scraping by, and if I didn't receive that check from the Zinkowski's soon, I'd be filing for Chapter 10. Wouldn't that make Mark happy to have me completely dependent on him? *Hell no. A sister can't even go out like that.* I needed to focus, and stop beating myself up. I'd done this before. All I had to do was think. *Think. Think, damn it! And that's an order.*

Three hours later, I reread the company's stock predictions two more times before returning to my presentation board. I fidgeted with some digits and altered a few bars on the graph so my proposal would look more appealing. If I was going to lose this account, it sure as hell wasn't going to be for incompetence. I took my place in front of the computer once again, and began to type. The words flowed fluently this time, and I had the speech written in less than thirty minutes. I reread my opening; it was an attention grabber. The body was filled with interesting facts, inspiring statistics, and the appropriate amount of humor and anecdotes. The ending, through my own tasteful modesty, served its purpose. It informed, educated, reiterated and motivated. I just hoped it would make those fat cats sign on the dotted line, because I'm way overdue for a new account—especially one that pays up-front and on time.

I looked over at the clock. It was half past two. Mark wasn't due home for another four hours, and I had already completed my work for the day. I might as well have some fun, because all work and no play made Roxy a crabby bitch. I saved my files and logged onto the Internet, humming a wicked tune. *I'm searching for adventure, or whatever comes my way. Born to be wild.* I checked into an adult chat room and started my customary midday romp. Today's cohort was Black Thunder, and our kinky sexual innuendoes were probably outlawed in twenty states, but we continued to inject our lustful fantasies anyway. I must say, he sure knew how to get a girl aroused. Before I knew it, I was trying to type responses in between my own self-gratification. Mental note: wipe down the keyboard with disinfectant. I wouldn't want Mark to know that thanks to the user-friendly luxury of cybersex, hundreds of other men have infiltrated his domain without the nuisance of prophylactics, or the actual exchange of bodily fluids.

I ended my tryst with Black Thunder and introduced myself to Queen Bi. Turned out she was a thirty-year-old, thrice divorced, mother of four, who was now expecting her fifth child. She told me she didn't *get down*, but was basically bi-curious. I abruptly ended our conversation, and moved on. Let somebody else pop her cherry. I was looking for a woman who was already experienced and aged to perfection. I shifted my attentions to Luscious. I asked if I could slide my tongue in and out of her crevice, and give her tits the attention they'd been longing for. Luscious responded with some well-known four-letter words, along with a few obscure ones. I guess she didn't *get down* either. I logged off, shut down the computer, and went into my bedroom.

My fingers grazed the alarm button on the clock radio next to our Victorian bed. I lied down and buried myself under the cream-colored satin sheets and black, silk down comforter. The one good thing about living with Mark was I no longer had to endure those cheap 180-thread-count cotton sheets I purchased for ten dollars from the street vendors on the corner of Park Avenue. Anything less than the crème de la crème for Mark Anthony Watkins was outright unacceptable. But I must admit, my falling for the three-P policy—prowess, paper and potential—only made me end up in the three-C mode—cornered, caustic and contemptible. My hatred seemed to have a counter-effect on Mark's ego. The more distance I tried to put between us, the more attached he became. Now, our relationship had boiled down to nothing more than one enormous power trip, with neither of us ready to admit failure. So our tumultuous journey continued…

The house phone, which doubled as my business line, rang, trying to charm its way into my thoughts. But I felt selfish today. I didn't want to be bothered by anything or anyone, especially not Mark. I heard the familiar beep of the answering machine, and was yanked to reality by the woman speaking on the other end. Her voice was low, sexy and full of panic and despair. She asked me to call her back as soon as I was able, cleverly leaving the ten digits uttered prior to her hanging up etched into my memory forever.

Ayana still had the same effect on me. I replayed the message in my mind several times as I masturbated to the sound of her syrupy voice. Despair, or not, she still sounded as sensual and inviting as she did all those years ago. And I'm quite sure I'd still want to fuck her on sight.

AYANA

After returning the antique telephone handset attachment to its cradle, I resumed pacing back and forth across the newly renovated parquet floors. I know I'm old school, but cell phones are just too small and uncomfortable. My cell phone's handset attachment was my accessory purchase of the century. I took a seat in front of my gold vanity and began reapplying my makeup. I moved closer to the mirror, inspecting the black and blue scars from last night's bout with Jasmine. For a prima donna, she sure as hell could throw a mean left hook.

How the hell am I going to disguise this one? I howled at my distorted reflection, snatching up my compact and dabbing around my eye with the overly powdered sponge. Frustrated, I hurled the compact against the wall, leaving a sizable blotch on the glossy enamel and a huge stain on the plush shag carpet below it.

"Great," I screamed, "more shit to clean up!" I looked around the room at the remnants from yesterday's match, and shook my head in disgust. "Ayana? Girl, when are you going to learn?"

#

I met Jasmine at a networking function my company was sponsoring for all the up-and-coming African-American public relations firms in the Hartford, Connecticut area. My old boss, Mr. Thomas J. Seagle, read in an issue of *Fortune* that the latest craze in business was hiring trendy, black PR firms for representation. I guess with the positive affirmative action vote, Euro-Americans figured they'd better jump on the bandwagon. So as not to upset his counterparts, Mr. Seagle leaped on, too. He thought it would be endearing to parade a bunch of educated Negroes in front of his cohorts, and elect the best black man for the job. He chose Robert Sampson Willowbrook III, of Willowbrook Public Relations. Since I was the only black person in a high-ranked position at the firm at the time, he appointed me to head the welcoming committee. My job was to cozy up to Mrs. Willowbrook and find out more about her husband so Mr. Seagle could make a good impression at their first official meeting.

Jasmine T. Willowbrook was a force to be reckoned with. Standing at a meager five feet, two inches, her athletic frame commanded respect. She wore a navy pinstripe pantsuit, and held a small navy handbag at her side. She mingled and socialized like a seasoned veteran, and never budged from her husband's side. After watching her from the sidelines for forty minutes, I decided to make my move. I slid up next to her, and lunged into a conversation she was having with one of the partners, Louis Silvers, on the invisible glass ceiling in corporations. I explained to Lou that he didn't realize there was a glass ceiling because it was transparent to his gender and concealed from his race, and as with God, you can't see Him, but you know he's there. Jasmine commended my rebuttal, and suddenly turned all her attention to me. Louis, who had now become a vibrant shade of red, used the opportunity to slink away. Jasmine smiled broadly and pushed a well-manicured hand in my direction.

"Jasmine T. Willowbrook," she said.

"Ayana V. Linden," I replied, grabbing her hand in a firm handshake.

"Are you always that candid?" she asked smiling.

"Yes. My mother always felt that people take up too much time beating around the bush, instead of just saying what's on their mind. She also told me that as a black woman, in order to rise above all the bullshit, I should just be direct and sincere, because people can spot a phony from miles away."

"Brilliant woman."

"And beautiful," I added. "I take after her in many ways."

We laughed wholeheartedly, and wound up spending the rest of the evening on the chaise lounge sipping champagne, enthralled in conversation.

She told me that her husband was a big Miles Davis fan, and was still a member of his first, official fan club. We spoke about how she and her husband built the company from a two-man operation, to a fifty-man conglomerate. I also found out that the "T" in her name stood for Tabitha, but if you asked me, nowadays that "T" stood for temper—and Mrs. Willowbrook's was vile. But that night, she was delicate and beautiful. Her complexion was the color of caramel and she had a heart-shaped face. Her lips were full and enticing, and what her bust line was lacking, her behind was more than making up for. After consuming four glasses of Dom Perignon, my tongue became lax, and I found myself inviting Jasmine to my place for dinner the next evening. To my surprise, she accepted.

"Come in," I said, as Jasmine walked past me and stepped into my apartment. After staring at the African art and paintings hanging on the wall, and fingering the Kente cloth upholstery of the furniture with adoration, she took a seat on the sofa and smiled at me. She looked stunning in her red, backless dress with signature handbag and pumps. She wore petite diamond studs on her earlobes, to match the larger rocks on her neck, wrist, ankle and ring finger. Her crimson lip color brought out the hazel flecks in her eyes.

"Ayana, you have a beautiful place." She gestured for me to take a seat beside her.

"Thank you, but before I get comfortable, let me check on dinner one last time."

"Okay."

"Would you like a drink?" I asked. "Cognac, perhaps?"

"That would be perfect."

"I'll be right back," I retreated into the kitchen. As I turned off the steamed vegetables and pulled the baked chicken from the oven, I heard my Isley Brothers CD come on. I sang along with Mr. Biggs about making love between the sheets. I filled two glasses and returned to the living room, handing one to Jasmine.

"If you don't mind, I thought it would be nice if we dined in the bedroom." I took a healthy sip from my glass.

"Well, that's original. I've never heard of dinner in the bedroom, but I'm game."

"Great, then follow me."

I held out my hand and led the way to my guest bedroom. I opened up the door to my fantasy chamber, and Jasmine stepped in, amazed. Lavender scented candles lined the walls. A king-sized air mattress was in the middle of the floor, and huge throw pillows were scattered on top of it. Two serving trays were strategically placed at the edges, with a long body pillow against the side of the wall for support. A bucket of chilled champagne was in the center, with two pink-tinted goblets inside. A platter of chilled shrimp cocktail sat next to it.

"This is beautiful," she said, as she bent over the edge of the mattress and sampled a shrimp.

"Thank you." I was mesmerized by her shapely ass, which rounded out nicely as she leaned over.

"Mmmmmmm, these are great," she held up the shrimp she had bitten into. "If the shrimp is this good, I can't wait for dinner."

And I can't wait for dessert.

We lay side by side on the mattress, rubbing our paunches, and savoring the flavor left in our mouths from dinner. Jasmine was going on and on about how boring married life had become.

"It's just lifeless, routine, stale, and Bobby just doesn't seem to do it for me anymore. Don't get me wrong, sex with him is still pleasurable, but now it seems like it's lacking something. I don't know, I just think I need more of a challenge in my sex life."

"Well, I think I can be of some assistance to you," I replied, hoping that she'd be game for this, too.

"And how is that?" she asked turning towards me. She leaned up on her elbow and smiled coyly.

"Well, you say that you want more of a challenge in your sex life, and I feel that I should be the one to indulge your cravings."

"My cravings?" She laughed wickedly. "My cravings for what?"

"What do you think?" I asked, partially annoyed, partially turned on. "You accepted my invitation to dinner, you approved my request to dine in the bedroom, and you haven't taken your eyes off of me since you got here. Ray Charles can see that you want more than just lively conversation."

"Oh, is that right?"

"Yes, it is," I whispered, placing my right hand on her breast.

The slap was an eye-opener. I mean I've had my share of unexpected reactions to my forwardness, but violence? I don't play that game.

"What the hell is wrong with you?" she screamed, pushing my hand away from her swollen nipple.

"Nothing is wrong with me, but you sure do need a reality check," I responded, close to tears from the force of her blow. "If you can't be a woman about this, then I suggest you leave and find another little girl to play with, because I'm not into mind games."

"You have some nerve putting your hands on my body, and then feigning injury. You better be glad the only thing truly hurt is your ego."

"Is that some sort of threat?" I asked, standing and preparing myself for battle.

"Take it any way you like. If you feel threatened by it, then it's a threat. If you feel cautioned by it, then it's a warning. If it pissed you off, as I can see it has, then my work here is done." She stood. "And it has served its purpose."

I walked towards her, and came within inches of her face. Our eyes met, our breathing was heavy and our lips were just inches apart. "Bitch, do you know who you're fucking with?" I asked icily.

"Yes I do," she said with a smile. "But technically, the fucking hasn't really begun yet. Has it?"

Her kiss was as powerful and sudden as her slap. Her tongue forcefully probed my mouth, and her hands caressed my body masterfully. I should have thrown her ass out right then, but no matter how hard I tried to resist her, I couldn't. I heard my father's voice echo in my mind, *"The difference with men and their sex organs, and women and theirs, is that men can only think with their heads, while women can say it with their lips. And a spoken word is much mightier than a thought."* I guess he was right. The pressure of my clasped thighs couldn't quiet my lower lips from screeching, YES, as the moisture oozed from my center, saturating my lace panties with my redolence.

#

Those were the good old days. And though Jasmine's outbursts have become extremely more violent, I still find it hard to resist her. Why I continuously allow myself to endure physical abuse at the hand of someone who claims to love me is beyond me. I know I deserve so much more, but my heart won't let me walk away. After my mother deserted me, I have these fucking abandonment issues, and I can never find the strength to leave until it's too late. I know if I don't get out now, just like every other time, I'll never be able to call it quits with Jasmine. The problem is there's only one other person who can help me withstand. Forever. I just hope she returns my call.

MARK

Roxy won't be expecting me for another half hour, but I think I'll surprise her. Maybe even break her out of her foul mood. I entered quietly and made my way down the hallway, towards the bedroom. Roxy was nestled under the covers, snoring lightly. I tiptoed across the room and kneeled beside her, gazing at her beauty. She is always complaining about her weight, and always thinks I'm bullshitting when I compliment her on how great she looks. Truth be told, for a full-size woman, Roxy is one sexy tigress. She has a confidence and aura about her that makes any skinny chick in her presence bow down and acknowledge her appeal. I'm in awe my damn self, always wanting to thrust my dick up in her heat and get lost within her moist folds.

"What are you doing home so early?" she whispered, opening her eyes slowly.

"I thought I would surprise you." I handed her the roses and candy I had hidden behind my back. "These are for you."

"Thank you," she said, grabbing the presents from my hand, and laying them on the nightstand. "What's the special occasion?"

"There is none. I just wanted you to know that I love you, and I will never take you for granted."

"Is that all?" she teased.

"No, I also want you to know that once we're married, I plan to live the rest of my life trying to keep you happy, because you are my life and I can't live without you."

"That is so sweet, Mark." Tears began to form in her eyes.

"What's wrong?" I asked suspiciously, because in the five years I've constantly professed my love to her, I've never seen her so moved. After five years of indifference, I had to wonder why she was so emotional.

"Nothing," she said, in her leave-it-alone-Mark pitch.

But, I didn't want to leave it alone. And why should I? "Why don't you talk about it?" I prodded. “It might make you feel better."

"There's nothing to talk about." She turned her back towards me, and buried herself under the covers once again.

"If you say so.” I stormed across to the bathroom.

I carefully undressed, placing my dirty clothes into the gold-toned hamper in the corner. While relieving myself, I observed how my urine changed the blue hue of the sanitized toilet water, to a vivid, bubbly green. I flushed, and watched as the emerald liquid drained out, and the bowl refilled with its previous aqua tint. I stepped into the shower, and let the hot water pound my nappy chest. After washing every inch of my body five times, I finally rinsed away the suds and dried off. There was no use in trying to postpone the inevitable.

I opened the door and exited the bathroom. Roxy was now propped up on the pillows, covers up to her neck, arms folded across her mammoth breasts, strategically contemplating our habitual confrontation. Tonight will be different. I'll let her blow off steam. I won't say a word. I'll just nod and agree. And occasionally, I'll slip into the closet and take a few quick swigs from the sterling flask I had hidden inside my old tennis shoes. I walked over to the bed, and spoke cautiously.

"How was your day, Roxy?"

No answer.

"Must have been a long one." I ignored her silence and positioned myself under the covers next to her. "Did you finish preparing for your presentation?"

Still no answer. Roxy just stared at me coldly. I turned my back to her and reached for the flashing message button on the answering machine. She grabbed my arm.

"Don't," she said.

"Why not?"

"Just don't, okay?"

"If it'll make you happy, I won't."

"Good."

"Well, now that I have you talking, did you have a chance to prepare dinner, or do I have to settle for takeout again?"

"What the fuck do you mean, again? Do I look like a maid to you?"

"No, you don't, but once in a while, I would prefer a home-cooked meal, instead of that fast food junk I have to digest five times a week."

"You don't have to do anything, but stay black and die," she huffed. "Besides, I'm not your personal chef. So, if you want dinner on the table every night, I suggest you take up a cooking class or hire a maid."

"Why should I hire a maid, when I have you?" Some things are better left unsaid, and by the look on Roxy's face, I'd have to guess that this was one of those things.

"You have me?" she screamed at the top of her lungs. "Mark, you don't have me, I have you and believe me—you're no prize."

"I'll just ignore that Roxy, because I'm not in the mood. So, if you want to argue, argue with yourself."

I slipped off the bed and entered my closet. I reached

for my much-needed reserve, as Roxy hurled numerous expletives in my direction, disparaging everything from my head to my toes. I tuned her out and concentrated on the warm Cognac flowing down my throat. It reminded me of the tasty liquid from Roxy's cavern, and I suddenly felt a telltale growth in my jockeys. I took one last swig from the flask, and returned it to its hiding place. I sprayed a generous amount of Binaca on my tongue, hoping to camouflage the pungency of the liquor, and emerged from the closet. Roxy was now outside of the covers, sitting up on the edge of the bed. She had replaced the frayed pajamas of this morning with a sexy, red, see-through teddy, and was talking on the telephone.

"And I'd like two egg rolls with the order." She turned her back to me.

Seeing her naked breasts underneath the chiffon, made my manhood stand at attention. Looking at her voluptuous bottom, which seemed to disappear into the softness of the mattress, was more than I could handle.

"I also want a two liter of diet coke," she continued, slighting my presence.

I walked over to the bed, and kneeled in front of her, parting her legs roughly. Her conversation ceased when my tongue pushed her mute button. The receiver dropped from her hands and fell to the floor, as she clenched the side of the bed and moaned softly.

"Hal-lo, hal-lo...," I heard the agitated Chinese man screech through the receiver.

I ignored him, and continued my oral exploration of Roxy's nether region. The dial tone reverberated through the room over Roxy's suppressed whimpers. I pulled the cord from the wall with one hand, while placing two fingers deep inside her with the other. After five minutes, I found the right spot, and within five more minutes, I coerced Roxy into a frenzied climax. Before she could recover from the impact, I spun her onto her stomach, maneuvering myself deep inside her. Her massive cheeks enveloped me, and their taut vibrations soon brought me to my peak. I withdrew and gave her ass a creamy shower then shivered with satisfaction, as all the day's tension drained from my body. I stood up without saying a word and walked into the bathroom. My jockeys were still around my ankles and a gummy discharge was running down my thighs. I shut the door behind me, jumped into the shower, and let the hot water pound my nappy chest once again.

AYANA

A*nother day, another penny*, I thought, as I crossed Madison Avenue and stood at the back of a never-ending patron line. It was Friday night, and since Roxy hadn't called back and I still hadn't heard from Jasmine, I went out on the town looking for some kind of enjoyment. With the help of three ice packs and a cut of top-choice sirloin, I finally got the swelling around my eye to go down. Now the makeup disguising my mishap looked passable, almost natural. I pulled a cigarette from my coat pocket and lit it. I took a long, refreshing drag just as a group of rowdy teenagers got in line behind me.

"Excuse me, Miss," I heard one of them say.

Miss? I knew this little girl wasn't talking to me. Then she tapped me on the shoulder.

"Miss?"

"Yes?" I asked curtly, blowing a cloud of smoke into her face.

"Can I bum a cigarette off you?" the tall, fair-skinned girl asked. She couldn't be more than sixteen. Her hair and makeup were overdone, and her skimpy outfit sagged terribly, showing off a very under-developed bust line.

"How old are you?" I asked.

"How old do I look?" she rebutted, as the juvenile giggles of her friends answered her question for me.

"Not a day over sixteen. Am I right?"

"No," she said in a dejected tone. "I'm celebrating my eighteenth birthday today."

"Is that so?" I asked unconvinced.

"Yup," a very petite pig-nosed girl, who looked like a miniature version of RuPaul chimed in. "We decided to take her out tonight so that she can get her groove on."

"Maybe even get me some," the birthday girl chimed in, slapping high fives with her allies. "Well, what about that cigarette. Can I get one?"

As I pulled another cigarette from my coat pocket and handed it to the birthday girl, I noticed a very handsome man approach the line behind the group. He was wearing a cream-colored cashmere coat, with a navy silk scarf tucked down into the neckline. His dreadlocks were long and full, falling evenly below his shoulders. His skin was the color of black coffee, and his lips looked like two ripe coconuts—rounded and chocolate. I caught his eye, smiled sexily, and broke the gaze. Moderation is rule number one.

"Move it in," the muscular bouncer shouted over the noisy patrons on the line. "Eight, nine, ten," he said, pushing me through the door by my waist.

"Stop right there!" he yelled to the underage teens behind me. "Can I see some ID?" he persisted as the door closed behind me.

Once inside, I checked my coat, and took a seat at the bar.

"What'll it be?" the bartender asked with a southern drawl.

"Hennessy on the rocks." I rested my purse on the bar, and lit another Newport.

"That's five fifty, Miss." He placed a napkin down and then my drink.

"There you go." I pointed to a twenty-dollar bill on the edge of the bar.

He took the money, and walked over to the cash

register. He returned shortly, handing me my change and an ashtray. The one thing I loved about this club was that although there was a smoking ban in New York City, they still had a small, private, extra-ventilated bar section tucked away in the back that catered to and welcomed smokers.

"Thank you." I sipped my drink.

"Is anyone sitting here?" I heard a deep voice say behind me.

"No." I gazed over my shoulder. It was Mr. Perfect from the line outside.

"What'll it be?" the bartender asked, appearing again from out of nowhere.

"What is she having?" Mr. Perfect inquired.

"Hennessy," I said seductively.

"Then I'll have the same, and she'll have another on me," he told the bartender. "That is, if it's all right with you, of course." He was now facing me.

"That'll be fine." I smiled back at the bartender.

"That'll be sixteen big ones." He placed the drinks down in front of us. Mr. Perfect handed the bartender two tens, and he disappeared to the cash register once again.

"By the way, my name is Marlon Fields and it's a pleasure to meet you."

"The pleasure's all mine." I shook his extended hand firmly. "I'm Ayana Linden."

"Here you go, sir." The bartender placed his change on the bar in front of him.

"Thank you," Marlon replied, leaving the singles on the bar.

I took another sip of my drink while I watched his lips embrace the rim of his glass. I followed the descent of the Cognac down his throat, watching the hugeness of his chest as it throbbed along to the beat of the Reggae music playing in the background.

"Do you come here often?" he asked, breaking me

out of my daydream.

"No, not really."

"What's not really? Every week? Every month?"

"Try four times a year." I knew it was better to lie than tell the truth. Well Marlon, not really means that I only come here when my girlfriend is acting up, and I need something of a wicked sexual nature—something that only a man can provide. "How about you? Do you come here often?" I countered.

"Nope. Actually, tonight is my first time."

"Oh, so you're a virgin of sorts." I outed my cigarette in the ashtray.

"Of sorts."

"And what sort of virgin are you not?" I continued.

"Are you always this forward?" he asked, laughing nervously.

"I don't consider asking questions being forward. For all you know, I may have been interested in ditching this place, and taking you to a church uptown in Harlem to play bingo. Something else I'm quite sure you don't do on a regular, if at all."

"True, but is that what you were really considering?"

"No."

"I didn't think so," he murmured, finishing off the last of his drink.

"What I really want to do is dance with you." I polished off my second glass. "Are you interested?"

"I'd be a liar if I said no."

He led me to the dance floor and we began to bump and grind to the pulse of the music. If he moved this good on the dance floor, I couldn't wait to get him back to my place. My hands ran the course of his back, and rested around his shoulders. He pulled my body to his gently, and held my waist tightly. Our bodies moved as one to the sensual music blaring from the overhead speakers.

"You're a great dancer," he whispered in my ear.

“So are you,” I whispered back, smiling radiantly. The hard-on he acquired had my name written all over it, and I couldn’t wait to unwrap my present. “Hey,” I heard myself say, “why don’t we vacate, and relocate to my place?”

“I thought you’d never ask,” he smirked, pulling me towards the coat check booth.

#

We undressed hastily, ripping at each other’s clothing like savages. I pushed him back on the bed, and mounted him like a cowgirl. I grabbed hold of his shoulders like reigns and used my groin and thighs to manipulate his body underneath me. I rocked gently up and down, teasing him with every motion, preserving our unavoidable fate. Too bad his date with destiny took place way before mine ever began.

"That was great," he moaned. He took a piece of Kleenex out of the box on the nightstand, and removed his overflowing condom. He then kissed me gently on the cheek, and nuzzled my ear. "Can I use your bathroom?"

"Sure, it's right through that door. Clean rags are on the shelf in the corner."

"Thanks." He stood, showing off two of the tightest cheeks I'd ever seen. *Bet he never needs a nutcracker.*

I heard the toilet flush and water begin to run against the porcelain basin. At least he's clean about his, I thought. Moments later he materialized, looking even sexier than he did from behind. My eyes plummeted to his midsection, and I was utterly pleased by the size of his penis. He was definitely down with the BDC—Big Dick Committee—and I couldn't wait to see if he could shake what his Mama gave him. He laid me back on the bed, and kissed me with an intensity I hadn't felt since the first night I was with Jasmine. I instinctively peeked over at my answering machine. No blinking light. *That's all right bitch, you don't have to call me. I'm not accepting your apology this time anyway. I've already found someone else.*

I shook my head, jarring Jasmine from my thoughts, and turned my complete attention to the chocolate Adonis, who had now found comfort between my thighs. He groaned loudly, clearly pleased with his own performance. The only thing on my mind was, is he for real? How can someone so well endowed be so ineffective in the dominant position? I felt myself losing interest, and knew that soon I'd be as arid as the Sahara.

Since it was apparent he was either too preoccupied with his own fulfillment, or just had no clue as to how to satisfy a woman the correct way, I knew I had to take matters into my own hands—literally. Reaching downward, I began rotating my fingers within my own moisture with one hand, and massaging my breasts with the other. If someone told me you could masturbate when you're not alone, I wouldn't have believed it. But here I was proof positive, that it was possible. Oh yes, it was very, very possible. I heard Marlon moan loudly, and I stole a glimpse of his expression. I couldn't believe this fool was actually beaming and grunting as he steadily pumped, thinking he was the reason my skin was glowing, and obscene whispers were escaping my lips. Shit, if his dick was as good as my fingers, perhaps he could garner the same response. Until then, I guess I'd just have to satisfy myself.

"Whose is it, baby?" I heard him call out softly between thrusts.

It's sure not yours, I wanted to scream, but that would be rude. So I said nothing. My silence either infuriated him, or made him think now he had to show me whose it really was. His motions became quicker, firmer, harder. His breathing heavier. His thighs tenser. His fingernails digging into my ass sharper. All this overtime he was putting in only to have me proclaim that he was the man. He could wait on it. Besides, after ten minutes of nonstop jabbing, he could no longer hold out. He started having convulsions like the Holy Ghost had taken over. I was waiting for him to jump up and start speaking in tongues, but he never did. With one last grunt, Marlon was off me and snoring in a fetal position at the foot of the bed. *Sorry ass!* My fingers started their rotation once again.

ROXANNE

I don't know what got into Mark last night, but whatever it was, I hope it enters him more frequently. Who knows, maybe this marriage thing could work out after all. Perhaps we could even start working on those three kids he kept telling me about. I wouldn't mind being someone's mother. Someone's wife. A Mrs., not just plain old Roxanne. Not that being me was such a bad thing, but I knew I was put on this earth for more important things, and bringing another human being into this world had to be the most momentous—or so I've heard.

I walked down the long hallway and entered the kitchen wearily, looking forward to my morning dose of caffeine and sugar. Some days I just needed to inhale the aroma from the opened coffee can for stimulation, but today that was not going to be enough. I needed motivation, and two cups of Java did the trick. I walked into the living room, and snatched my to-do list off the desk. 1. Call the messenger. 2. Rework the Sampson Springboard folio. 3. Contact the media about the Avalon press release. 4. Call Ayana.

My fingers began dialing the memorized number way before my brain could stop them. I started to hang up after the first ring, but my arm wouldn't cooperate. After the third ring, I was really about to give up hope when a muddled voice came through the receiver.

"Hello," the voice said.

"Hi, hello. May I speak to Ayana Linden."

"This is she. Who's calling?"

"Ayana? It's me, Roxanne."

The silence was deafening.

"Yana, are you still there?" I asked.

"Um. Yeah, yeah. I'm still here," she replied. "I was asleep, and I was just making sure I wasn't dreaming."

"Well it's no dream, honey. You're wide awake, and I'm just returning your phone call. You sounded worried. Is something wrong?"

"Yes and no."

"Care to elaborate?"

"Sure, but I'd prefer if we met in person. How about we have lunch at Evelyn's around two o'clock? My treat."

No. NO. NO! "Okay," my heart said, before my mind had a chance to decline.

"Good. I'll see you then."

I stood in the doorway holding the receiver, hearing loud bells ringing. I hung up the phone when I realized that the loud ringing was coming from the detached handset. I placed it back in its cradle, and walked into my bedroom. As I rummaged through my closet looking for an outfit that was elegant, yet hid my flaws and accentuated my shape, I tried to think about something other than my last sexual encounter with Ayana.

I arrived at the restaurant twenty minutes late, happy to be making an entrance. I sashayed over to the table where Ayana was seated. I wore a black v-neck flowing silk tee with a matching mini skirt. I was dressed to thrill, and although I hated to admit it, Ayana was, too. She wore a black one-piece pantsuit with a silver belt draped around her thin waist and signature silver sunglasses to complete the ensemble. I could tell she still got her workout on, because she looked better than I remembered her. Seeing her again after all these years made the bad memories and deep-seated hatred I once felt suddenly fade away. As we kissed each other on the cheek, I felt her hand graze my waist and I shivered inwardly. She was still beautiful, still sexy and still off limits.

"You look better than I remember, Roxy. How have you been?" she asked, watching amorously as I took a seat across from her. God Bless her and Mark's penchant for big women. It worked wonders for my self-esteem.

"I can't complain," I replied, picking up the menu. "And you? How's it going?"

"Okay, I guess. How's Mark?" she asked, with a hint of disgust.

"Oh, he's wonderful. Life with him couldn't be better," I laid it on thick. At least I remembered how to get a rise out of her. "And how's your love life? Meet anyone new?"

"As a matter of fact I have."

"That's nice. What's her name?"

"His name is Marlon."

"His? Did I hear her right?"

"Yes, you heard correctly." She smiled wickedly. She was happy to hear my reservation, as my innermost fears seeped from my lips.

"Sorry, I didn't know I was thinking out loud."

"It's okay. I just thought you would have outgrown that habit by now."

"Well, you know what they say, weather changes, not people. I guess it's true, because you haven't stopped ogling my breasts since I walked in."

"Touché." She motioned for the waiter. "Would you like a drink?"

"I'd love one," I replied, as the waiter appeared by her side.

"I'd like two Grey Goose apple martinis, straight up," she said.

"Sure Madame, anything else? An appetizer, perhaps?" he asked with a muddied French accent.

"Fried calamari and shrimp cocktail would be fine," I interjected.

"I'll be back shortly." He turned on his heels and disappeared behind two large swinging doors.

"You do still like apple martinis, don't you?" she asked.

"Yes, I do."

We exchanged pleasantries over the appetizers and halfway into our entrees until I thought my curiosity would swallow me whole. I could no longer hold my tongue.

"Ayana, why did you call me after all this time?" I blurted

out, while dabbing the corners of my mouth with the white linen napkin.

"Because I needed to talk to you." She let her fork rest against her plate, removed her shades and raised her eyes to meet my gaze.

"Well, I'm here now. What did you need to talk about?"

"Roxy, maybe this isn't the right place. Do you think we can go back to my place after lunch?"

"Hell no!" I exploded through gritted teeth, "If this was your sick way of trying to get me back, you blew it. I knew you had something up your sleeve the minute I heard your voice on the answering machine. But I just wanted to believe you changed. Now you've gone so far as to pretend to be in some kind of grave danger, just so my dumb ass will rescue you."

"First of all, this isn't make-believe. I *am* in danger. Sort of. Second of all, I'm not trying to get you back, well not exactly. All I want is to be friends again, because if you put all that other bullshit behind us, that's what we started out as—friends. Best friends. I'm sorry, but I miss that, and I miss you. Is something wrong with that?"

"Yes. We can't just pick up where we left off. Too much has happened, and my lifestyle is different. I've changed, and honestly I don't want to go back. I'm about to be married..."

"When?" she interrupted. "Have you even set a date, Roxy?"

"Yes. No," I stammered. "We're working on it."

"You've been working on it for five years now. You seem to find time for everything else in life, Roxy. You've undoubtedly committed to living this lie, so why can't you commit to one simple date?"

"That's none of your business."

"That's not entirely true, Roxy. I do consider it to be my business, since we both know *I'm* the reason why."

MARK

I was finishing my fourth hand of poker on the handheld game Roxy bought for my birthday when I heard a light tapping on my door. I placed the game in my drawer, and picked up some of the papers strewn over the top of my desk so I could pretend to look busy.

"Come in."

"Sorry to interrupt you," Myrtle, my secretary—oh excuse me, my *administrative assistant*—said as she entered cautiously, "but there's a gentlemen here to see you, and he doesn't have an appointment. I think his name is Royal, or something like that, but, he...," she trailed off, unsure if she should say what was on her mind.

"Yes, Myrtle? Spit it out," I muttered, trying to build up my composure. Knowing full well it would diminish as soon as I was face to face with Royal T. Roaman again. And that's pronounced Ro-yal-ty, because he thought of himself as King. I, on the other hand, knew the "T" stood for trouble.

"It's just that he doesn't look like your average businessman," she continued. "If you know what I mean."

I knew exactly what she meant, but I wasn't going to indulge her. That's part of the reason I usually sent her on errands on Wednesday afternoons. I wouldn't want her to find out about my covert lifestyle. It was nothing to be ashamed of. I just didn't want her to get the wrong impression and think I had a legitimate business relationship with a thug like Royal. Quite frankly, Royal was a street pharmacist, but not your average corner-to-car type dealer. He ran a more prosperous operation, and had laundered his felonious resources into several very profitable establishments. Though I hated anything that had to do with drugs and their poisonous effect on the hood, I couldn't help but envy the fruitfulness of his trade. But not all money was good money. That was the main reason Royal's constant attempts to try and lure me into his craft had been unsuccessful. After seeing someone with as much hope and promise as my first true love fall victim to its toxic influence, I perceived his profession as nothing more than street-ordained assisted suicide—perpetuated and destructive. I knew by his coming to see me this early in the day and not sticking to our regular four o'clock appointment, Royal had ulterior motives. But as always, I would just reject him before he had a chance to lay it on me, because a man was but so strong. One of these days, if I was not careful, I knew I'd become a part of the business he chose to pimp. Turned out like all the others. Just another whore. A rich whore, but a whore nonetheless.

"Should I show him in? Mr. Watkins," Myrtle inquired, eyeing me strangely.

I nodded.

"Mr. Watkins," Royal said, entering my office and closing the door behind him. He walked towards me with his hand outstretched.

"Mr. Roaman," I replied, grabbing his hand in a down-home, black power handshake routine. "What's the good word?"

"C.R.E.A.M. my man. Cause cash rules everything around me." He smiled, showing off three gold crowns on his upper row of teeth. "Can I have a seat?"

"Be my guest." I surveyed his 24-karat presidential Rolex, and the two diamond-clustered pinky rings he donned. Ten or twenty gold chains, all of different lengths and styles, hung around his thick neck, and rested on the open neckline of his tailored Armani suit. "What's up?"

"Nothing much, Mark-O. I was just wondering if I could interest you in a...a...a business venture, per se. YouknowwhatImean?"

"Yeah, I think I do, and as always, I think I'm going to have to decline this time Royal, my man."

"Decline? You haven't even heard what I have to offer."

"Whatever it is, I'm sure it's not legal. So..."

"There you go again," he interrupted. "Why do you always think the worst of me?"

"Maybe because the worst of you is all I ever experience."

"Are you still holding a grudge, Mark-O?"

"Does it matter?"

"No, I just thought that after seven years, you would've forgotten about her. That's all."

"Well, obviously she meant more to me than she did to you, although that's not what you used to tell her. Is it?"

"Mark-O, Mark-O, Mark-O. Let's not go there, okay? That's history. What's done is done. YouknowwhatImean? I can't change the past. I can only live for the here and now. So, do you want to hear me out, or not?"

"Not."

"Suit yourself." He stood and walked over to the

door. He opened it slightly then closed it again. He turned around and walked back over to my desk. "Oh yeah, before I go. I know it's early, but do you got that?"

"Yeah, I got it." I reached into my desk drawer, and flung a small manila envelope on the desk in front of him.

"I think you should hear me out on this one Mark-O. I mean, look around you. Your office is just screaming for some modern renovations."

"I think it's time you leave, because I already told you man, I'm not interested." Besides, I thought, the only thing that needed some modern renovations was his gold wearing, played out ass.

"Okay, but next week when I roll up in here with a bank roll of Presidents, sporting more of my iced-out jewelry and tailored suits, don't say I didn't reach out, my brother."

"Well, I appreciate the offer, but next time, you can save yourself the trip."

"Save myself the trip? Well, this doesn't look like five grand." He eyed the envelope. "It doesn't feel like five grand," he continued, holding up the envelope and squeezing the contents between his fingers. "And it sure don't smell like five grand." He held the packet up to his nose. "So, I guess I won't be saving myself that trip after all. I'll see you next week, man. Same time, same place, same Benjamins. YouknowwhatImean?"

I didn't answer him. I stood up, walked over to the door, and watched as he slipped the envelope inside his jacket pocket.

"Nice doing business with you, Mr. Watkins."

"I wish I could say the same, Mr. Roaman, but as always, the pleasure is obviously all yours."

I slammed the door behind him, and smashed my fist into my open palm. The son of a bitch still knew how to get under my skin. I leaned against the wall and envisioned my ex-fiancée, Rachel Nesbitt. She was beautiful, and we were in love. We were both working towards our masters in business, and were planning to be married two months after graduation. Just as finals week approached, and things between us couldn't get any better, in walked Royal T. Roaman, and his miracle cure for the jitters. We both declined, because we were strongly against drug and alcohol use of any kind and volume, and we made a solemn promise to keep our distance from it. She also vowed she would steer clear of Royal when it became apparent he had a secondary interest in her. I later found out her word wasn't good for anything, and after two weeks of being hooked on Royal's home-cut remedy, she had given back my ring, dropped out of college, and moved in with him. Two months after that, I was awakened from my own self-induced inebriated coma by Royal himself. He had come to tell me that the woman I thought would be my wife and the mother of my children was now dead. The autopsy concluded it was a drug overdose.

The funeral was beautiful, but the makeup couldn't hide the damage and decay of her $500 a day habit. All her hopes, her dreams. Our hopes, our dreams. Gone. Dead. Buried with her diminutive shell. For the first and last time, Royal T. Roaman did something for someone other than himself. Even though he was the reason for her demise, and because I sure as hell couldn't afford to, he sent Rachel to her final resting place in magnificent fashion. For that, I was forever in his debt, or so it seemed. Especially, when the son of bitch hitched on interest of 200 percent to the already exorbitant funeral costs, plus an additional fifty percent for regulatory costs—whatever the fuck that was supposed to mean—bringing my total obligation to a whopping $200,000 dollars. Which in simple terms meant that for the last seven and a half years, I had been graced with his presence, and have helped finance many of his corrupt ventures with my $500 a week pay-up-or-get-fucked-up stipends. What’s more fucked up is that he won’t accept anything more, or less. It’s $500 a week even, no matter what.

I wiped the tears falling down my cheeks with the back of my hand, and walked over to the intercom. “Myrtle?”

“Yes, Mr. Watkins,” her voice screeched through the box.

“I’ll be leaving early today. Do you need anything from me before I go?”

“No, Mr. Watkins. Are you okay?”

“Yes Myrtle, thanks. I’m just a little tired that’s all. As a matter of fact, why don’t you get your things together, and take off, too.”

“You sure?” she asked excitedly. I heard the computer shut off, books close, drawers slam shut and pens being placed in their holder before I could answer.

“Yes, I’m sure. Good night, Myrtle.”

“See you tomorrow, Mr. Watkins.”

The main office door slammed shut as I turned off the intercom. I put on my coat, smiled to myself sadly and shook my head.

Once I made it home, I shuffled through the door, downtrodden and drained. I secretly prayed Roxanne was out. I didn't feel like arguing, and I wasn't in the mood for her shit. I just wanted peace and quiet. Not to mention a stiff drink. I entered and walked straight over to the bar. I poured myself a glass of scotch, and grimaced as the liquid burned my throat. I finished two glasses, poured another, and readied myself for combat. I crept into the room on tiptoe, hoping not to wake Roxy from her evening nap. To my pleasant surprise, the bed was made and she was out. I turned on my favorite Usher CD full blast, and finally found solace in a steaming bubble bath. I had some confessions of my own to think about.

AYANA

I turned the key in the lock, and pushed the door to my apartment wide open.

"I can't believe you convinced me to come over here," Roxy shook her head from side to side as she walked inside.

"I'm just glad you finally agreed. Have a seat." I walked over to the liquor cart and poured us drinks. I handed her a glass and sat down on the sofa beside her. "Roxy, what happened to us?"

"You already know the answer to that Yana, so why are you asking me again?"

"I don't know. Maybe because I wasn't really looking for an answer."

"Then what were you looking for?" She sipped her drink and then placed her glass on the end table behind her. "Now stop with all the games Yana, and tell me why you called me after all this time."

I took a long sip from my glass, and sat it down on the wood floor. "Roxy, I need you. I'm miserable right now, and only you can make me happy."

"What about Marlon?" she asked and raised her eyebrow. "I thought he was your sunshine."

"*You're* my sunshine. Marlon was a one-night stand. I just threw his name at you because after hearing about how great you and Mark were getting along, I was hurt. And you know me, I needed to strike back. Do you forgive me?"

"Only if you forgive me."

"For what?" I grabbed my glass and took a hearty gulp.

"For lying to you, too. Mark and I are barely making it, Yana. We are constantly at each other's throats. I don't even know why we're still together."

"Could it be the sex?"

"Lately? Yes. But before that? I just think it was fear. Fear of the unknown. Not wanting to start that whole *can I get your number* dating bullshit again."

"I hear you. That's where I am now, and I tell you, it's for the birds. I just want something real, something like what we had...," I trailed off when I sensed annoyance in Roxy's gaze.

"Yana, you'll never change. Stop wasting my time, and tell me what's going on. You can't hide that scar forever."

"What scar?" My eyes opened wide and I tried to move away. Leave it to Roxy to find a fucking needle in a haystack.

"I was talking about this one." She pulled me to her, as her finger skimmed the outline of my cheekbone. "But now, as I look more closely, I can see that there's definitely more than one. Is that why you called me?"

I looked away, too ashamed to face her. I had always been the strong one. Now the tables were turned. I was now the victim, and I sure as hell was not used to that role.

"Answer me, Yana!" She forcefully pulled my chin around so that I would be facing her.

"Yes," I said weakly, feeling tears behind my closed eyelids.

As soon as she grabbed me, I began wailing like a

baby, and gushing like a faucet. She held me tight and rocked me gently as I told her all about my myriad one-night stands and gave her the in-depth details of my abusive relationship with Jasmine. I made sure to leave out the fact that I seemed to be a domestic abuse magnet, since Jasmine was just following the cycle I had come to accept. My mind clouded over as her lips came down upon mine. Gentle, but firm. Pained, but reassuring. Indulgent, yet controlled. I couldn't compose the fire building inside me, and I surrendered. We explored each other's mouths and bodies for all of twenty minutes, until she pulled herself away.

"Why did you stop?" I asked. Not wanting the feeling to end.

"I'm sorry. I just can't go there with you again. I don't want to start all over..."

"And why not?" I asked. "I need you right now, Roxy. More than I needed you before. More than I've ever needed anyone in my life."

"I know that, but I'm scared."

"Scared of what?"

"Scared that this time I won't be able to walk away. Yana, we've been through this before. We're sisters, and this isn't right."

"We are step-sisters, Roxy. Nothing more. We don't have the same blood running through our veins. We are friends, whose parents just so happen to be married to each other. Evelina is not my biological mother and Joseph is not your biological father, no matter what it says on those adoption documents. So, why are you holding back when you know you still love me?"

"Who says I still love you?"

"You didn't have to say it. I could feel it. Or were your lips lying to me, too?"

"This has nothing to do with my lips, or my lying, or my love for you. This is about me taking charge of a situation that had spun out of my control once before. Something that I refuse to let happen again." She stood.

"Where are you going?"

"Home."

"Your home is here." I placed her hand on my heart.

"Not anymore, Yana." She pulled her hand away. "Not anymore."

Ten minutes passed by, and I still hadn't moved from in front of the closed door. I knew Roxanne would come to her senses, and come back to me. I knew she was going to get halfway home, realize what a mistake she was making, spin that car around, and come back home where she belonged. That's what she told me with her kiss. That's what I saw in her eyes. Even though that's not what her mouth said, I refused to listen to her words. That was her head talking, not her heart. Her heart was going to bring her back to me. I just knew it. I just hoped it. I just prayed it. Please God, send Roxanne back here to save me from my own self-destruction.

The doorbell rang catching me off guard. I stripped off my clothes and opened the door, revealing the French-cut thong and bra set I bought for our reunion.

"I knew you'd change your mind." I opened the door widely. My sunshine turned to rain.

"Change my mind about what?" Marlon asked, as he eyed me affectionately. "How did you know I was on my way up? Did the doorman call you?"

"No, but he damn well should have," I fumed, grabbing my jumpsuit off the floor and wrapping it around my nakedness.

"Well, if you weren't waiting on me, who were you waiting on? You look just about ready for action, and I thought you said you weren't seeing anyone..."

"I'm not." I tried to lighten my tone.

"So, why the sexy get up? I know you're not dressed like that for the mailman."

"And what if I were?"

"Were you?" He grabbed me in a bear hug and kissed my neck.

"No," I said softening.

"Then whom were you waiting on?"

"You," I lied. "The doorman called up just as you rung the bell. I hope I'm not being too forward." I let the jumpsuit fall to my ankles.

"No, you're not. As a matter of fact, I just so happen to like forward."

He picked me up and carried me into the bedroom.

As we kissed, my encounter with Roxy clouded my thoughts. I pretended his lips were hers and acquiesced to his urgency until flashbacks of the previous night's escapade invaded my mind. I could no longer make believe the hands exploring my body were hers. They were no longer soft and tender; they were now huge, strong man hands. His scent was masculine—not like the flowery smell Roxy embodied. His tongue, which was thrashing in my mouth, seemed to be snaking down my throat. Choking me. I pushed him up roughly, and gasped for air.

"What's wrong?" he asked.

"Nothing. I just..."

"What Ayana? Tell me. Is it something I did?"

"Yes. No. It's just..."

"What? You can tell me."

You asked for it. "Marlon," I began, looking deep into his eyes, "it's just that, I wasn't exactly pleased with your performance last night." I saw pain take the place of confusion in his expression, but I continued anyway. "And tonight, I want perfection. I'm really not in the mood to settle for anything less."

"So what are you saying? You don't want to be with me?"

"No, it's not that. But if we are going to do this, I just

want it to be done right. Do you have a problem with that?"

"If it means having another chance to feel what I felt last night, I have no problem whatsoever. Just tell me what you want me to do."

"What I want you to do is take your time. We have all night, and I'm in no rush. I also want you to be gentle. I'm no virgin, but I don't like it rough all the time either. I want you to be considerate, because last night, you were at the finish line way before the gun went off. If you catch my drift…"

"Yeah, I catch it," he replied in a measured tone. "Is that all?"

"Not exactly. I still want to walk you through. Will that be okay?"

"Sure, but I just have one question for you."

"Shoot."

"Did I do anything right last night?" he asked with a nervous laugh.

"Yes. You came into my life when I needed you most, and I'm thankful for that. Now, come here." I pulled him down to me, and kissed him softly.

ROYAL

It was a normal Thursday night at Royalty Bar & Grill. The regulars seated at the bar were getting drunker, and the clump of teenagers in the corner booth were enjoying what they thought was an even mixture of gin and juice. It was actually only five percent gin to ninety-five percent juice. I made sure waitresses circled their table regularly. Refilling empty tumblers with the watered down concoction I invented for this very purpose. I didn't have a problem charging them extra for my diluted blend either. The way I saw it was, if they didn't mind sneaking in here and risking my being busted for serving minors, then I didn't object to having the little fuckers finance my bond. YouknowwhatImean?

I continued to survey the crowd from my mirrored cage overlooking the bar, as I sat perched on my golden throne. I smiled approvingly as the waitress pulled out a detector pen and scribbled on a bill that was handed to her by one of the teenagers. I had to call a second emergency meeting just three months ago, when it became apparent that some of the younger customers were still doling out counterfeit twenties. I remembered reading about similar occurrences in some of the other bars near campus, and I recalled seeing a few stories about it on the news years ago, but my first warning to the waitresses went unheard, and somehow the fake money still slipped into the loop. I liked to think the detector pens were actually the waitresses' idea, but Rita, one of my more aggressive waitresses, told me in so many words they didn't have a choice. I think they did. The second time around, I just informed them any fake cash accepted would be taken out of their pay, along with a 200 percent penalty. The next day, the pens emerged and the problem was immediately rectified. I called that excellent management skills, but Rita called it extortion. So I called her ass a cab, and told her to get the fuck out of my establishment. She was the first and last sister I'd hire. Fuck all that uplift the race garbage. Sisters know nothing of subservience, and there would only be one monarch in my institution. YouknowwhatImean?

I looked over at the bar and noticed Martha, the unruly white woman I most recently hired, looking around suspiciously. I moved closer to the glass, and watched as she pulled a twenty-dollar bill from the cash register, and pushed it in between her surgically augmented breasts. The same boobs that got that bimbo the job were the same ones that were going to cost her the job. I fumed, rising to take care of some necessary business. I was on the top step, about to descend the gold and red accented staircase, when She walked in. She was beautiful. She had bright, moon-shaped eyes, lips that looked like a heart and a full-framed body with curves in all the right places. *A gift from God,* I thought. My eyes followed her into a side booth, and I secretly wished my face could take on the formation of the red velvet booth cushions. I had to meet her, but my feet were anchored to the floor. I watched as the waitress sat a drink down in front of the woman. She then pulled an ashtray from the front of her apron and placed it down beside the drink. My mind drifted back in time, and I visualized my first sweetheart. Her name was Rachel Nesbitt, and I truly loved her. I swear I did, but she didn't want anything to do with me. The more I pursued, the more she backed away, and I would have done anything to make her love me. I felt the same way when I looked over at the cocoa-colored woman in the booth, but the aftermath of Rachel's addiction eclipsed her image. I shook my head and stared at the woman again. *This time will be different,* I thought, as I continued down the staircase. I had just cleared the last step, when Martha passed by carrying a tray with an empty decanter on top. My anger returned, and I placed destiny on hold. I grabbed her by the arm.

"Why is this decanter empty?"

"I was just going to fill it, Mr. Roaman."

"There won't be any need for that, YouknowwhatImean?" I took the tray and placed it on the bar. "Come with me upstairs for a minute." I gently pushed Martha up the steps ahead of me.

Before following Martha's ascension, I glanced over my shoulder to make sure She was still there. She was. As the waitress refilled her goblet, she began to make herself more comfortable. I rushed up the steps, and entered my office. Martha was standing in front of the two-way mirrors, scanning the crowd. I walked over to her, and glanced down over her shoulders. The corner of a bill was sticking out the neckline of her jumper.

"Martha?"

"Yes, Mr. Roaman."

"Would you consent to a strip search, per se?"

"Well that all depends on who's going to be doing the stripping, and who's going to be doing the searching." She smiled seductively. "But since we're the only two here, I guess we'll be the only two involved. So-o-o-o, Mr. Roaman, I'd have to say that when it comes to you, I'd consent to just about anything." She now had both arms draped around my shoulders, and her breath was hot on my earlobe. She began to kiss my neck.

"What are you doing?" I jerked away from her.

"Exactly what you want me to do. Isn't that what you called me up here for?"

"Look Martha..." I was about to tell her she was fired, but she closed my mouth with one hand and opened my zipper with the other. Within seconds, she was on her way down. As she dropped to her knees in front of me, I stared out into the bar and zeroed in on the lady in black. She was now on what seemed to be her third drink, and it didn't look like she had any intentions on leaving anytime soon. She lifted her glass to her mouth, just as Martha placed me inside hers. As she sucked and caressed me into a vehement frenzy, I pictured Her on her knees before me. Savoring the flavor of my spirits, as they streamed down her throat. I looked down at Martha's chalky complexion, and withdrew myself abruptly. Not only was I betraying my race, but I was also forsaking my authority.

"Look Martha, a blow job's not why I had you come up here." I pulled up my zipper.

"Well, I didn't hear any protests ten minutes ago and I sure as hell didn't hear any complaints when you came."

"That's only because you made sure you didn't leave me any mess to clean up, YouknowwhatImean?"

"No, I don't know what you mean." She said this with a little more attitude than I was used to.

"Well, let me put it to you this way. Since, I've been paying you for the last two weeks, and all you've managed to do is screw me, how about you pull my money from between your tits and consider the two of us even? YouknowwhatImean?"

"No, I don't know what the fuck you mean, Royal. Simple english, motherfucker."

"Fine." I tried to figure out where this bitch found the balls to call me a motherfucker. "I want you to take the bills you copped from the register, place them in my hand, then get your shit, and get out. You're fired. Is that simple enough for you?"

"Fired? You can't..."

"Martha," I said, now a little irritated. "Save yourself the embarrassment. Wipe the cum from your mouth, and pay me for my motherfucking services."

ROXANNE

I drove around for a few hours, and was about to make a left on Third Avenue, when I saw an enormous bar to my right. I pulled into the parking lot, and rushed inside for a drink. When the waitress pulled an ashtray out of her apron and placed it in the center of the table next to the candle, I smiled gratefully. I had given up smoking when I ended my relationship with Ayana, but tonight, as I inhaled the vapors from the Capri Indigo 120 dangling between my fingers, I found solitude. I washed down three Jack and cokes and chain smoked about a dozen cigarettes before my problems became individualized, and I was able to dissect them one by one.

I couldn't believe I let myself get sucked in again by Ayana's wiles. She almost had me right where she wanted me, and for a moment there, I had to remind myself that's not the place I wanted to be. I'd been there, and done that. Contrary to what she was trying to make me believe, it wasn't always roses and sunshine. I used to drive myself crazy with all the sneaking, whispering and secrets. Not to mention, the dementia I caused my boyfriends, who were always trying to figure out ways to make me feel whole, since I constantly complained about feeling incomplete with them. I knew I was the main cause for their bitterness, and knew I was the reason for their subsequent failed relationships. I was also the one behind all of the broken hearts they've administered, but I didn't ask them to fall in love with me. I didn't ask to be saved; well, not outright anyway. My weight problem was my own. Still was. None of them could convince me it didn’t matter and that their love was real. Not when the only thing a size ten in my closet were my shoes, and definitely not when they were glomming onto the first skinny, light-skinned bitch that crossed their path after I called it quits.

That brought me to problem number two. Mark, my Savior. I loved him. I just didn't like him sometimes, but I knew I incited my own disdain. If I weren't so temperamental and difficult, we could probably make it. I truly didn't want to be, but I was torn. My being in love with a man, with future promises of marriage and children was a fantasy. My strong proclivity for those bearing the same physical makeup as myself was a reality. Although I could continue to front it off, I felt my facade deteriorating, along with Mark's dignity. I really didn't want to hurt either of us, but it was too late. Our feelings were far beyond mere injury. We had moved on to malice, becoming the other’s willing recipient.

I was so enthralled with my own mental combat I didn't notice I now had a guest sitting in the booth across from me.

"Are you okay?" he asked, placing his right hand on my arm.

“Yes, thank you.” I looked past him and answered to no one in particular.

"You sure? You look troubled."

"Yes, I'm sure." I reached for yet another cigarette. Mentally calculating that I was up to number fourteen.

"My name is Royal," he said.

Silence.

"I'm not really in the mood for the usual barrage of

can you buy me a drink lines, YouknowwhatImean," he continued. "So, I figured if I shared this booth with you, we could pretend we were together. Friends even. I hope I'm not imposing, and I hope you don't mind."

"No, I don't mind." I finally gave in. "Really, I can use the company. My name is Ro...Rhonda." I knew there was no way in hell someone would actually name their child Royal. To be honest, I found it somewhat intriguing. For once, I didn't have to be good old-fashioned Roxanne Emile Linden. I could be this other woman, Rhonda, and Rhonda could be whoever the fuck I wanted her to be. It was just what I needed—a viable escape.

"If you don't mind me saying so, you don't look like the singles bar type. You seem way too classy to even be in a place like this. YouknowwhatImean? So, what brings you here?"

"Four wheels and a V-6 engine." I batted my eyelashes and smiled. "And you?"

"A $500 pair of gators." He laughed.

"Well, if you can pay $500 for a pair of shoes, why do you feel it necessary to hide from a eight-dollar tab?"

"Maybe because my feet have earned the $500 price tag, but some of the less attractive clientele who frequent this place, don't even come close to deserving the eight-dollar charge. YouknowwhatImean?"

I gave Royal the once over, and wasn't very pleased by what I saw. He was huskier than I liked, and had on enough gold to put Mr. T to shame. I was never into the cocky type, but tonight I wasn't me—I was Rhonda, and Rhonda was into whomever I wanted her to be into. Besides, after I washed down my fifth Jack and coke, Rhonda started enjoying his pompous attitude. YouknowwhatImean? "Well, since I'm of a classier variety, I guess I've more than warranted that amount."

"Mmm, sexy and clever. I like that. I'd be more than

happy to buy you that drink, but first I have to ask you for your car keys."

"What?" My neck rolled. I know I didn't hear him right.

"I said I need your car keys."

"Is that some sort of joke?"

"Not at all." He was stone-faced. "I wouldn't be able to live with myself if I were to allow you to walk out of my establishment in your condition, and then get behind the wheel of a car. There's no telling what can happen to you, or an innocent bystander. I'm not going to let you take that chance. YouknowwhatImean? Furthermore, if you weren't so intoxicated, I'm quite sure you would agree with me."

"Intoxicated," I slurred. "Who the fuck is intoxicated? I've only had a couple of drinks."

"And a couple more and then another, and you've only been here for a little over an hour. So, I'm sorry to tell you Rhonda, but you are intoxicated, and I do need those keys."

I stood up and tried to steady myself. "You won't be getting anything from me tonight, my brother. My keys included." I moved to turn away, but suddenly became faint. I tried to sit in the booth again, but I felt myself sinking instead. Then darkness.

MARK

As soon as my head hit the pillow, my cell phone rang. "Hello?"

"Hello, Is this Mr. Watkins?"

"Who wants to know?"

"This is Beverly, of Royalty Bar & Grill. I'm looking for Mark Watkins."

"May I ask what for?"

"Well, it seems his girlfriend, Rhonda...I mean, hold on." I heard keys clanking, and someone rummaging through papers. And then, "sorry, that's Roxanne..."

"Roxanne. Did something happen to her?"

"No, not yet. We have her in our back room, resting. She blacked out in the bar, and we found you as the last dialed number on her cell phone. I just wanted to call to see if someone would be able to pick her up."

"Pick her up? Isn't she driving?"

"Well, yes sir. She drove herself here, but it's the policy of the bar not to allow intoxicated patrons to drive themselves elsewhere. So, will you be coming for her, or should we put her in a cab?"

"I'm coming for her." I sighed. "What's the address?"

I stepped out of the cab and was amazed at what I

saw. A thick red, Persian carpet, surrounded by solid gold enclosures, lead the way to the front door of Royalty Bar & Grill. I smiled as one of the doormen, in a crimson and gold uniform that matched the exterior perfectly, held the door open for me. Once inside, I gawked at the lavish spread. The furniture and fixtures were all solid gold, and the floors, bar stools and booth cushions were covered with plush red velvet. The entire staff was white, including the deejay. The deejay was stationed in a glass chamber above the bar, bedecked in a gold pantsuit, spinning Rhythm and Blues Oldies over the elaborate sound system. The all-female floor crew were dressed in red leotards, and each held gold trays, with gold decanters on top. I walked over to the counter, and caught the attention of the very attractive bartender behind it.

"Hi, are you Beverly?" I shouted over the music. I gave her the once over and liked what I saw. My eyes stopped at her bulky cleavage. They weren't real, but they still looked good.

"Yes." She leaned down to meet my gaze. "Do I know you?" she yelled viciously.

"Yes, I mean, no." I tore my eyes away from her bosom and looked into her eyes. "I'm here to pick up Roxanne."

"You must be Mark Watkins. She's in the back." She sized me up, smiled seductively, and ran her tongue back and forth across her scarlet lips. "You have to excuse my cold reception, but you never know what type of weirdo you'll find lurking around in a place like this. With my job, you've got to be on your P's and Q's. YouknowwhatImean?"

"Yeah, strangely enough, I do."

I followed Beverly into the back, my eyes automatically dropping to her backside. She had an hourglass figure, and one of those coffee table asses. Boy, what I wouldn't give to be naughty with this little red devil. I lifted my eyes, and started thinking about the old wrinkled lady I saw crossing the street on my way over here. Anything to deflect the hard-on growing in my cotton Dockers. My anxiety was curtailed as soon as I saw him standing over her motionless body. Deja vu. It all made sense to me now. Royalty Bar & Grill, as in Royal T. Bar & Grill.

"Mark-O." He walked over to me and waved Beverly away. He placed his hand on my shoulder and started grinning like he had just stolen someone's virginity. "I didn't know what I would find when I went through her cell phone. But when I saw your name next to the last dialed number; well, you can understand my shock and embarrassment."

"Though I can see why you'd be surprised, I don't feel you have anything to be embarrassed for..."

"Me neither. The embarrassment was for you, Mark-O. It looks to me like if you're not careful, you may be leading yet another one of your pretty little ladies into temptation. YouknowwhatImean?"

I snatched away from his grip, and walked over to Roxanne. I shook her gently. There was no response.

"Looks to me like she needs to spend the night, and she's more than welcome. That's if you trust she'll come back to you tomorrow."

"It's you that I don't trust Royal. Not her." I tried to support the dead weight of Roxanne's lifeless body. "I wouldn't be surprised if you didn't slip a few roofies in her drink."

"Mark-O, I've been without the assistance of aphrodisiacs since college. You, of all people, should remember my rite of passage and she was just as beautiful as old Rhonda, here..."

"Her name is Roxanne."

"Sorry, force of habit. I mean, Roxanne. Although, Rhonda is the name she gave me. Who knew it was an alias? Maybe your new girlfriend has something to hide, too. Youknowwhatlmean?"

I didn't bother to answer. I pushed by him, struggling with the weight of Roxanne's drooping body as I tried to lead her out the room. It was a slow crawl past Beverly as well. She gave me a knowing smile. Or was that seduction? Whatever it was, it was fleeting, and I didn't want any parts of it. Well, that's not entirely true. I would love any part of her, but that would mean that I'd also have to endure parts of Royal. With my last payment coming due in a little over two months, that was something I would no longer have to bear.

I pushed Roxanne through the bedroom door, and dragged her onto the bed. I took off her shoes and clothes, and was caught off guard by her fiery red undergarments. It was the same red that enveloped Beverly's massive ass cheeks. A vision of me bending Beverly over the bar, and fucking her straight through her spandex played in my head. I felt my hard-on coming back and there was no need for diversions this time. I flung Roxanne over on her back and ripped off her panties. Within in seconds, I was out of my boxers and in her warmth. I began moving gently inside her, until I heard Royal's voice over my shoulder. *You may be leading yet another one of your pretty little ladies into temptation.* My thrusts became more intense, and I began fucking Roxanne with a vengeance. *You have to pay for the humiliation you caused me*, I thought, as I pushed deeper inside her. You will not end up like Rachel, Roxy. I won't let you. You hear me? I won't let you. I continued to hammer away at her, letting all my anger build and my frustration expand, until my body felt like it was going to explode and I let it. I jerked violently with each pulsation, as I filled her with my creamy elixir. I smiled to myself, pleased at what I had just accomplished. For the first time, I was king of my castle, and it felt good. This was the first fight with Roxanne I had ever won. Although mainly due to the fact she was out cold, a victory was a victory. I now had to take control of my own destiny.

I turned Roxanne onto her stomach, and entered her once again, grinding purposefully. I quickly came to the point of no return. The point where it was all or nothing, and I usually withdrew myself from her just in time. But tonight, everything was different. I had to preserve our virtues. I had to create a bond that no one could break. We will call him Junior, I thought, as I erupted inside her. I screamed out with anguish, pleasure and relief, as the thick liquid gushed from my body and found a new home within hers. At last, Roxy, you are whole. You are complete. I'll tell you all about it when you wake up in the morning.

AYANA

I didn't know if one could honestly be taught the art of making love. But let's just say if my body were an empty canvas, Marlon certainly filled it with his own personal spirit and color. Using bold strokes and unique detail to make his masterpiece come alive—and alive I was. After years and years of looking for a competent replacement for Roxy, my search was now complete. But one could never be too sure. I mean, was I on some type of rebound here? Was it great only because I couldn't have who I truly wanted, and fantasy had somehow vanquished my better judgment? What if he had already forgotten all the hands-on training he received last night, and would need constant reminders as to the magnitude and manner in which I preferred to be pleasured? Could he truly take my mind off of Roxy and Jasmine, and fulfill my multifarious appetite? I mean, I've heard women talk about making love to a man, and being in love with a man, but I've never experienced either. That is, until now. I think. But in my perfect world, I always imagined Hers and Hers towels lining my bathroom walls. Shared wardrobes and similar tastes in shoes. Light, sugary scents and delicate contact. Intense heart-to-hearts with my analogous mate. A woman, who will love me completely, because only another woman truly knew what it was I craved. But just as I carved out this compliant, inexplicable sexual wonder, I found myself questioning the possibility of sculpting a perfect HeShe—a man with all the characteristics, sentiments and compassion of a woman. One who not only knew the meaning of love, but also knew the countless ways in which to express it.

I was suddenly extracted from my reverie by Marlon's fingers creeping upwards towards my geographic triangle. I guess there was only one way to know for sure if the night before was merely a fluke. If it was—sorry Marlon, but Peeeeeaaaace! If it wasn't...

For sanity's sake, I just hope it was.

It wasn't.

Marlon was gone. I was on my third glass of wine, and it was only seven o'clock in the morning. I reached for my cell and called the office. The answering machine picked up after three rings.

"Hi Virginia, it's Ayana. I had two last minute confirmations last night, so I'll be at meetings most of the morning. You can text me with anything urgent. Otherwise, I'll see you around two."

I ended the call and set my alarm for twelve. My one and only appointment was with Mr. Sandman.

I hit the snooze button as soon as the alarm sounded, but the damn thing wouldn't shut off. I smashed it repeatedly with my fist to no avail. I opened one eye and stole a glance at the time. It was only ten thirty. The alarm went off again. Now fully awake, I realized that it had been my cell phone all along. I pressed the answer button.

"Hello."

"Promise me you won't hang up," the voice said.

"I don't make promises that I can't keep."

"Come on, give me a chance to explain."

"There's nothing to explain, Jasmine. We're through."

"You don't mean it. You're just upset right now. Why

don't you take some time to think about it, and..."

"I don't need any more time. I mean it. We're through." I pressed the end button and pulled the covers over my head.

My cell phone rang again. I didn't move. I couldn't. All I had to do was hear those three little words, and I'd be right back to square one. After two years of abuse, I'd had enough. The phone continued to ring. The more I tried to ignore it, the louder it echoed. The sound was deafening. I snatched it up.

"What do you want?" I screamed.

"Did I catch you at a bad time?"

"No. I'm sorry. I just got a barrage of junk calls, and I was trying to sleep in. But that's not important. I didn't think I'd hear from you after yesterday."

"I know, but I've been thinking..."

"And?" I was now sitting up in my bed, anxious to hear what Roxanne had to tell me.

"I think we need to talk. My intention was to leave a detailed message on your voice mail, because I didn't think you'd pick up. Since you did, I guess I can just tell you."

"Tell me what?"

"That I miss us, too, but not the way you do. Ayana, when we were found out, and the shit hit the fan, I felt like I lost a part of me—a very important part. For years I couldn't figure out what it was, until I heard your voice again. Now I'm not saying that I want to continue where we left off, because that would be impossible. I just want to work towards repairing the damage our relationship caused. Hopefully, the two of us can survive through it all. That is, if you're willing."

"I'm not saying that I'm not, but it's something I have to think about. I know I was the one to reach out to you, but after seeing you it just brought back so much. We're talking about a lot of pain and humiliation, and I'm not sure I'm really ready for all that. Just give me some time, and I'll let you know. Okay?"

"Good enough, Ayana. And before I hang up, I just wanted you to know that you were right."

"About what?"

"About me. I was stringing Mark along all this time, because I was senselessly dreaming about a union between the two of us. But I know now that it can never be, and I just want to make everything right again. Ayana, I want my life back."

"I do too, Roxy, and I think I'm finally on that road. I just want to take it one day at a time. So, just bear with me."

"Do I have a choice?" she asked. I knew she was smiling.

"Do you ever have a choice?" I asked. “Now stop getting on my nerves, and hold your fucking horses."

We laughed, and it was just like old times. We were both teenagers, lying across my bed, prattling away about the insignificant details of our lives. I knew I missed her, but after all these years, the gravity of my longing was now magnified. I knew she could hear it in my voice, but I didn't give a damn. Nothing else mattered to me at that moment. No one else existed. I closed off the rest of the world and immersed myself in conversation. When I finally peeked up at the clock, I saw that it was now eleven thirty. We had been on the phone for an hour already, but I still didn't want to hang up. My prayers were finally answered, and Roxanne was back in my life—temporarily. My only mission was to make it permanent. Which meant I finally had to do what I had been putting off. A confrontation that would be nothing less than consequential—and very, very dangerous.

ROYAL

It was twelve fifteen. I had a very important two o'clock meeting with the president of the Fifth Avenue Bank of New York branch and I didn't want to be late. I picked up my tailored navy blue suit from the cleaners and had my white shirt pressed and starched the previous morning. Everything was laid out on the bed in my guest room, along with my tie, blue gators and matching rawhide attaché. My gold cufflinks and presidential Rolex were on the marble stand near the bed, and my gator-skinned belt was hung across the door. I looked over at the bulky mass beside me under the covers.

Beverly was a nice girl, with a born-to-be-fucked figure. I liked her, because she understood her role in my life and she didn't press me for anything more. I even enjoyed the way she took charge in the bedroom, especially because she was sure to take orders in the workplace. Our little arrangement was working out fine, until yesterday. I didn't know why, but she was jealous of Roxanne. She didn't have to say it, because I could see it for myself. Well actually, I didn't fully realize it until my traditional thirty minutes of fellatio was cut down to an infinitesimal thirty seconds and her usual unquenchable sexual voracity was appeased in ten minutes. To top it off, I had to administer my own self-alleviation when she made it crystal clear that she had already reached her destination and wasn't interested in traveling any farther.

"Beverly," I whispered loudly, nudging her awake.

She sucked her teeth. "What?"

"I'm leaving soon."

"What does that have to do with me?" She pulled the covers up to her chin and turned away from me.

"Nothing. Just make sure you lock the door on your way out. I wouldn't want to be the victim of a chance robbery. YouknowwhatImean?"

"Whatever."

From the backseat of the yellow cab, I watched the different sights and sounds of the city, and smiled at my own cleverness. I asked the concierge to go up and check the door locks once my company left, and gave him a $100 tip for incentive. I learned my lesson the hard way a few years back, when an old girlfriend staged a robbery and took off with $500,000 of my most precious possessions. The police said it was an inside job, and Susan's mysterious disappearance backed up their claim. When she resurfaced, she was too doped up to even realize who I was, or what I wanted. So with the assistance of a Brompton cocktail, I proclaimed myself the Messiah and sent Judas to the New Jerusalem. I promised myself she was the last white woman I'd get involved with, and I'd never stray too far from my religion. I've kept at least half of that promise. Although Beverly was white, she wasn't Jewish. She was Baptist, like me, and I didn't really consider her a girlfriend or an involvement. She was merely someone to do until the right person came along. YouknowwhatImean?

My mind reflected on Rachel. She was the kind of woman who could make a man like me settle down and leave all the bullshit behind. And I would have. All she had to do was say the word, but she never did. Instead, she contributed to my flaws, and I became her supplier. When it was clear all my money, cars and jewelry couldn't make her happy, I ultimately found something that did. Heroin. I knew she was only with me for the drugs, but with a beauty like Rachel by my side, I figured it was okay to pretend. If it were drugs she wanted, then drugs were what she would get. Plentiful doses. Limitless reserves. Complimentary rations. All to win her heart. But her heart belonged to someone else. Even the drugs couldn't cure her longing to be elsewhere whenever I was around. When I came in one evening, and caught her staring at Mark's picture with tears in her eyes, reality hit. She would never be mine, not completely. I could no longer make believe that one day she would. So I did what any other man would do in my situation, I took away her happiness. Tit for tat. YouknowwhatImean? She spent the next few days lip-locked with a bottle of Southern Comfort, begging me for a hit every now and then, but I wouldn't oblige her. After a week of binging, she came to me one night and crawled into my arms like a child. She kissed my lips so gently.

"Why are you doing this to me?"

I didn't answer. I felt myself softening, and knew that any words I uttered would be half-hearted and weak.

"Royal, I love you." She looked deep into my eyes.

I knew in my heart she was lying, but I wanted so badly to believe she really did. Rachel was a virgin and had vowed to stay celibate until she was married. When she finally gave herself to me that night, she convinced me that I was the one. It was all I ever wanted. In return, I gave her what she needed—a fix. She polished off her newly opened bottle of Southern Comfort, and disappeared into the bathroom. When twenty minutes passed, and she hadn't returned to our bed, I began to worry. I busted the door open, and gagged. Rachel was lying on the floor. A frothy white liquid was oozing from her nostrils. The syringe was hanging from her vein. The tourniquet was still in place on her arm. Her eyes were wide open. I reached over, pulled down her eyelids and cried.

"That'll be twelve-fiddy," the driver's words cut into my memory. He reached an unclean, ebony palm over the back seat.

I paid him, stepped onto the curb and looked down at my watch. It was one fifteen. I walked into a coffee shop next to the bank, and sat down to a piping hot cappuccino. I let my mind wander again. It was unfair what happened to Rachel, but Roxanne was my second calling. She had to be. It all added up now. It was kismet. The fact that Mark Watkins was a part of her life was some sort of omen. YouknowwhatImean? This time, I won't fuck it up. I knew now she walked into my bar for a reason. It was time for me to make amends. *I'm going to make it up to you Rachel. I promise.*

ROXANNE

When I hung up the phone with Ayana, it was going on five o'clock. Mark would be home soon, and I still hadn't gotten out of bed for the day. I looked over at the picture of him on the nightstand, and smiled. I must say, when he first told me he had unprotected sex with me while I was passed out, I wanted to choke the shit out of him. I would have, but his sincerity stopped me. He not only told me how much he loved me, he actually showed me. His dick game screamed forever and commitment. Everything I'd ever wanted, and for once, I stopped fighting him and gave in. I forgot about Ayana and Royal and concentrated on his love and devotion and let it all go. I reminded myself that forgiveness begins with me, and I wanted so badly to be forgiven. After so many years of misery, I was finally going to allow myself redemption. See Mama, I told you that you *could* grin when you're thinking about salvation.

I crossed over to the bathroom and turned on the water in the shower. I leaned against the sink, inhaling the vapors while the steam rose above the curtain rod. The doorbell rang just as I slipped out of my gown. Damn, who the hell could that be?

The doorbell rang again.

"Coming!" I yelled, as I grabbed my robe off the door hook and exited the bathroom. "Who?" I screamed, looking through the peephole. I couldn't quite make out the figure on the other side of the door, especially because whoever it was made sure they were off-centered.

"Delivery for Roxanne Linden," the male voice said.

I opened the door, and looked up at the familiar face. I stared deep into his dark, piercing eyes and shuddered. "How...how did you find me?"

"It wasn't too hard. YouknowwhatImean?"

I pulled the robe around my body, and nearly cut off my circulation as I tied the belt tightly around my waist. I looked back up at Royal and tried to stop my body from shaking. He was grinning, obviously enjoying my uneasiness.

“Can I come in?” he asked and entered before I had a chance to object. He moved into the room and spun around. Taking in everything from the champagne glasses Mark and I left on the table to the stack of crumpled papers on the floor beside my computer desk.

“Are you a writer?” He turned to face me.

“What? Um, no. I’m not.”

“Then what is it that you do?”

I shook my head, and wiped across my face with the palms of my hands. I exhaled and tried hard to gain control of this awkward situation. “Excuse me, Mr...”

“Royal.” He moved closer to me. “The name is Royal. However, I’m not sure if I should call you Rhonda or Roxanne. YouknowwhatImean?” He smiled again, showing off his gold-encrusted teeth.

“It’s Roxanne, and I don’t know what happened between us the other night, but you seem to have gotten the wrong impression. Now, I don’t want to seem ungrateful or rude, but you’ll have to leave before my husband comes home and finds you here.”

"Your husband? I didn't know the two of you were married." He smirked.

"There's a lot you don't know about me, and unfortunately, there's a lot you never will."

"Unfortunately?" he questioned, turning towards my laptop. He clicked on the power button, and watched as the screen came to life.

"What are you..."

"Shhh." He held a long, dark finger up to his lips and winked. "Be patient. I have only one last thing to share with you, and then I'm gone. I know when I'm not wanted, and I'm not about to stick around trying to convince you I am. YouknowwhatImean?"

He typed a few words on the screen, breezed past me and walked over to the door. He blew a kiss towards me and exited. I shrugged off his gesture, ran to lock the door, and stared over at my laptop. The screen appeared ten times bigger, and I heard his voice calling me. I moved towards the table slowly. Almost afraid to look at the message sprawled across the screen. But curiosity got the best of me. If I were a cat, I'd be dead by now.

The Way To A Woman's Heart Is Through Her Soul. P.S. Check Your E-Mail.

That was what Royal's message said. I didn't quite know what it meant, but I was logged onto the Internet, examining my e-mail before I knew it. The first message was from Mark. *I'll check that one later.* My eyes canvassed the files searching for Royal's message. It wasn't too long before I found it and displayed it on the screen. The subject line read: *Virtual Florist Bouquet Delivery*. I wasn't sure what that meant either, but I couldn't help but smile. I opened up the e-mail and was soon directed to the Virtual Florist website, where I could pick up my bouquet. I entered the pickup code, SXB5703, and was amazed at the sight that greeted me. Royal had sent me a Virtual Flower Bouquet, which consisted of a dozen long-stemmed, red roses, and the following greeting: *ABOUT LAST NIGHT...BEAUTY COMES IN MANY SHADES. MY SHADE OF BEAUTY IS YOU. I WOULD LOVE TO GET TO KNOW YOU BETTER—ONE ON ONE. HOW ABOUT TONIGHT? SAME PLACE, SAME TIME.*

"Is he for real?" I asked the computer as I clicked the icon for a return message. Just as I readied myself to type, my cell phone rang. "Hello," I answered.

"Well, are we on?"

"What are you psychic?" I asked, already knowing how he got my cell number.

"No, I just figured you to be the inquisitive type, and I guess I was right."

"Well, maybe you were, but you were wrong about us..."

"So we're not on?"

"No Royal, we aren't. As I was going to say, I was just about to e-mail you to tell you that I have to decline your offer."

"Is that so?"

"Yes it is."

"What? You didn't like the flowers? I thought all women loved roses."

"Well, many women do love roses, and I'm no exception to the rule. I just don't think it would be wise to see you again. I'm sorry."

"Don't be. You declined this time, but maybe next time you'll say yes."

"I doubt it."

"I don't. See ya, Roxanne."

"Don't count on it, Royal."

"And don't count against it. YouknowwhatImean?"

MARK

I didn't feel like the normal commute today, so I grabbed a taxi from Times Square and made my way uptown via the West Side Highway. I looked down at my watch. It was a little after five and I was already home. I should definitely do this more often. As I exited the cab outside of my building, I caught a glimpse of a man that favored Royal entering a taxi across the street. No, it couldn't be. I tried to get a better look, but a large moving van blocked my view. By the time it cleared the taxi it was too late. I stood motionless watching the cab move down the street until it was completely out of my sight. *Mark, get a grip,* I thought, as I entered the building.

Inside the elevator, I looked up at the lighted numbers, counting off the floors as the bell rung with each passed stop. I found myself smiling. Roxanne and I had an unforgettable night, and I couldn't wait to make her my wife one day. In a couple of months I'd also be out of debt. That meant no more weekly visits from that low-life, Royal. *What was he doing here anyway?* I couldn't stop obsessing over the man in the taxi. If it were Royal, what the hell was his purpose for being here? I thought Roxanne and I had an understanding, or maybe it was just a front. She did give in pretty easily, and that wasn't like her at all.

I stepped off the elevator, and moved towards the apartment with a vengeance. This wouldn't be the first time Roxanne played me, and if I let it go like I'd done in the past, it sure as hell wouldn't be the last. *Well, at least this time it's with a man*, I thought. I turned my key in the lock and entered the apartment. I heard the shower running, and all kinds of crazy thoughts flooded my mind. *She's in there scrubbing off all the evidence, my man. What are you going to do now?*

I walked down the hall, and sat on the edge of the bed facing the bathroom door. I knew there was going to be a confrontation, and it sure as hell wasn't going to be pretty. But unlike all the other times, I was ready.

The shower turned off and moments later Roxanne emerged dripping wet. She had a terry towel over her head, drying her hair with one hand. The other hand clasped a second towel she had wrapped around her body. It barely covered her assets and I could feel my Johnson slowly rising. Focus, man, focus. She pulled the towel on her head down around her shoulders and was startled by my presence. The other towel dropped to her feet, showing off that sweet cavern that made me blind with lust and insane with passion. My Johnson was at full tilt and I felt like I was about to explode.

"I didn't hear you come in." She walked over to the vanity nonchalantly and took a seat. She didn't even bother to replace the towel that had fallen at her feet. Instead, there she was—bare-ass to the world, brushing through the tangled mass of wool growing from her head. "Hard day at work?" she asked with her eyes closed, enjoying the feel of the bristles against her scalp.

"I should be asking you that question," I tried hard to sound angry, when the only thing I wanted to do was replace my face with the vanity's stool.

"What's wrong with you?" She turned towards me, giving me her full attention.

I was speechless. All the nasty accusations that lingered on the base of my tongue refused to come to the surface. Sitting there, looking at her shapely bosom and thick, moist thighs was more than a man like me could handle. In one motion, I transported her from the vanity to the bed. Two seconds later, I exited my business suit and entered heaven. On the verge of euphoria, a vision of the man getting into the taxi popped into my head, and my dedicated private now stood at ease.

"What happened?" Roxy whined, as I slid out of her and fell to my side of the bed.

"Nothing."

"Nothing?"

"Yes, nothing. I just fell out of the mood."

"You fell out of the mood?" she asked, getting louder. "While you were in the middle of the mood, you fell out of the mood? What's the problem?"

"There is no problem, just leave it alone."

"Leave it alone? You get me all hot and bothered waiting for the thrill of a lifetime, and then you pull out in mid thrust and expect me to leave it alone? Either you're going crazy or you're trying to make me. So, what the fuck is the problem?"

"Don't curse at me, Roxy. I'm warning you!" I felt all the venom from half an hour ago rebuilding in my system, and I was ready for action.

"Warning me? You have the nerve to start shit up, don't finish, and then cop a fucking attitude. What the fuck am I missing here?"

"I should be asking you that question, Mrs. Clean."

"And what the fuck is that supposed to mean?"

"Cut the shit, Roxy." I calculated my next phrase so that it had the right amount of anger, with just enough sadness to maintain my status as victim. "I saw when he left. Now, all I want to know is how long it's been going on?"

"What are you talking about?"

Oh, she's good, I thought, as she stared at me emotionless. I didn't sense any betrayal, or surprise or any feeling whatsoever. Be that as it may, I wasn't going to stop there. "Did you think I'd never find out about the two of you?"

"The two of who? Mark, if you don't stop fucking with me, you're going to wish I'd pull my dick out of *your* ass. Now, what the fuck are you talking about?" She asked this through gritted teeth.

"Nothing." I stood and entered the bathroom.

Once inside, I sat my bare bottom down on the edge of the tub and listened as Roxy slammed drawers and closet doors. I scanned the room, and my eyes became fixated on a pair of hot pink, satin panties lying in a ball by the toilet. Before I knew it, my private was back in gear, ready for that ten-mile hike.

I found myself on my knees, sniffing at Roxy's panties like dogs sniff at each other's asses. Smelling my territory. Familiarizing myself with the scent. Making sure it was safe to enter. I picked up the panties, brought them to my nose and inhaled the vapors. The aroma was that of red cinnamon and black molasses—thick, rich and sweet. Not since my teenage years had I felt so naughty and deceptive. It dawned on me, this scent belonged to Roxy. It didn't embody the musty funk of a man's fiery groin. It was flowery and feminine and it was turning me the fuck on.

I kept the panties to my face, as my free hand embraced my genitals. There I was. A grown-ass man. Butt-naked on the bathroom floor. Jerking off to the scent of my girlfriend's essence, and I didn't give a flying fuck who knew it. I caressed my member gently at first, increasing the power of each stroke as Roxy's fragrance invaded my nostrils. I moaned with pleasure, as my hand taunted me into a frenzy. I crunched into a semi-fetal position as the force of my blows intensified, and I found myself on the verge of orgasm. I finally let the panties drop from one head to the other, wrapping it tightly around my private. Readying him for the approaching storm. Oh, what a glorious storm it would be. My body jerked violently as the panties seemed to take on a life of its own. Enclosing my penis inside its warmth and bringing me to new heights, as my love spurted viciously into its silky material. I moaned with delight. Not only for the task at hand, but also for getting away with it.

I lie on the bathroom floor with the panties around my member and smiled. Roxy wasn't cheating on me after all.

AYANA

When will I ever learn? I thought, as I put the finishing touches on my baked ziti. I invited Jasmine to dinner when I already promised myself I wouldn't travel down that road again. But this time would be different. At least I hoped it would. I now had a purpose, and with Roxanne back in my life, I also had focus. I would simply tell Jasmine there was someone else, and I no longer wanted to see her. This time if she put her hands on me, I'd call the police.

The doorbell rang right on time. I popped the ziti back in the oven, pulled off my apron and placed it on the hook. I walked over to the door and opened it nervously.

"Chocolates for my chocolate princess." Marlon handed me a box of candy and a cute, pink teddy bear.

"What are you doing here?" I asked, exasperated. Jasmine would be here any minute, and the last thing she needed to see was Marlon—and vice versa.

"What kind of greeting is that? Aren't you glad to see me?"

No. Now move the hell away from my door before I call security. "Of course, I am." I surrendered to his powerful embrace.

He bent to kiss me, and his tongue probed my mouth masterfully. I wanted to take him right there at the threshold—door wide open and all. I lost myself in the tenderness of his kiss, and it threw me completely off guard as a familiar voice boomed behind him.

"Is this why you invited me to dinner?" Jasmine asked, pushing her way past Marlon, and entering the living room. "Ayana, who is this?"

I was too frightened to turn around. My feet were locked in their position, and I felt weak. Then complete darkness. I guess Marlon caught me before I hit the floor.

The scene I awoke to was definitely an unexpected one. Marlon and Jasmine had taken it upon themselves to start dinner without me. They were seated side by side at the foot of my bed, sipping champagne. Completely engrossed in conversation—and each other. I coughed loudly to make my presence known. They both turned to face me.

"I thought we lost you for a minute there," Jasmine said. She stood, placed her plate on the top of the dresser, and walked over to me. "Are you okay?"

"I guess so," I whispered.

"Well, you really had us worried," Marlon chimed in. He placed his plate next to Jasmine's and sat on the edge of the bed opposite her.

Here I was stuck in the middle of the two people who truly loved me, and I was confused. I didn't know what either of them knew, and I sure as hell didn't want to be the one to have to bring the truth to light. Imagine. Jasmine, this is Marlon, the man I've been fucking, and Marlon, this is Jasmine, the woman I've been fucking. There was just no sweet way to put it. So I stayed silent. I pushed my head deeper into the pillow, and brought the covers up around my neck for protection. I looked from Marlon to Jasmine, from Jasmine to Marlon and then up at the ceiling. Lord, please help me get out of this one.

"Are you going to be all right?" Jasmine asked.

"Yes," I murmured.

"Good, because Marlon and I were talking, and..." She trailed off.

"And...," Marlon continued. "We figured since you seem to want the best of both worlds, why not have the best of both worlds all at once?"

You've got to be kidding me. "What?" I managed to ask.

"You heard us," Jasmine said, stepping out of her shoes and kneeling down on the edge of the bed.

I couldn't believe this was really happening. I looked up, and Marlon and Jasmine were slowly undressing themselves, while flirtatiously ogling each other. Jasmine bent to kiss me, and the taste of champagne rolled off her tongue onto mine. Marlon gently pulled the covers off of me, and took his usual position at the foot of my bed. He inched my panties down off my waist, past my thighs, slowly down my knees, and quickly off my feet. He spread my legs with his and buried his head between my thighs. I writhed with pleasure as Jasmine began fondling my breasts, and suckling my nipples.

Moments later, I felt Marlon's penis take the place of his tongue and I could feel my opening moisten and contract as it enveloped him. Jasmine was working double time on my breasts, and the only thing I wanted to do was taste her. I positioned her backwards on my lips, and delved my tongue deep into her milky triangle. She was facing Marlon, and he now had her breasts clasped and they were kissing. The sound of our moans was too much for me to handle. I began moving my hips underneath Marlon with a vengeance. I grabbed hold of Jasmine's waist and pulled her further into me—taking all of her into my mouth. We all shook in unison with the satisfaction of well-deserved orgasms. I fell back on the bed and Jasmine bent to kiss me. Then she asked the unthinkable.

"Do you mind?" She took residence atop Marlon's lap.

Well if I did mind, it sure as hell didn't matter now. I watched in horror as Jasmine made love to my man in my bed, using all the moves she used on me. Marlon was falling victim to Venus' flytrap, and there was nothing I could do about it. Jasmine had undoubtedly taken over my sacred territory, and by the looks of things, Marlon sure as hell didn't mind a bit.

"Oooh," she cooed, as Marlon hit the spot I trained him to locate. All of his moves were impassive. Methodical even. But it didn't seem to matter. As the two of them swayed to their own jungle beat, my mind ran rampant with disillusion and doubt. Why in the hell did I allow this to happen?

"Oh, Marlon, you're wonderful," she purred, as he bent his head to nurse her breasts. She arched her back into a perfect angle, and curled her legs tightly around his back. His strong arms lifted her up and down on top of him. My bed pulsated with each elevation and release, and I was beginning to feel nauseated.

"Come here, sexy," I heard Marlon say and knew he must be talking to Jasmine. To my surprise, he had already pulled me up and bent me over the edge of the bed. He filled up my anal opening in a matter of seconds and was thrusting like a wildebeest before I even had a chance to object. *For Heaven's sake, at least change the fucking rubber.* As I opened my mouth to protest, Jasmine crawled through my open legs, and began licking my vagina like it was a melted ice cream cone. Her tongue went up and down the inside of my lips. Canvassing my clitoris. Taking stock of each and every pubic hair. Feasting on my love as if it were her last supper.

Moments later, Marlon let out a ferocious moan and shivered with relief behind me. He slowly released himself and staggered over to the bathroom. I wanted to jump off the bed and run inside with him where it was safe, but I was too afraid to move. I was paralyzed with anxiousness and I didn't know what to expect. For the first time since the big revelation, Jasmine and I were alone. I knew she was a ticking time bomb ready to explode.

"Is this your way of saying good-bye, Ayana?" she whispered, as she took her usual position atop my torso.

"I don't know."

"You don't know? Either it's good-bye or it isn't. Are you sure you're ready to let me go?"

"I don't know that either." I was certain any other response would have caused a scene I was not prepared for. "Why are you asking me that now?"

"Well, when am I supposed to ask you? After Superdick tries to cut me in half a second time? If it was dick I wanted Ayana, I would have stayed at home with my husband."

"Well, if it wasn't dick you wanted, Jasmine, why the hell did you fuck him? Was it to satisfy me? I don't think so. From all the fucking oohs and aahs, I know it wasn't."

"Ayana, are you jealous?" She laughed.

"As a matter of fact, I am."

"Of whom?" she asked, seriously. "Him or me?"

"I don't know." I heard the change in her tone and knew the truth would just offset the fucking timer.

"What do you mean, you don't know? Either you're upset that you had to share me with him or you're upset that you had to share him with me, or is it both?"

"Jasmine, I said I don't know. Now leave it alone."

"Fine, if that's the way you want it. But hear this, I will not be taken for granted, and I will not sit idly by and watch you and Romeo live happily ever after. You said you want the best of both worlds, and you just got the best of both worlds. But if you don't keep partaking in the best of my world, then I'll just take your place in Marlon's."

"Is that a threat, Jasmine?"

"No, Ayana, it's not a threat. It's a motherfucking promise."

Great. Here I was, in the midst of some shit that I couldn't get out of as easily as I thought. I was caught between two of the three people in my life that I loved. One of which I knew I had to let go immediately, and the other whom I could continue to lead on until I had Roxanne all to myself. My perfect picture was now blurred, and I wasn't sure which route destiny had chosen for me to take. I finally reached my fork in the road, and I still didn't have a clue as to what I was supposed to be—a woman who loved women, but fucked men, or a woman who loved men, but fucked women. I'll tell you one thing, this bisexual shit was not all it was cracked up to be.

ROXANNE

I didn't know what had gotten into Mark tonight, but I had enough. Accusing me of shit that I hadn't even done. Well, at least not yet. I could say his behavior led me back there, but I would be lying to myself. I couldn't put a finger on it, but it was something more. It was like a strong force that I had no control over. No matter how much and how hard I tried, I couldn't fight it. I knew I was making a big mistake the moment I walked in, but I couldn't stop myself from going all the way. I stepped inside, and saw him immediately. My feet led me straight to his table. His face brightened, and he smiled radiantly.

"I'm glad you made it," he said.

I looked down at the table. Two dozen long-stemmed white and red roses were in a gold vase. A bottle of champagne was chilling in a gold ice bucket, and matching flasks were hanging to each side. "By the looks of things, I see you were sure I would."

"I wasn't sure at all. It was just wishful thinking. Hoping to God that my prayers would come true."

"You sure don't seem like the religious type to me..."

"Well, looks can be deceiving, youknowwhatImean?" Royal smiled at me seductively, and gestured towards the champagne. "Can I pour you a drink?"

"How about if I pour you a drink?" I reached for the champagne, popped the cork, and took a seat at the booth across from him.

"You must have known that I like a woman who can take charge."

"You must have known I was that type of woman." I handed him a glass. "However, we can't let ourselves forget I am involved, and very much in love."

"If that's how you truly feel, I'll keep that in mind. Although it's not really me that you're trying to convince with that line."

"What exactly does that mean?"

"What exactly does it sound like?"

"I don't know, but tonight, I can do without the bullshit. YouknowwhatImean?"

"Yes I do." He laughed loudly. "And I can oblige."

And oblige he did. Within the next four hours I found out a lot about Royal T. Roaman, and I had to admit I was sort of turned on. No, his enterprises did not start out on the up-and-up, but he managed to turn something negative into something positive. By the look and sound of it all, it had truly been lucrative. I mean, a condominium on Park Avenue, a timeshare in the Bahamas, a beach house in Puerto Rico, and various other properties was not bad for a man who started out as a petty thief and street hustler. Royal had street smarts, turned them into business savvy, and transformed my drunken ass into a groupie. There I was—lock, stock and barrel—hanging onto every word this motherfucker had to say, hoping like hell he was feeling half as horny as I was. I knew it was wrong to be there and for me to feel this way, but I didn't give a damn. My mind was telling me to get up and go home, especially because Mark didn't even know I left out. But just the thought of how he fucked with me earlier in the evening, kept me planted in my seat. Let that son of a bitch worry about me for a minute. I'm tired of always going along with his flow. Shit, I need a flow of my own. And perhaps, Royal here can help me find one. YouknowwhatImean?

"You all right?" he asked, cutting through the silence.

"Yes. Why do you ask?"

"I don't know. You just seemed deep in thought. You must be thinking about the husband, and he must be worried about you, too. Don't you think it's time you started heading home little lady?"

"Royal, I'm a big girl, literally and figuratively. I don't go home until I'm ready. Are you trying to get rid of me?"

"Of course not. I just don't want you to feel taken advantage of in the morning. YouknowwhatImean?"

"I'll put it to you this way, Royal. I may be a little smashed, but I know my limitations. If anything happens tonight it's not because I was impaired, it's because I wanted it to. Okay?"

"Okay then." He reached for my hand across the table. "Roxanne, I'm going to be straight with you. I would love to spend the night with you, and before you protest, sex is not the issue. I just feel very comfortable around you, and with you knowing my background and not giving me the heave-ho, it tells me that you like being around me, too. I just don't feel like sharing you with anyone anymore. I want your complete attention, in a comfortable, quiet atmosphere. So I'll just cut to the chase, and come out with it. Roxanne, would you please do me the honor of accompanying me home tonight?"

Hell no! What kind of woman do you take me for? "Of course, I will Royal."

I'll be a good girl, I promise.

Well, I was a great girl and Royal was no slouch either. "Here you go." I passed him a Kleenex off the end table.

"What's that for?" He kissed my shoulder.

"The condom. What do you think?"

"The condom? You know I took that off." He made wet circles on my neck with his tongue.

"What? You took it off?" I sat up and looked at Royal like he was crazy.

"Hell yeah. I asked you if it was okay, and you said yes."

"I said no such thing. What are you talking about? Please, don't fuck around like that." I tried to laugh it off, but Royal's expression told me he wasn't joking. I moved away from him.

"I'm not fucking around. I asked you if you wanted to feel all of me, and you said yes."

"That was supposed to mean that you were pulling off the fucking condom?"

"What else is it supposed to mean? I know you felt the difference." He reached for me and I pulled away.

"How the hell can I feel the difference? A dick is a dick—condom or no condom. It's the same fucking feeling once I'm wet and you're in there. Why the fuck would I tell you to take the son of a bitch off?"

"Listen, calm down...,"

"Don't tell me to calm down, Royal. I'm pissed off, and I'm going to stay pissed off. Okay?" I jumped up and pulled on my dress.

"Roxanne…" He stood and grabbed me tightly around the waist. "It was just a matter of miscommunication. Believe me, everything is going to be all right. I didn't mean to upset you. I just wanted to be with you so badly that when you said that you wanted to feel all of me, I just went with it. I'm sorry. I just don't know what else to say. YouknowwhatImean?"

"Save it, Royal. I fucked you, and now I'm fucked. I guess I'll just have to pay for my sins and ask God's forgiveness on Judgment Day."

"What's that supposed to mean?"

"Did you cum in me?"

"Of course, I did, but…"

"Then you know what it means," I countered. "Good-bye Royal." I walked out of his bedroom. It was too dark. I was in a rush to leave and I couldn't find my panties, but that didn't stop me from slamming the front door behind me, and running down the stairs.

Once outside, with my ass out to the wind, I ran around the corner down a few blocks, around another corner down a few more blocks, around two more corners and ended up at Central Park. It would have been just my luck that some maniac would have pulled me in and raped me. Well, at least that would be the reason Mark's baby wouldn't look like him. My mind clouded over with all types of thoughts. What if Royal managed to do in one night what Mark had been trying to do for the last three years? It would be like a Maury episode or some shit. All I could do as I stood on the corner trying to hail a cab was think of my options. The only thing that popped into my mind at the thought of me being pregnant by Royal was abortion. At the rate I was going—lesbianism, lying, adultery and now abortion—I knew my ass was going straight to hell with gasoline drawers on.

ROYAL

What just happened here? One minute, I was making love to my second calling. The next minute she was gone. What the fuck went wrong? I did everything she asked me to do. I moved with her, screamed out her name. I even went downtown and that was something I never did. Fuck that. Let these bitches scrape up their knees blowing me, not vice versa. Besides, I was never big on sucking out some shit that pisses daily and bleeds once a month. And that's not regular blood either. That's that real internal film. That fleshy, could have been a baby shit. So, thanks, but no thanks. That was, until Roxanne—and she still wasn't satisfied. But I wasn't going to stop at that. I got her once, and if she turned out to be pregnant with my seed, then I'd have her forever. You could bet on it.

I don't know what time I fell asleep, but I awoke at five thirty completely naked and aroused. The thought of having sex with that erotic godsend weighed heavily on my mind, and I couldn't stop my hand from reaching downwards to stroke my taut erection. I reflected on the way her bosom slid across my chest as her hips engulfed my manhood. The way she bellowed my name so sweetly when I positioned her on her back and inserted myself into her caramel crock pot. I could still feel the power of her thick legs holding my waist in a vice grip, her heels digging into my back, and her fingernails cutting into my shoulder blades as she professed her lust and longing for me. My ejaculation was pure bliss, and I was careful to cum directly into the same Kleenex Roxanne had passed me hours earlier. Not only because of the eroticism of where the Kleenex came from, but because cum stains were almost impossible to remove from satin sheets. YouknowwhatImean?

I turned to put the Kleenex in the garbage, and saw a black object peeking out from behind the wastebasket. I stepped down off the bed and retrieved what turned out to be black lace panties. Roxanne must have left them behind for me. A token of our night together. I held them to my heart and smiled. Roxanne was to be my redemption for all the fucked up things I'd done in my life. She was to be my new Rachel, and I had already messed up. I had to make amends. I just wasn't sure where to start.

My cell phone vibrated loudly, cutting into my thoughts. Who the fuck could that be this early in the morning?

"Hello."

"Where the fuck have you been all evening?" It was Beverly and she was heated.

"Home."

"Then why haven't you been answering your phone?"

"Beverly, what do you want?"

"I want to know why you were ignoring my calls. Were you too busy fucking your new black bitch?"

"What are you talking about?" My mood darkened instantly and my voice took on a heightened tone.

"Royal, what the fuck am I? Your token white pussy? Don't you think I have feelings, too? Isn't it enough that you paraded that bitch in my face all evening in front of everybody? Then you had the audacity to go home with that black whore, leaving me to lock up your fucking bar. That's supposed to be our job, and I'm supposed to be the one leaving with you."

"First of all, locking up the bar is the job of whoever I say it is. If I tell you to do it, then you just do it. As far as you being the one who is supposed to leave with me, yes you are my token white pussy, to use your own words."

"Royal, I…"

"Beverly, I never said I was in love with you. I never told you that I was going to be committed to you. As a matter of fact, I thought your place in my life was already etched in stone. YouknowwhatImean? When the fuck did all that change, and when the fuck did it turn around to me having to answer to you about my whereabouts."

"Royal…"

"Shut the fuck up! If I choose to fuck Roxanne, then that has nothing to do with you. The only time my dick should be your concern is if you're sucking it, or I'm fucking you. Now, if that is too much for you to handle, you can come by tomorrow, clean your shit out my bottom drawer and be gone."

"Just like that Royal?" I could hear that she was now crying, but I didn't give a fuck. Who the hell did this bitch think she was to be badmouthing the love of my life? If she were lying here next to me, I would have slapped the taste right out of her mouth. "Don't I mean anything to you?"

"No Beverly, you don't." With that, I hung up.

I needed a drink and remembered I was all out of brandy. I had forgotten to take the two bottles from my office when I left earlier with Roxanne. Fuck it. I quickly got dressed and made my way back over to the bar. I had to figure out a way to win Roxanne back, and Paul Masson was definitely going to help me figure it all out.

MARK

When I finally emerged from the bathroom, Roxanne was gone. I threw on my pajama bottoms and lay in bed. I tossed and turned for hours trying to figure out where she could have gone. My only thought was she had run into Royal's awaiting arms. *If you're not careful, you may be leading yet another one of your pretty little ladies into temptation.* I could hear his voice. See his face. Even smell his breath. I couldn't take it.

I walked into the living room and drowned my sorrows in a bottle of whiskey. I either fell asleep outright, or passed out from the liquor. Either way, I was sprawled out in the middle of the living room floor when I heard Roxanne's key turn in the lock. I sprung to my feet.

"Where the hell have you been?" I screamed, before she even had a chance to enter the apartment. I was ready for one of her smart-ass responses, and stood stoically awaiting my little tigress to chew me up and spit me out. But as Roxanne entered, I saw a tamer animal stood before me. I could see lines of salt trailing her cheeks, her crimson-colored eyes mere slits, and there was a look of despair on her face I had never seen before.

"Oh Mark," she cried as she fell into my arms. She grabbed me and clung to me as if she were hanging on for dear life. I searched her face for an explanation, and in her eyes all my questions were answered. Roxanne had reached the brink, and she needed me to save her before she took her final plunge into a sinful abyss. "Baby, I'm so sorry. I'm so sorry."

"It's okay." I walked her into the room and laid her back on the bed. I went back to the living room to fix her a drink.

Five drinks and two screaming matches later, the truth had come to light. I had lost yet another lover to Royal's wiles, and there was nothing I could do about it. He won. I lost. It was just that simple. I got dressed and walked out the door. My destination was unclear, but I knew I had to get away. I stepped out of the building, and hailed a cab.

"Where to?" the driver asked, with a thick Hindu accent.

Good question. I gave him directions to the only place that would have me.

As I walked the path of the fiery carpet to the front door, I knew that I would be face-to-face with Satan in a matter of moments, but this was something I had to do. I had to stop running, and learn how to face my problems like a man. I also knew the moment I stepped inside those doors, I'd be just like all the other so-called men who had come before me. To Royal, I'd be just another bitch. Another whore. Another piece of ass that he would surely have his way with. But it didn't matter to me. Nothing mattered to me anymore. It had to be done. Unlike all the rest, it would be at my request and not forced upon me. I was the ruler of my destiny, and this time around, I was looking forward to being fucked. I had a deep-seated compulsion to experience him completely—and I wasn't going to leave until he gave me everything he had. Once it was given to me, I could claim it and he and I would become one, thus giving me back all that had been taken away from me. I didn't quite understand what all that meant myself, and I knew that I was no longer making any sense. I was insane and irrational, but where the fuck could I find sanity and rationality in my situation? My life had been stolen from me a second time, and in order for me to get it back, I had to take it back. In like a lamb, out like a lion.

"Surprise, surprise," a drunken Royal said, as I approached his table. He looked as disheveled and fucked up as I did, and I couldn't understand why. Didn't he accomplish all that he set out to do? Didn't he make my life his? "I would ask you what the fuck you're doing here, but by the look on your face, I guess I already know the answer to that. YouknowwhatImean?"

I didn't say anything. I couldn't. Outside, I forgot how intimidating Royal really was. In the parking lot, I was a take-charge kind of guy, but standing here in front of his burly physique, staring into his dead eyes and smelling the alcohol seeping through his pores, I became that same little pussy from college. It was just he and I in the bar, and I still couldn't muster up enough courage to fuck him up. I wanted to smack the glass of brandy from his hand, and crack the bottle on his skull. I stood motionless, blinking back tears as I realized I would never beat Royal at his own game. Shit, if I wasn't careful, I'd meet the same fate Rachel did, although it wouldn't be from any kind of high. Unless, of course, they invent a new way for someone to become high off of gunpowder.

"Take a load off." He moved over in the booth, and patted the seat across from him. "I think it's about time that we talk all this out, anyway."

I sat down, just like a good, little boy. Where was my fucking spine? "Royal!" I trailed off. What the fuck was there to say? What the fuck was there to discuss? Why the hell did I come here anyway?

"Mark-O, listen to me."

"No, Royal, you listen to me." I had newfound power. "I don't know what you think is going to become of you and Roxanne, but you'll have her only over my dead body."

"Now Mark-O, you and I both know that can be arranged."

"Fuck you and your threats, Royal! I'm not scared of you anymore. There's nothing else you can do to me, you son of a bitch."

"Calm down, Mark-O." He handed me a drink.

"I don't want anything from you, Royal." I stood and smacked the glass out of his hand. It crashed to the floor and shattered, and for once I felt like a man. I hovered over Royal and looked down at him. He just stared back at me. He didn't say anything. He didn't blink. It didn't even look like he was breathing. I felt a yellow line creep up the base of my spine once again, as I anticipated the worst. It happened when Royal began to laugh in my face. Not a simple chuckle, but one of those rambunctious, side-splitting, teary-eyed laughs that stripped me of the one little piece of dignity I was still helplessly clinging to. His mission was accomplished, I felt like a fool. I walked out, as his laughter reverberated from the walls behind me.

AYANA

"Hello," I screamed into the receiver. There was no response. I slammed the phone back on its cradle and peeked over at the clock. It was going on six in the morning, and I still didn't get a wink of sleep. I wasn't sure of the exact time my company left, but I had to admit, I was happy to see them go. I just couldn't take it anymore, and I knew that it must have been Jasmine on the other line, making sure I hadn't trailed Marlon back to his place for seconds.

The doorbell rang. I remained still. What if it were Jasmine coming to do all she couldn't when Marlon was here? I surveyed the room, looking for a weapon, but there was none to be found. The doorbell rang a second time, then a third. A fourth. A fifth. Then whoever it was began to bang and kick erratically. I ran to the door, and swung it open.

"Oh, Yana." Roxanne fell into my arms. Tears streamed down her cheeks. She hugged me with such desperation that it caught me off guard.

"Roxy, what's wrong?"

"Everything, Yana. Everything."

"It's going to be okay, Roxy." I held her with one hand and locked the door with the other. I led her into my bedroom, and we sat on the edge of the bed. "What happened? Is it Mark?"

She shook her head "no" and sniffled, grabbing a wad of Kleenex from the box on my nightstand. "It's me, Yana. Once again, Roxy fucked up. And I mean I fucked up big time."

"What did you do? What happened? Talk to me Roxy…"

"I cheated on him, Yana."

"You've done that before, and he's forgiven you. So, what's the big deal?" I spoke matter-of-factly, because she and I both knew that Mark was a big pushover. "You say you're sorry. You tell him you love him, and everything will be okay. Mark loves you Roxy. Believe me, he's not going to let one night's infidelity jeopardize what the two of you have."

"But you don't understand, This is different. Before, it was..."

"I know. Before it was with a woman, and that woman was me, but since we are also considered family, our relationship doesn't exactly count. But it does—to me, to you and to Mark. And if he stood by you then, he'll definitely stand by you now. Was it another woman?" I was hoping like hell it wasn't.

"No."

Thank God. "Was he a friend of yours?"

"No."

"A stranger? A one-night stand?"

"No."

"Then who? Tell me something, Roxy."

"There's nothing to tell, Yana. I don't even know anymore. See, I met this man named Royal, who owns a bar on Third Avenue. Mark told me he and Royal had a past, but he never did elaborate. All he said was for me to stay away from him because he was bad news. Well last night, Mark and I got into our usual argument, and to get him back I returned to the bar. All I can say is one thing led to another and..."

"And, what? You're in love with him?"

"No, Yana, I'm in love with Mark. I know that now. I'm truly in love with Mark, but it's too late." She blew her nose loudly and grabbed for more tissue.

"Do you want a drink?" I asked, knowing that after these revelations I certainly needed one.

She nodded.

As I stood in the middle of my kitchen fixing drinks at the counter, I reflected on the evening's events. First, there was Marlon—sweet, fine Marlon, with his chocolate skin and strong embrace. I wanted so desperately to be with him, to live like a normal woman, but I still wasn't sure if that were possible. At least I knew now it definitely wasn't possible with Jasmine. Even if she wasn't married, I could not see myself committed to her for the long run. She was just too domineering. To think, the same thing that drew me to her in the beginning is the same thing that was making me hate her towards the end. Not to mention the fact that she was also abusive, and that was something I would no longer tolerate. Then God, in His infinite wisdom, straightened it all out for me. I knew He was the reason Roxanne showed up at my door. He wanted me to guide her into the light. Even if that light was at the end of my own personal tunnel. I returned to the bedroom and handed Roxanne the drink.

"Here you go."

"Thank you." She sipped the drink slowly, and looked up at me. Her eyes were red and her skin was pale and worn, but somehow she was still beautiful. "Ayana, I need your help."

"My help? In what way?"

She sighed loudly.

"Let it out, Roxy. You didn't come all the way over here at this time of morning to clam up on me." I pulled her towards me, and stared into her scarlet eyes. "Roxy, I love you, honey. No matter what it is, I'll do it. Okay?"

She nodded and began to cry against my shoulder. By force of habit, my hands began caressing her back. They moved up and down systematically, loving the feel of her plump flesh under my fingertips. I pulled her closer to me with each stroke. She returned the gesture, and we were soon kissing. Her tongue probed my mouth with force, searching for a purpose. Hoping to find a place she belonged. I didn't want to move too fast, so I eased up on my tongue gyrations and followed her lead. Her hands were soon on my breasts, and the softness of her touch ignited my sexual fire. I could feel the burning between my legs, and I pressed my thighs together tightly trying to smolder the flame. She gnawed softly on my ears then my neck, and her mouth soon took the place of her hand on my left nipple. She encircled it with her tongue, and ignited the blaze I tried so desperately to suppress. I quickly pulled away from her.

"What's wrong?" She tried to kiss me and I pulled away again.

"This is. I don't think we should do this. Not right now. It's not the right time."

She hung her head, and tears began to roll down her cheeks again.

"Roxy, don't cry." I held her closely. "You know I'm right. You always look to sex as your way out whenever you're upset, pissed off or confused."

"That's why I'm crying, Yana, because you're right. Even though it's something I've been dying to do since seeing you again, sleeping with you tonight would just make matters worse. I mean, I'm already fucked, and fucking you tonight would truly screw me."

"In more ways than one," I chimed in. For the first time that morning, I saw promise in Roxanne's eyes. We burst into laughter and continued to laugh away our blues until the sun finally seeped into my room through the closed blinds.

Roxanne was on her way to recovery, and I was simply caught up. How deep I'd be willing to go was beyond me, but I had already promised to do whatever she needed. If there was just one speck of a possibility that Roxanne and I would be together in the end, then I would do anything she wanted. Whatever it took.

ROYAL

Mark's visit meant one of two things. It was either a warning, or a plea for me to stay away from Roxanne. Either way, I couldn't guarantee that I would. Why should I? I mean, yes, I asked her here, but she came of her own free will. I told her to go home, and she wouldn't. When I invited her back to my place, she had every opportunity to decline my offer, but she didn't. I was not the villain here. Nor was I the victim. Circumstances just worked in my favor, and I had a chance to make love to my Angel, and it was well worth it.

"Good evening," Beverly said, as she entered my office, cutting short my trance. "I'm sorry I'm late. I was out with a male friend, and lost track of time."

"Is the fact that you were out with a friend supposed to matter to me? You never give me excuses any other time; don't feel the need to now. YouknowwhatImean?"

"Well, excuse me for trying to be professional here."

"Professionals are paid by the hour. You're paid by the day. Don't make this day your last."

"Royal, what has gotten into you?" She walked over and grabbed my arm.

"It's more like, who I've gotten into. Isn't it?" I pushed her hand away.

"Yes, it is."

"Well, that has nothing to do with you. End of conversation."

"End of conversation?" Her hands were now on her hips. "Royal, what about me? What does that mean for us?"

"It means that you're more than welcome to continue to pleasure me if that's what you would like to do, but if you were thinking along the lines of living out the American Dream with the first qualified Negro to sling the dick your way, I'm sorry baby, but it's not going to happen."

"First qualified Negro? Royal, when the hell did race become an issue?" She rolled her neck and folded her arms across her chest.

"When you made it one, Beverly. If Roxanne is a black bitch, what kind of bitch am I?"

"Royal, you're taking that completely out of context..." She threw her hands up.

"No, you're saying it was completely out of context." I jabbed the air as I said each word. "Or did you forget that she and I share the same skin color?"

"No, I did not forget. And that was just an expression." She fanned her hand at me.

"Well, here's another expression for you. Get your shit, and get out." I motioned towards the door.

"What?"

"I said get the fuck out of my office, and don't stop until you reach the pavement." With that, I spun around in my chair, and looked down on the crowd below.

"Don't you turn your back on me, Royal." She placed her hand on my shoulder.

I looked over at her, and hated myself for even getting involved with her in the first place. I stood, grabbed her hand roughly, and threw her down on top of the desk. "Don't you ever put your hands on me again. Do you hear me?"

"Yes," she said, weakly. She was now crying hysterically. I let her go and moved back an inch. "Why are you doing this to us, Royal?"

"Beverly, don't. Okay? It was fun while it lasted, but the moment has passed."

"How can you say that?" She reached for my belt. "Don't I make you happy, Baby?"

Before I could answer, she was on her knees, trying to suck the skin off my shit. Why is it when the going gets tough, white girls get on their knees? I let her pleasure me for a good half hour, before I finally relieved myself. Though I usually allowed her to pull away just as the liquid rushed out, I pulled her head firmly to my groin this time and made her swallow all of it just for spite. Besides, I wasn't really in the mood to clean up after myself. I had more important things to think about. "Are you through?" I asked her, as I withdrew myself from her lips.

"I don't know. Am I?" She stroked my penis.

"Yes you are." I pulled away, adjusted myself in my boxers and closed up shop. "Now, make sure you leave the keys with Susan on your way out."

"What! After I just..."

"Yes. Since you seem to take so much pleasure in it, I didn't think you'd be satisfied if I let you leave before the job was done. YouknowwhatImean?"

"Fuck you, Royal!"

"No, thank you, Bev. Now that you've sucked my dick, there's really no need for all that, is it? Now, if you'll excuse me." I turned my back to her.

"I can't believe I..."

"Beverly!" I jumped up. "I'm giving you three seconds to get the hell out of here on your own, before I escort you out personally!"

"Fuck you, Royal, I'm not going anywhere! This shit is far from over. You can't just play with my emotions, and think it's okay. You have not seen the last of me..."

"Hopefully for your sake, I have. Don't force me to fire you from existence, too. YouknowwhatImean?"

"If that's a threat, then hear this, I know everything about your dirty dealings motherfucker, and I'm not afraid to talk."

"You don't have to be afraid, but it's going to be kind of hard to talk when you're dead."

"Royal…"

I couldn't take it anymore. I stood up, pulled her by her mangy, brown hair, and snatched her out of my office. I pulled her down the stairs and ripped my keys from her bra. Her breasts were now exposed from the tear I made in the material, but I was oblivious to it. I didn't even hear the blood curdling screams Susan would later tell me she unleashed. My mission was to get her the fuck out of my establishment, and it wasn't until I tossed her ass out on the concrete that I was happy.

I returned to my office, hung my *Do Not Disturb* sign on the knob, and locked the door behind me. I kicked off my shoes, and layed down on my gold leather sofa. I readied myself for a much-needed nap, but sleep wouldn't come. I was too distressed, and didn't understand why I was in so much turmoil. Today should have been the happiest day of my life, but instead I was dealing with a bunch of bullshit. First Roxanne. Then Mark. Now Beverly. What the fuck was going on?

I thought I made Roxanne happy. I knew I did. I saw it as her body curved into mine. I felt it as she held on to me while I was inside her. I heard it as she moaned my name in ecstasy. It wasn't a dream. It was real. No matter what guilt or remorse she must now endure for Mark's sake, her feelings for me could not be denied. What I felt last night was love. For two hours of my life,

I could honestly say I was truly loved. Not because of what I could do for her, but for what I did to her. YouknowwhatImean? After the passing of my initial beloved, this feeling was something I couldn't take lightly. I sure as hell couldn't let the same tragedies befall Roxanne. I had to step in and take over. I had to achieve atonement. The only way for me to do that was to face up to the cold, hard facts. The most important being the reality that Rachel's murderer was still out there walking free. Worst than that, he and I were one and the same.

ROXANNE

I showered at Ayana's and put back on my same outfit. I couldn't fit into a damn thing in her closet, so I gave up trying to squeeze my big ass into her made-for-Barbie wardrobe. I wasn't ready to go back home to face Mark, but on a Saturday, where else could I go? I walked slowly down Lexington Avenue weighing my options, and then dipped into a small coffee shop on the corner. I took a booth in the back, and ordered a small breakfast and a large cup of cappuccino. As the frothy liquid warmed my throat, I recounted the events of the last twenty-four hours of my life.

I wasn't sure if I brought all the grief to myself, or if it was unavoidable. If Royal would have never showed up at my door, would Mark have come in with his accusations anyway? If Mark hadn't started the argument, would I have found some other excuse to sneak out to be with Royal? Perhaps in some abstracted state, I started the argument so I could have reason to leave. Maybe I was so smitten with Royal that I forced Mark to lunge at me. Maybe he knew for himself, even before it was apparent to me, that I was preoccupied with another man. That other man just happened to be someone from his past.

That was another thing. Just what kind of past did the two of them share? A shady one, no doubt. Especially because Royal was so corrupt and Mark was so virtuous, it couldn't be anything on the up and up. Maybe it had to do with money, or drugs. Shit, it could be a number of things, and I didn't have a clue. But I did have a plan. If everything went over smoothly, I would know exactly what that past consisted of. Perhaps I could even use it as leverage against them when the shit finally hit the fan, because I knew it undoubtedly would.

Just then my mind returned to Ayana's kiss, and I smiled. Ayana was going to help me find out just what Mark and Royal were hiding from me. I told her all I knew about Royal, and what he went for in a woman, and she said she would handle the rest. Exactly what that meant and what it entailed, I didn't know. All I knew was Ayana said she would have an answer for me as soon as possible, and she'd do whatever it took. I just hoped it didn't take her to the same place it took me, because I hated to think of the two of them together intimately. I guess that information would just make me angry. Jealous even. But once she got to know Royal the way I knew him, I couldn't blame her if she dabbled. Royal was like an Oreo cookie—dark and hard on the outside, but light and fluffy on the inside. His brutish physique hid the fact he was truly a gentleman. If I had met him before Mark, who knows? But since that was not the case, I had to put those feelings behind me and move towards reconciling with my man.

I looked down at my watch. It was going on two o'clock. I still wasn't ready to go home. As I finished off my last piece of toast, I tried to figure out my next move. I could go back to the bar and confront Royal, but I didn't think I was ready for that. I could go back to Ayana's and hide out for another night, but that wasn't an option. Especially because I couldn't guarantee we wouldn't wind up making love to each other. Sex would just confuse things even more, and open up a whole new can of worms. I could spend the day out and about and keep postponing the inevitable. Or, I could be a woman and just face the consequences of my actions.

I decided to go to the movies.

When I finally got home it was a little past two in the morning, and I wasn't drunk but I was tipsy. I figured if I had to throw myself to the lions, I might as well be feeling good. I walked into the house, and grabbed a bottle of whiskey off the bar that had about two swallows left in it. I made my way down the hallway and walked into the bedroom. Mark was lying on his side, fast asleep. I crept past him, and entered the bathroom. When I emerged, I was completely naked and smelling of perfumed lotions and bath oil. The bottle of liquor was gone, and I was feeling a bit frisky.

I crawled in bed behind Mark, and rubbed my breasts softly against his back. He moaned slightly, and continued to snore lightly. I rolled him onto his back gently, making sure not to wake him and pulled the covers down below his waist. To my surprise, Mark was completely naked too, and his staff was at full mast. *Guess I can cancel the blowjob.* I crawled on top of Mark and started moving rhythmically. He awoke with a groan.

"Roxy, is that you?"

"Who else would it be?" I asked throatily, lifting and releasing my body above him.

"What are you doing? Where were you all night and all day?"

"Fucking you and out, to answer your questions respectively," I moaned loudly.

"I mean, wha..." He trailed off as my gyrations became more powerful, and my pelvic muscles began to contract. He grabbed my ass cheeks and pounded them into his groin.

We kept up that sweaty episode for all of three hours, and then collapsed at each other's side with exhaustion. If making up always felt this good, then we sure as hell should argue more often.

MARK

Roxanne was snoring by the time I made my way back into the bedroom. We had just finished a three-hour sex marathon, and she was done. I stood over her sleeping frame and felt the tears well up in my eyes. I tried everything I could to stop them, but they were soon streaming down my cheeks, and I began bawling like a baby. Why was I always being hurt by the women who claimed to love me? Why didn't I stand up to Royal?

That night taught me one thing about myself that I had been trying to deny since day one—I was weak. Weak against the sins of the flesh, and weak in protecting myself from those who were trying to do me harm. I didn't know if Roxanne was as intentional as Royal in bringing about my downfall, but they were both doing a bang up job on my ego. It was time I put my foot down and took control of my life. Over the years, I had been able to do quite well for myself, despite many setbacks. I also had a little cash stashed away for a rainy day. Perhaps that storm had come, and it was time to reap the rewards of my success.

It felt close to 100 degrees in the elevator, as it descended to the basement. I felt like the Devil sinking into his fiery chasm, damned for all eternity. As the elevator doors opened, yet another rush of heat entered from the dryers in the laundry room. Customarily, I would lie in bed on Sunday's while Roxanne did the laundry, but today I needed to get away. I had to. I felt like my world was crashing in on me, and I couldn't take it.

As I was pouring detergent into the last machine, a sexy sister entered pushing a small cart of laundry. I took a seat on the bench and pretended to read the magazine I brought downstairs with me. In reality, the photos of the scantily clad women were no match for the real thing. I found myself watching this Nubian princess as she bent to load the two empty machines at the end of the row. She was close to naked, and I didn't consider the one-piece dress she was wearing to be a complete outfit. Not with all that flesh exposed. She pulled various shapes, sizes and forms of lingerie from a black, silk laundry bag, shaking them firmly before placing them into the machine. The stench of stagnant Egyptian musk invaded my nostrils. *She must be a stripper*. I couldn't help staring as she pulled a pair of sequined thongs and what appeared to be a matching bra out of the bag.

"Interesting magazine?" she asked, in a husky, sexual tone that made the hairs on the back of my neck stand, and caught me completely off guard.

"Um...yeah, very interesting." I turned the page and tried to concentrate on the magazine's contents.

"Well, if it's that interesting, why aren't you reading it?"

"I was. I mean, I am."

"No, you're not. In actuality, you've been watching me ever since I walked in here, and you haven't given that magazine any of your attention. But I ain't mad at you." She smiled.

I smiled back.

"Would you like to see more?" She closed the washing machine door and poured detergent and fabric softener into the marked compartments.

"Wh-what?"

"Since you seem to enjoy watching me so much, I asked if you would like to see more." She walked over and stood in front of me.

I was speechless. Standing before me was this gorgeous sister with a booming figure and cleavage for days, propositioning me. What exactly the proposition was, I wasn't quite sure. But it was a proposition nonetheless, and she was directing it towards me.

"Follow me," she said.

Fifteen minutes later, I was lying down on her white shag carpet butt-naked, with my Johnson stiff as a board. It turned out I was right. Monica Evans was a stripper. Her stage name was Mocha—and she was definitely a piping hot cup of something. She gyrated in front of me in a royal blue g-string and matching pasties. Rihanna's "Birthday Cake," was playing loudly in the background and with each bass drop, she rotated her pelvis and bounced her huge ass to the beat. She reached into a little box on top of her TV, and pulled out a condom. She kept with the rhythm of the music as she opened the wrapper and placed the condom in her mouth. She then bent down on all fours, and crawled towards me slowly and deliberately. She kissed my neck, spiraled down to my navel, and stopped at my midsection. I didn't know how she did it, but in the midst of blowing me, she had the condom securely wrapped around my penis, and she didn't even use her hands. The radio was now blasting French Montana and Nicki Minaj's "Freaks" and Mocha was in full thrust. She mounted my lap and took over.

"Do you like it rough?" she half grunted, half whispered in my ear.

"What?" I was a little taken aback. I mean, I don't mind being dominated when I'm on my back, but I don't want to be hurt either. Shit, I'm not the one to associate pleasure with pain.

"I said, do you like it rough?"

"What's your definition of rough?"

Instead of answering, Mocha laid flat on top of me squeezing her thighs together tightly, making sure that my manhood wouldn't slip out of her passage. With her toes resting on the floor, she reached down through my legs and palmed the carpet on either side of me. She then lifted my legs by the back of my knees and held their weight with her muscular arms. Her movement was now an up-and-down motion as opposed to in-and-out, and she tensed and released her pelvis with each movement. Although I felt like a bitch lying there with my legs in the air, and my knees parallel to my shoulders, I had to admit it felt damn good. I reached down and grabbed Mocha's ass cheeks, pulling her hips into mine. I could feel my manhood tensing, and I knew that I would soon be on the verge. Mocha must have felt it, too, because she eased up on her movements and released my legs.

"What the hell did you do that for? I was just about to cum."

"I know," she said as she kissed my neck. "I wasn't ready to join you. Besides, I'm not finished with you yet."

Mocha descended to my waist. Her mouth came down on my shaft with such force, that I shuddered from the impact. She gritted her teeth along its edges while she suckled me in and out of her throat. Her hands lifted my legs into an arc, and once again I found myself in another compromising position, but I didn't mind. Not until I felt Mocha's tongue thrusting into my rectum. I wanted to push her off of me, and slap the shit out of her, but I couldn't. The feeling was so intense, I couldn't move. Now I'm not gay or anything, but if a dick in the ass feels as good as a tongue, I can damn sure understand the infatuation. I started moaning loudly, pulling at hair, screaming out to the Lord and grabbing up shards of carpet, but it all didn't seem to faze Mocha. She just continued her oral audit of my forbidden cave. Licking me into a thrashing, groaning rage.

I couldn't take it anymore. I forced my legs down and pinned Mocha to the carpet. My Johnson slipped itself inside her, and I began thrusting powerfully. Then I had a change of heart. I withdrew from her vagina, and inserted myself into her rectum with timidity at first, and once I was completely inside, full force. Mocha's toes were practically touching the floor above her head, as I bent her into a pretzel-like position, and continued to ram myself deep inside her.

"Yes," she moaned. She dug her acrylic-tipped fingernails into my back. "Yes, you're hitting my motherfucking spot, Daddy."

Daddy? Now that's a first. I must admit, the incestuous vision she implanted in my head with that one epithet was too much for me to bear. "Whose is it, Baby?" I asked, increasing the pressure of my jabs.

"It's yours, Daddy."

"And who are you?"

"Mocha, Daddy," she yelped, squeezing my back tightly.

"No, you're Daddy's Lttle Girl." I eased up on the pressure. "And if you don't want Daddy to stop, then I want to hear you say it."

"Daddy, please don't stop." She grabbed my hips and pulled me into her.

"Then let me hear you say it. Who are you?"

"Daddy's Little Girl," she whispered.

“Who?” I increased the pressure a bit.

“Daddy’s Little Girl,” she said a little louder.

“I still can’t hear you, baby. Now unless you scream it, Daddy’s going to have to stop.”

“No Daddy, please don’t stop.” She moaned.

“Then scream it. Who the fuck am I?”

“Daddy,” she howled, digging her nails into my back again.

“And who are you,” I asked, pressing her toes onto the carpet.

“Daddy’s Little Girl! I’m Daddy’s Little Girl!”

“You’re damn right you are, and don’t you ever forget it.”

She began to climax. Her orgasm must have lasted all of ten minutes. I was inside her so long that I had a chance to cum, grow hard and cum again. Now, that’s what I call a good fuck.

AYANA

Roxanne acted like she was throwing me to the lions or something. The way she went on and on about Royal, she had me believing he was this supernatural, untouchable being. But the man who stood before me now was quite the opposite. He did have a somewhat barbaric appearance, but he had friendly eyes. Although he practically blinded me from the golden glare of his smile, I had to admit he sure was something to look at and I was definitely attracted. I had to pinch myself to regain my composure, because I was there for Roxanne. It was not a social call. As I followed Royal upstairs to his office, I had to hold myself back from reaching up and grabbing one of his ripe ass cheeks.

"Do you have any experience?" he asked, once we were behind closed doors.

"Yes and no." I pivoted to my right side, showing off just the right amount of thigh.

"Well, what don't you have experience in?" He sized me up then grinned.

"Bartending."

"Bartending?" He chuckled.

"Yes, bartending."

"Why are you applying for a position in which you have no experience? I'm a busy man, and..."

"And..." I quickly interrupted. "I am a very quick study, and I'm not adverse to working long hours. Especially when I have the right company." I licked my lips with intent and stared him dead in his eyes.

"I see. And what kind of salary are you looking for?"

"Whatever you're offering, I'm game. Besides…" I let each word roll sweetly off my lips. "Beggars can't be choosy, and I'm very easy to please."

"Good answer."

"I hope it's good enough to land me the job." I bit my bottom lip and hit him with bedroom eyes.

"Well honestly, I think you're just what I've been looking for. YouknowwhatImean?"

"I think I do, and in that case, I just hope I live up to your expectations."

"You already have." He reached over and rubbed my arm. "When can you start?"

"Two hours ago." I shuddered from the warmth of his touch.

Two hours later, I found myself behind the bar in a red leotard, beset with crimson fur and a plunging neckline. Royal himself stood beside me, pointing out the myriad variations of liquor and spirits. He gave me the rundown on prices and phony discounts, and taught me the correct alcohol measurements, ad nauseam. After an hour of practicing contrived orders, Royal put my skills to the test.

"I think you're ready to start little lady. Show me what you got."

"Yes sir." I saluted him and returned his hungry gaze.

I turned towards the bar just as a handsome, chocolate brother took residence on a barstool and summoned me over. Royal stepped back, and watched as I went to work.

"May I help you?" I asked sweetly.

"I certainly hope so," the gentleman smiled.

"What'll it be?"

"The seven digits I need to contact you with after your shift is over."

"I'll tell you what." I leaned over, showing off my glistening cleavage. "If you can last until my shift is over, the digits are all yours. Now, what can I get for you in the meantime?"

"A rum and coke, my love, and an ashtray." He unbuttoned his suit jacket and made himself comfortable at the bar.

"Coming right up." I placed an ashtray before him. I turned to fix his drink, and Royal sidled up behind me.

"I thought you said you didn't have any experience." He stared at me through the bar mirror.

"I don't." I looked over my shoulder into his eyes and almost melted. Damn, he was sexy. "I also said I'm a quick study. I guess you're just a great teacher. YouknowwhatImean?" I winked at him then went back to fixing the drink.

"Well, keep up the good work." He gave my ass a squeeze.

I quickly removed his hand, and returned to my customer. "Here you are, sir." I placed the drink on top of a serving napkin. "That'll be eight dollars."

"Keep the change." He passed me a crisp bill.

"Are you sure?"

"Yes I am. Since, I'll be here to closing, you can think of it as a very generous tip."

"Thank you." I looked down at the fifty-dollar bill in my hand and smiled.

Man, I can learn to like it here. I looked up at Royal, as I retrieved the change from the cash register. Shit, I can learn to love it here.

ROYAL

I know I said I'd never hire another sister, but there was something about Imani Daniels I just couldn't put my hand on. She was a classy lady, with a hint of tramp and she sure was a sight to look at. If I could have her and Roxanne, why, I'd be the happiest man on earth. From my office, I watched her closely as she served my customers with a finesse that had been missing from this place ever since I had to let Rita's ass go. But unlike Rita; hell, unlike any sister I've ever known, Imani understood her place. She was careful not to overstep her boundaries. At least not yet. But every woman had a breaking point, and it was my job to find out exactly where hers began.

As I watched one of my regulars take his usual residency on barstool number two, I knew I would have to look no further for the answer. Imani had been on her feet for close to eight hours, and she still didn't seem fazed. After one comment from this asshole, I knew her sweet façade would soon turn sour. I wanted to be standing right there when her bubble burst.

I opened my office door and began to walk down the steps. I reached the landing just as Imani turned her attention to Kent. Kent was a rich, white kid with too much money, too little ambition, and a tendency to find trouble wherever he went. The problem was two years ago, my bar had become his stomping grounds, and his problems always turned out to be my problems. If it weren't for the $700 bar tab he ran up nightly, I would be inclined to kick his ass out once and for all. But in this business, money talks, and I sure did love his conversation. YouknowwhatImean?

"Well, hello there," Imani said to him, with a smile. "What can I get for you?"

"A waitress that doesn't smell of watermelon and fried chicken," Kent slurred. Imani raised her eyebrows, placed one hand on her hip and leaned her other elbow on the bar. I just knew the shit was about to hit the fan.

"What did you say?" Imani furrowed her brow, and stared Kent down.

"I said, I want me a waitress that doesn't smell of watermelon and fried chicken." By this time, Kent had the attention of most of the patrons at the bar, and we were all readying ourselves for the blast.

Well it was an eruption, but not quite the one we were looking for. Instead of reading, writing and erasing him like most sisters would do, Imani burst out laughing, taking everyone by surprise. "I thought that's what you said, but I wasn't quite sure." She chuckled. Like a seasoned veteran, Imani flashed her pearly whites and gave him all of her attention. "Now why would such a handsome man limit himself to pork?"

"What?" Kent's jaw dropped.

"Why are your limiting yourself to coffee and cold cuts?"

"What?" His eyes drifted away from Imani as he surveyed the onlookers.

"Have you ever been served by one of the chicken-eating persuasion?"

"No, and..."

"Well," Imani cut him off. "There's a first time for everything." She backed up a little and gave him the once over.

Kent squirmed on the stool from all the attention.

"Now with a physique like that, I know you wouldn't want some watered-down concoction. I can see you take it straight up. As a matter of fact, you look like a Jack Daniels man to me."

"And how do you know that?"

"Because Jack is my brother. Imani Daniels at your service." She extended her hand to him.

He tilted his head, sized Imani up, and stared at her open palm.

"I know you're not going to leave me hanging." She said loudly. "Especially not with all these men sitting around you. You don't want them to think you're scared of me, do you?"

"I'm not afraid of anything." He shifted on the stool once again. "Where'd you come from anyway?"

"Here and there, but this isn't about me. It's about you and my handshake. Now are you going to oblige me?" Imani leaned over, letting all of her cleavage show. "Or, are you going to turn me down?"

A few of the customers snickered as Kent looked around nervously. He quickly shook her hand. "Now, what about my Jack Daniels?"

"What about it?" Imani folded her arms over her chest and shrugged her shoulders.

"Are you going to serve me, or not?"

"Would you like for me to serve you?" She asked him sweetly.

"I don't see anyone else standing back there."

"Well, I'm not so sure I want to serve you. You know, me smelling of watermelon and chicken and everything. I just can't bring myself to fix you that drink.

Sorry." Imani turned to walk away, and Kent touched her arm. She glanced back at him.

"Listen, can we start over?"

What? If Imani Daniels got this crackpot to change his tune, she was definitely a keeper.

Imani turned around, stoically. "I don't think that would be possible. Am I supposed to just forget that you insulted me?"

"I'm sorry, Mrs. Daniels. I didn't know who I was dealing with," Kent put his head down and pouted.

"It's Ms. Daniels, and now that you do know?" Imani smiled.

"Let's just say that in this case," Kent lifted his head and smiled back at her. "I hope my first impression won't be a lasting one."

"For your sake, let's hope it's not." Imani walked over and pulled a tumbler out from under the bar. She turned to the wall and pulled down a newly opened bottle of Jack Daniels. With her back to Kent, she began filling the glass with the liquid. With the tumbler halfway full, I watched as Imani lobbed a ball of spit into his drink, and then continued to pour. She shook the glass slightly to mix its contents and walked back over to Kent. "Here you go." She sat the drink on a napkin in front of him. "I hope it's to your liking."

"I know it will be." He smiled and tipped his glass to her then to himself. He downed the drink in one swallow. "I think I'm going to keep you on your toes tonight, Little Lady." He pushed the empty tumbler towards her.

"It'll be worth it." She winked then filled his tumbler once again with Jack *an*d Imani Daniels.

It must have been one hell of a mixture, because Kent outdid himself. By closing time, his tab skyrocketed to $950. He bought at least six drinks for every lady in the place, and was still nowhere close to scoring when I decided it was time to call him a cab.

When I finally came back inside the bar, I was shocked to see Imani still lingering on. Only two or three patrons were hanging around, and all of the other workers were long gone. I took a seat at the bar and watched as she tried hard to look busy. She rearranged and straightened all of the bottles on the shelves, and refilled the empties. She organized the cash register, wiped down the bar, and restocked the napkins and straws. She even placed the uneaten nuts and crackers in the mini refrigerator underneath the bar. She finally emerged when everything was spotless and to her liking.

"So, how was your first night?" I was amazed that she still looked terrific. All of the other women left out of here bedraggled and tore down. Imani looked refreshed and brand new, like she just walked in the place.

"Not exactly what I imagined, but I can't complain." She pulled a wad of bills from her bust line and wiggled them in front of her face before placing them in her apron pocket.

"So, what do you plan to do with your morning?" I asked.

"Spend it with me, I hope," I heard a man's voice behind me and turned to see who was talking. It was the brother from earlier, Imani's first customer. At first, I couldn't see how he lasted until closing, but then I looked over at Imani. She was beaming and radiant, and I understood fully. "So, how about some breakfast?" I heard him ask her. To my dismay, she smiled and accepted.

"Royal, is there anything else you need for me to do?"

"Nope Imani, you're free to go." I tried to hide my anguish.

"Okay, I'll see you tomorrow."

The guy extended his arm, and she took it. I watched angrily, as he walked away with the only woman who could be Roxanne's replacement. Fucking cockblocker.

ROXANNE

It took Mark close to six hours to wash and dry one load of clothes last night, but I didn't bother to ask him why. Today was a new day, and I was turning over a new leaf. Really, I had no choice. After what I had done, I didn't have room to question him on his whereabouts. Though I couldn't change anything that happened over the weekend, I was going to make sure as hell it didn't happen again. Now with Ayana in my corner, I was certain it wouldn't. Besides, Mark's ego took a beating, and I knew he had to regroup. I didn't expect him to do it in one night, no matter what he said. I mean, he may have forgiven me, but he will never forget what I did to him. Not a second time.

Ayana and I had just come back from spending the day shopping, and we stopped at a neighborhood bar and got smashed. She didn't want to trek all the way across town in her condition, so I invited her to stay at my place. Well really Mark's place, because I surely couldn't afford the $2,900 rent they were asking for. Mark was away on business, so we had the whole place to ourselves.

We hadn't experienced one another in over two years, and I thought that part of my life was over. We had managed to put our intimacy on hold, and regain the friendship that was almost lost due to our discretionary behavior. We sat beside each other on the bed and began talking. The conversation soon turned sexual, and it wasn't long before we were tearing each other's clothes off. I was flat on my back on the bed, legs bent at the knees, and my feet resting on Ayana's shoulders. Her head was buried deep in my lap when the light sprung on.

Mark's jaw dropped along with the bags he was holding. "What the fuck is going on here?" His voice could've cracked plaster. He watched us with disgust as we scurried for something to cover ourselves with. Something to help us hide our shame. Not so much for the situation, but more so for being caught.

"Mark, what are you doing here?" I managed to ask.

"I should be asking her that question." He pointed to Ayana, who was now cowering in the corner looking helpless. "How long has this been going on, Roxy?"

"Mark listen..."

"I'm not listening to shit. How the fuck can you claim to love me, and the whole fucking time, you're still fucking your sister. Is this some sort of sick joke, or something? What the fuck is wrong with you? Are you a fucking dyke for real?"

"Mark..."

"Never mind, Roxy. I don't even want to know." With that, Mark picked up his bags and left the room.

It took a week for him to finally resurface. When he did, just like a dead body in the bottom of the ocean, all the shit I was hiding from him floated right to the top, and I was discovered. For a second time.

The first time was when our parents found out. Joseph outright disowned the two of us. He had no choice. He was just as guilty as we were, even though he and Mama chose to ignore it. Since our actions were an abomination in the eyes of the Lord, it didn't take long for him to convince my mother to do the same. Why she didn't disown his ass, too, was beyond me, but that was her husband, and she loved him more than anything in the world. I just wished she felt the same about her own fucking daughter. Instead, she threw my scandalous ass to the fucking wolves, not once looking back. Not once calling to see if I was all right. Not once giving a damn if I survived it all, or if the whole situation ate me alive.

Mark, on the other hand, gave me an ultimatum—Ayana or him. Though I loved Ayana with every fiber of my heart and soul, I chose to stay by his side. In return, I got his undying love and devotion, and a year later, a huge rock on my ring finger to seal the deal. Ayana disappeared from existence for a while. I always knew where she was, and vice versa, but due to all the pain we caused, we made certain to steer clear of each other. That is, until her call.

I peeked over at the clock. It was going on one, and I still hadn't heard from Ayana. This could mean one of two things—either she spent the night at Royal's and didn't get home yet, or she was still asleep after being up all night. I was secretly hoping it was the latter, as I carefully dialed her number.

"Hello." She yawned loudly.

"Yana, it's Roxy. How was your evening?"

"Fine I guess." She cleared her throat. "What time is it?"

"Almost one. What time did you get in?"

"A little after seven." She yawned again. "I'm exhausted."

"I know you are, girl. Being up on your feet all night is no joke."

"Enough shit already, Roxy. Ask me what you called to ask me so I can get back to sleep."

"You never were one for tact, Yana."

"And you never were one for small talk, bitch. So, spill it."

"Fuck it, did you fuck him Yana?"

"What kind of question is that, Roxy?"

"An honest one. I just want to know how far it went between the two of you. I mean, can you speak freely this afternoon, or does he have his ass curled up beside you?"

"What the fuck do you take me for Roxy? I must admit, Royal is a nice looking brother, and he does have the charm to match, but I'm doing this shit for you—not me. Any feelings I have for him are irrelevant. Believe me, I know how important all this is to you, and I sure as hell wouldn't jeopardize it for a fuck."

"Yana, I'm sorry."

"No, you're not."

"No, I'm not." We burst out laughing. "Listen girl, I have no right to question you about that. I asked you to find out by any means necessary. I pray you don't have to resort to that, and I'm not saying that I think you would, I'm just saying that I hope you don't. But if you have to, it's better to be safe than sorry, and I'd appreciate being the first to know."

"You will be. That's if I decide to go there."

"Well, have you decided?"

"No, I haven't and just to make sure that I won't have to make that decision any time soon, I've enlisted some help of my own. You remember Tyrone from uptown, right?"

"The cutie with the fuck me eyes?"

"The one and only." She laughed. "Well, he's pretending to be interested, and will be picking me up for the next few days, just so I can avoid Royal. Because I tell you, a girl can be but so strong."

"Tell me about it. One look from that gold-toothed heifer and my drawers dropped quicker than Grandma's in *Nutty Professor II*."

"You are one sick bitch."

We went over our game plan for another hour or so, and then I laid down for a nap. It was only twenty-four hours since my last sexcapade, but it felt like an eternity. I was horny as hell. I hoped Mark was up for what I had in mind.

MARK

When I left Mocha's the previous night, I returned to the basement, retrieved my laundry and then headed back upstairs. I was waiting for the latest confrontation, but there wasn't one. Roxanne was sitting up in bed reading a magazine, and to my surprise, she wasn't upset. She didn't even complain when I told her I wasn't in the mood for sex. I didn't know if it was out of pity, or what, and I really didn't care. I knew after fucking Mocha, I barely had the energy to wash my own ass, let alone try to satisfy hers. I was just grateful for a peaceful night's sleep.

Thankfully, today was uneventful, too. Work came and went and all I wanted to do was go home and crawl into bed. I hopped off the elevator and made my way down the hall. I stopped short as I caught a glimpse of two figures standing in front of my door.

"You're early." Mocha walked towards me. "I'd like you to meet Khandi. She's a good friend of mine." Khandi extended her hand, and I shook it.

"What are you doing at my door? You know I live with my fiancée."

"Seems like you answered your own question, Daddy." She hugged me around my neck. "I can't call, and I miss you. Don't you miss me?" She slipped her tongue into my ear.

I grabbed her arms and pushed her back slightly. "Listen Mocha, you can't be here right now."

"And neither can you." She held up a pair of handcuffs.

"What the hell are those for?"

"You." Mocha clicked one side to my arm, the other to hers, and she began to lead me towards the elevator.

"Wait a minute, I have to go home."

"And you will. As soon as we're finished with you."

Once again, I found myself butt-naked at Mocha's, but this time we were in the bedroom. Just the three of us, Mocha, Khandi, and me—the pussy in the middle. While Khandi took residence atop my lap, and Mocha's thighs found their niche upon my face, Roxanne was weighing heavily on my mind. *What the hell am I doing here?* I thought, as I felt myself quickly reaching my point.

"Not yet, baby," I heard Khandi say as she lifted off of me. "We've only just begun."

After hours of prodding, poking, grinding and sucking, I was a disheveled mess. My dick felt tight, my jaws ached and even my balls felt inflamed. I was so exhausted that the thought of sex made me sick to my stomach. I walked through the door, praying that Roxy would at least let me make it into the shower before she started her regular tirade. No such luck.

"Where the hell have you been?" Roxanne screamed as I took my first step into the apartment. "Do you know what time it is?"

"As a matter of fact, I don't." I rubbed my eyes and made my way towards the bedroom.

"Oh, and now you feel you have room to be a smart ass," Roxanne fumed. "You come waltzing in here five motherfucking hours late, with no fucking explanation, and all of a sudden you want to try out for the got-damned *Kings of Comedy* tour? Let me tell you one motherfucking thing..."

I have no idea what else was said. I was exhausted, and I just didn't give a fuck. I zoned Roxanne out and headed for the shower.

AYANA

I finally crawled out of bed in time to start getting ready for work. It had been a long time since I'd stayed up all night, and it was going to take some getting used to. I slipped into a pair of jeans and a T-shirt, and pulled on my Nike cap. I figured the less attractive I looked, the less tempting I'd be. Lord knows I needed all the help I could get to keep Royal at arm's distance. If not for his sake, then at least for my own. I was just about to walk out the door when my phone rang.

"Hello." I cradled the phone on my shoulder.

"Ayana, we need to talk."

"Can't right now. I'm on my way out." I grabbed my keys off the table.

"Out? That'll make it two nights in a row," Jasmine said viciously.

"Yes it does."

"Well, do you mind telling me where you're going to be spending your evenings from now on, since it's obviously not with me?"

"Jasmine, I…"

"And it damn sure better not be with Marlon, because you know I'm not playing with you Ayana."

"I swear I don't need this shit right now, Jasmine." I sucked my teeth. "I have to go. I'll talk to you in the morning." I unlocked the door and walked out into the hallway.

"Whatever, but don't be so sure that I'll be here to take the motherfucking call."

Jasmine abruptly disconnected the call. I just shook my head and locked the door.

"Good evening, Sunshine," Royal said with a huge smile, as I entered the bar. "You're dressed down today, I see."

"Yeah, last night was a rough one, so comfort is of the utmost importance right now."

"I hear you. So, how was breakfast?"

"Fine, thanks." I moved towards the back of the bar. "I'll be ready in a minute."

I walked into the back room, sat down on one of the chaise lounges, and began undressing. Pull yourself together, girl. I felt my body tensing from the impact of Jasmine's words. She was a real piece of work. One minute she wanted to fuck me, the next she wanted to fuck me up, and it was a scenario I was getting a little tired of. Why couldn't everything be black and white with that bitch? How many times did I have to tell her that it was over, before she realized it was really over? Then again, it was my fault, too. Roxy always told me no one could do to you what you didn't allow them to do, and she was right. I mean, a person can make mistakes, but the idea was to learn from them. My ignorant ass just kept repeating the cycle, and if I wasn't careful, Jasmine could be my most costly mistake ever. She was already starting to prove it.

"Everything all right in here?" Royal asked peeking his head inside the door.

"Just fine." I tried to tie my apron behind me.

"Let me help you with that." He walked over and took the straps from my hands. I could feel the heat emitting from his body, and the smell of his cologne was almost intoxicating.

"Thank you."

"No problem." He tied the straps and placed his hands on my hips, smoothing out the material. "All done." He turned me towards him. His face was solemn. He stared into my eyes.

"What's wrong?" I instinctively touched his cheek.

"Imani, are you happy here?"

"Of course I am, Royal. Why, are you planning to let me go, or something?"

"Never that. I just want to make sure that you plan to stick around for a while, YouknowwhatImean?"

"Well, I'm not going anywhere. At least, not without a fight." I smiled.

"You won't have to worry about that, because I see a very bright future ahead for the both of us. Hell, with your skills behind that bar, who knows how far you'll take us."

"I'm happy you're pleased with my performance, Royal."

"I most certainly am. Here, this is for you." He handed me a small white envelope.

"What's this?" I took it from his hand.

"A token of my appreciation. Now get your ass to work. I expect to see you behind that bar in five."

I opened the envelope as he was talking and smiled at the crisp $100 bills staring back at me. "With incentive like this," I said, holding up the envelope. "Fuck five, you'll see me out there in two."

He smiled and closed the door behind him. I looked at my image in the mirror in amazement. I counted out $378 in tips this morning, and Royal just handed me an additional $500 just to pour drinks. Hell, I've been in the wrong profession all along.

ROXANNE

Mama always told me if it looked like a rat, and smelled like a rat, then it was most likely a fucking rat. I truly believed I was living with Mighty Mouse himself. In all the years I've been with Mark, he had never been late once. Not without a phone call. He had never refused me sex. Not without a viable excuse. And he had never been distant. Not unless I demanded more space. Now all of sudden, he couldn't seem to find his way back home, and when he did, he still couldn't manage to find his way back home—if you know what I mean. I'm not saying I'm a nymphomaniac or anything, but if we live together, routine sex is a given. If I wasn't receiving, then I wanted to know who was. I snatched up my cell phone, scrolled down and clicked his office number with determination.

"Hi Myrtle, is Mark in?"

"Yes Roxanne, one moment please." Myrtle's thick, Caribbean accent always made me smile.

"Thank you."

"Roxanne? Is something wrong?" Mark said, panicked.

"Is there?" I asked icily.

"I don't know. You never call me at work. What happened?"

"That's what I'd like to know."

"Roxy, what are you talking about?"

"I'm talking about the fact that you've been avoiding me like the plague recently, and I don't know why. I was honest about Royal, because I didn't want to lose you. If what I did is going to cause you, or us, major problems, then let me know right now."

"And then what, Roxy? You can't change anything, and who said that I'm having a problem with that anyway?"

"Well, you're damn sure having a problem with something, and I want to know what it is. What? I don't turn you on anymore?"

"Roxy, don't be silly. Of course, you do."

"Well, you could've fooled me, Mark."

"What are you wearing right now, Roxy?"

"What did you leave me wearing?"

"Whatever it was, take it off. I'll be home in forty five."

"Mark, you can't be serious."

"I'll show you how serious I am. Bye, Baby."

Break up, to make up, that's all we do. Mark got home in thirty, and proceeded to rock my world. I was right in the midst of my fifth orgasm, when the doorbell rang. Mark deflated faster than a balloon.

"Are you expecting someone?" I asked, as Mark jumped off me, searching the floor frantically for his pants.

"Um...no, no...are you?"

"No, bumbling Bill, I'm not."

"Then, I'll go see who it is, and I'll get rid of them." Mark picked up his pants and put them on quickly.

"How about if we both go..."

"No," Mark shrilled, pushing me back down on the bed as I began lifting up. "Don't move. I'll be right back to finish you off."

With that he left the room. Moments later, his body returned, but I could tell he had left his mind at the front door.

"Who was at the door?"

"Wrong door," he said, pulling off his pants. He sat on the edge of the bed and turned to me. "Roxy," he began and then trailed off.

"Yes Mark, what is it?"

"Nothing." He looked down at the floor and shook his head from side to side.

"Mark," I said, grabbing his chin and pulling him to face me. "What's wrong with you?"

"Nothing, baby. I love you, and I just want to make you happy." With that, he plunged his tongue down my throat, and continued to pleasure me until my vaginal walls were dry and chafe. I don't know who was at that door, but if it turned him on this much, I sure hoped they would keep coming back.

ROYAL

It was only her second night, and Imani already had every man in the bar wrapped around her perfectly manicured finger—myself included. I was mesmerized by her simple beauty, and sexually aroused by her curvy figure. Imani represented the total package—looks, brains, charm and class. She had the ability to make any man fall to his knees, and I wanted to be the one she chose to be her Mr. Right. To be honest, I'd even settle for being her Mr. Right Now. YouknowwhatImean? I sidled up beside her as she poured a drink for a sexy vixen in blue that was unreservedly checking her out.

"It looks like you have the same effect on both sexes," I whispered in her ear.

"What are you talking about, Royal?" she asked with a smile, as she placed the bottle on top of the bar.

"You figure it out," I said as she walked towards the woman, and placed the glass in front of her.

"You're new," Ms. Blue said.

"So I am," Imani replied. "That'll be..."

"Six fifty," she interrupted, passing Imani a twenty-dollar bill.

Imani walked over to the register and retrieved her change. “Here you go,” she said, placing it in front of her.

“Keep it.”

“Thanks,” Imani said, sliding the coins into her apron pocket and the bills between her ample breasts.

“Would you be offended if I asked your name?”

“Not at all. It’s Imani, and yours?”

“Well, my friends call me Delicious, but you can call me tonight.” With that, she placed a business card on the bar.

“To be honest with you,” Imani said, placing the card in her apron pocket, “I’m not sure I’ll be able to call tonight, but you’ll definitely hear from me soon.”

“Good enough,” Delicious said, “I know you’ll be worth the wait.” She stood, blew Imani a kiss and then walked away, shaking her majestic ass to the rhythm of the music. I noticed Imani watching Delicious, too, and I suddenly became aroused.

“Looks like someone has turned both of your heads,” Imani whispered in my ear, as she moved in close to me. “You better be careful with that, you can cause some serious damage.” She rubbed her breasts against my chest. I didn’t know if it was intentional, or not, I just knew it was turning me the fuck on. This gorgeous woman, whispering sweet obscenities in my ear and giving me a sample of the flesh. It was too much for me to handle.

“Um, excuse me,” I managed to mumble, as I brushed past her and rushed up to my office.

Safely inside, I walked over to the glass and stared at Imani, who was now tending to another customer. As she bent over the bar, reaching for a bottle of Bacardi, I could feel the tightness in my slacks returning. My hand was soon inside my waistline. As I watched this Nubian Princess interact with both men and women alike, I brought myself to the most satisfying climax I could in all of five minutes. Five minutes after that, I lay comatose on my leather sofa. When I finally awoke, Imani was standing over me.

"For a moment there, I thought you were dead," she said, as I sat up wiping the crust from my eyes. "You've been sleeping for seven hours straight. Must have been one hell of a night."

"I wish." I cleared my throat, stood up and walked over to the mirror. To my surprise, the bar was empty. "Where is everyone?"

"In bed, I would guess. It's six thirty. I closed up shop about half an hour ago. I was on my way home, but I just wanted to make sure you were okay."

"I am. How about you? Long night?"

"I guess, but I'm fine."

"You sure are."

"Royal, if I hear one more come-on line tonight, I think I'm going to scream."

"Well, get those lungs ready, because I was just about to ask you if I could buy you a drink."

"Buy me a drink? Isn't this your bar?"

"Yes, it is, but you're worth the tab. So, how about it?"

"Why not?" She followed me down the stairs.

Imani took a seat at a booth near the bar, as I slipped behind it and fixed us two drinks. I returned, catching Imani in mid-yawn.

"You okay?" I asked.

"Yeah, just a little tired."

"Well, don't worry, I'll have you in bed in no time," I placed her drink in front of her.

"What?" she asked, with a smirk.

"That didn't come out right." I smiled. "What I meant is, I won't keep you out much longer."

"Now that's better," she said, picking up the glass and taking a sip of the liquid. "This is delicious. What is it?"

"A special mixture I came up with about two years ago. It's Hennessy, 99 Bananas and Malibu Rum. It's pretty, but watch out, it's one of those silent killers."

"I can tell," she said, polishing off the concoction.

Three drinks later, Imani and I were chatting like we were old friends.

"So, you mean to tell me you didn't inherit this from anyone. You built it from scratch?"

"I'm afraid so," I slurred. "Hard work and determination."

"I hear that. Not to mention a prolific side gig."

"Ain't nothing wrong with cleaning up dirty money."

"Not unless you're a cop. Then it would be considered money laundering."

"Well, I'm not a cop, and I like to think of it as a wise investment. Something like the stock market. Except, instead of trusting someone else with my money, I'm doing the leg work myself."

"I see. Well, why isn't there a Mrs. Roaman yet?"

"I don't know." I shook my head. "I just haven't met the right person, but I'm beginning to zero in on one of two options."

"Is that right?" She finished off her drink and peeked down at her watch. "Boy, it's going on nine o'clock and I need some sleep, but I almost hate to leave."

"You don't have to, you know." I placed my hand over hers.

"Yes I do." She pulled her hand away gently. She stood with her glass and walked unsteadily towards the bar. "I'll just wash this out, and I'll be on my way."

"Don't worry about that." I stood and followed behind her. "I'll do it. You go ahead home and get some rest."

"You sure?" She turned to face me. I didn't realize how close we were until I felt her warm breath on my chest. She looked up and stared into my eyes. "Royal," she whispered.

"Yes, Imani," I whispered back.

"Would you mind if I kissed you?"

"Not if you don't mind if I kissed you back."

"I don't." She planted the sweetest kiss on my lips. She delicately pushed her tongue into my mouth, and let it linger there for a while. Our tongues intertwined, and our hands explored each other's bodies. I could feel the tightness in my pants once again. I pulled away slowly.

"What's wrong?" I could tell she was just as aroused as I was.

"Nothing." I tried not to sound too anxious. Although it took everything out of me not to pick her up, and whisk her off to my office. "Listen, I think you better go, before we do something we'll both regret."

"Believe me, you won't regret a thing." She kissed my neck.

"I'm quite sure I won't," I said, softly pushing her back. "But I want to make sure we want to be together because we really want to be, and not because the liquor in our system is telling us we should be. YouknowwhatImean?"

"Yes, I do." She smiled, shook her head and moved back slightly. She began to laugh softly.

"What's so funny?"

"Just when I thought I had you all figured out, you turn around and surprise me. You know, any other man would have jumped at the opportunity to have sex with me."

"Maybe because sex is all they want from you. That's not me. Imani, I want to make love to your mind, as well as your body, and I can't do that if I'm inebriated. It's not the same, and you deserve much more than lust. You deserve to be loved, and the only way I can make sure it's really what you want, is to let this liquor ease its way out of our systems. If tonight finds us in the same predicament, then I promise you, I'll make love to you in a way no one ever has before." I planted a kiss on her forehead, and stared into her eyes. "Is that okay with you?"

"Yes," she said, breathlessly and delicately pushed her tongue into my mouth once again.

AYANA

I awoke with the hangover of a lifetime. I was so fucked up my skin ached. It was going on six in the evening, and I was in no shape to face Royal. I pried myself from the bed, and walked into the bathroom. This was definitely a Calgon moment. I fixed myself a steaming milk bath, and found solace on the toilet. This liquor had to come out of my system one way or another. The phone rang just as I submerged myself into the bath water. Who the fuck could that be? *Maybe it was Royal*, I thought, as I dashed into the room, wet and naked, snatching my cell phone up.

"Hello."

"I'm beginning to think you don't love me anymore. Why haven't I heard from you lately? I've left messages, and..."

"Marlon, I'm sorry. I've been very busy helping out a friend, and I just haven't had the time. As a matter of fact, I was just on my way out. So, let me call you later this week, and we can get together then. Okay?"

"If that's all you can offer me, I guess so. I'll be waiting for your call."

"I know. Bye, Marlon."

"Bye."

I took two steps towards the bathroom, and the phone rang again.

"Hello."

"Ayana, we need to talk," Jasmine said.

"I know, but I'm sorry, I just don't have the time."

"You never seem to have the time lately! I thought it was because of Marlon, but after last night, I know it's not him either…"

"After last night? What happened last night?"

"What didn't?" Jasmine chuckled. "You don't know what you're giving up, Ayana. Marlon is definitely a keeper. If you don't want him, or me, we'd be happy to take care of each other from now on without you."

"Is that supposed to make me clear my schedule, and pencil you in? I said I was busy Jasmine, and I meant it. Now, if you'll excuse me, I have to go. Perhaps, Marlon has time for you tonight, since I turned him down two minutes ago, too." I pressed end, slammed the phone on the bed and left the room.

I sighed as I settled back into the tub. The water was now frigid, and so was I. I turned on the faucet, and let the steamy water ease my misery. I reminisced about my encounter with Royal, and felt a moistness between my thighs I couldn't blame on the bath. My mission was to wear him down and find out the truth about the past he shared with Mark, but I was nowhere close to the answer. I knew he was a drug dealer at one time in his life, but Mark was never into that sort of thing, so it couldn't be drug related. I also knew he was a thug, but Mark was too wimpy for that type of profession, so that couldn't be it either. I had to get closer to Royal somehow, and tonight would be the night I took it where I promised Roxanne I wouldn't go. But I knew if I wanted Royal to trust in me, I had to let him in me to do it. YouknowwhatImean?

"Sunday nights are a little extreme, but don't worry, you can always take a break if you feel too uncomfortable." We were sitting in Royal's office, going over the night's events.

"I think I'll be all right," I said, not knowing fully what I had gotten myself into. "Will there be added security?"

"Of course, but they'll be worrying about the others. My job is to protect you, so I'll be by your side all night. I hope you don't mind."

"I don't. I just hope the other girls don't get jealous."

"Too late, they already are."

We laughed loudly, and stopped abruptly when he touched my cheek.

"No drinking tonight," he said, softly. "If this were meant to be, then I have to know now. I can't wait any longer."

"Don't worry. With the hangover I harbored earlier, it's not going to be a problem."

It was two minutes to midnight, and nothing extreme had happened yet. I was beginning to wonder if it was all a ploy just so Royal could stay by my side, when suddenly all the lights went out. I heard screaming and cheering, and then felt an arm around my waist. My body tensed.

"It's all right, Imani. It's me," Royal said, holding me close to him. "It's about to start, I just want to make sure you can handle it."

"Handle what?"

"This," Royal said.

Just then, a dim, red light came on and a cage now sat in the middle of the bar. Inside the cage was an extremely sexy sister in a waitress uniform. She was definitely something to look at, and I could feel myself drooling. I wiped my lips secretly, and continued to watch her as she began to gyrate to the music.

"You okay?" Royal asked. "I don't want you to take offense to all this."

Offense to what? Don't you know this type of shit turns me on? "I won't. I'm okay with it."

"You sure?"

"Positive," I said, demurely.

"If you want her to take it off," the deejay screamed into the mike, "you have to scream her name. Let me hear you say, Mo-cha."

"Mo-cha," the crowd chanted.

"I can't hear you, motherfuckers!" the deejay screamed. "Where are all the real men in this place? Let me hear you say, Mo-cha."

"Mo-cha," the crowd chanted, even louder.

"Say, take it off, Mocha, take it off!" the deejay screamed.

"Take it off, Mocha, take it off," the crowd repeated.

They went back and forth like this for a while, until Mocha was down to nothing but a two-piece, sequined thong. She looked fabulous, and had everyone in the bar aroused—Royal and myself included. I looked over at him and smiled. Oh yeah, he was definitely going to get fucked tonight. He must have read my mind, because he gave my waist a little squeeze. He then moved behind me, letting me feel that he couldn't wait either. I looked back up at the cage, and watched as Mocha relieved herself of her bra. Her breasts were huge, supple and semi-saggy. They weren't perky and hard looking. Oh no, her tits were the real McCoy—she got those from Mama. I watched in disbelief as Mocha stepped out of her g-string and then began to pleasure herself with a bottle of Alize. The crowd went wild, and so did my private parts. There I sat in a puddle, leaning into Royal's huge erection, all the while wondering how I could get close enough to Mocha to get her phone number.

It was now a quarter to four and Mocha had been upstairs with Royal for extremely too long. Well, it wasn't even five minutes yet, but I still didn't like it. Hell, I knew what I could do with her in five minutes, and it made me sick to my stomach to think how she was pleasuring Royal in that same time span. I looked up at the closed door and began seething.

"You okay?" I heard a voice say from behind me. I turned around and came face to face with Susan, one of the girls who worked the tables.

"Yeah, I'm fine," I said, with a fake smile. "What can I get for you?"

"Two gin and tonics."

I reached under the bar and began fixing the drinks. My eyes couldn't help but wander back up to Royal's closed office door.

"Hey," Susan said, placing her hand on my arm. "Don't worry about that. It's all business. He has his eyes on you."

"I'm not worried." I could tell Susan wasn't buying it.

"Listen, Imani. I've seen the way you two look at each other, and outside of one other sister who has visited this bar recently, I can tell you no matter what that trollop attempts, it's not going to work. Besides that, for some odd reason Mocha can't seem to stand Royal. So believe me when I say she's not going to try anything."

After the crack about the other sister who visited the bar, Susan lost me. "What other sister?" my heart blurted out, before my mind could catch it.

"I think she gave the name Rhonda, but once her husband came to pick her up, Royal confided in me that her name was Roxanne. I don't know what happened to her. He was obviously smitten, but she just suddenly disappeared."

"I see." I exhaled. Then it hit me. "Why the fuck did Royal confide in you?" my heart blurted out once again.

"We're good friends, Imani. Nothing more. Royal gave me a legitimate job three years ago when I was hooking for the money to support my two kids, and for that I'm forever loyal. There's nothing there. He frowns upon my old profession, and even if I tried to go there, he would never let me take it any further. In his eyes once a whore, always a whore. But for me, he's at least given me the benefit of the doubt, and learned to bear with me anyway. He's a good person, Imani. Give him a chance."

"Why are you so concerned?" I handed her the two drinks.

"Because I can see that you have eyes for him, too, and he needs a good person in his life. He deserves the best, and from what I've witnessed—if you aren't it, it doesn't exist."

"Thank you." I was close to tears.

"Don't mention it." She walked towards the cage.

My eyes automatically went back up to Royal's office door, which was now open. Mocha exited and descended the steps. She walked towards me and took a seat at the bar.

"May I have a glass of water, please?" she asked, sweetly.

"Sure you don't want something stronger?"

"No thank you, water's fine."

I fixed her a glass of ice water and placed it on a napkin in front of her. "That was some show you put on tonight."

"It pays the bills," she said, defensively.

"There's nothing wrong with that. If I had your body, I'd have enough to pay Trump's bills."

"I needed that." She laughed loudly. "To be honest with you, I could use something stronger."

"What will it be?"

"Surprise me."

I fixed her the same mixture Royal gave me only hours earlier, and watched as she downed it in one gulp.

"How much do I owe you?"

"Don't worry about it. I'll put it on my tab. Let's just say, I wasn't close enough to throw any dollars in the cage so I'm making up for it now. This second drink should just about cover it." I refilled her tumbler.

"Hey there, Mocha," a drunken man said, throwing his arm around her neck. "How's about I take you home and fuck you like you need to be fucked?"

I reached over and pushed his hand off of her shoulder. "That's my job. Now, if you don't get your hands off of my girl, there's going to be trouble."

"Sorry," he said, raising his hands apologetically. "I didn't know she was a dyke bitch."

"Well, now you know. So beat it." He staggered off and Mocha looked over at me smiling.

"Thank you so much."

"Don't mention it. I know how it gets. Just because you're working here, guys think you're an easy target. I'm sure you get it more than me in your line of work, but we both get it just the same."

"Tell me about it. You know, I'd love to hang out with you sometime." She pulled out her cell phone. "I don't really have a lot of friends in the city."

"No need to explain." I recited my name and number. "Call me whenever you're lonely, or whenever you're just tired of all the other bullshit in this world."

"I will." She stood. "What time are you off tonight?"

"It varies, I couldn't tell you."

"Well, do you want me to wait for you?"

"Unfortunately, I made plans for tonight, but I would love to meet up with you tomorrow. Would that be possible?"

"Sure, I'll call you around noon."

"Tell you what, call my phone now and that way I'll have your number, too. If you don't call me, I'll definitely call you."

ROXANNE

I put on my black see-through teddy, lit a few candles and reminisced about the lovely evening Mark and I shared the previous night. He had me so open that I greeted him earlier with breakfast in bed. And not your usual okie doke shit either. I made French toast, with Spanish omelets, sausage, bacon, flapjacks and some freshly squeezed orange juice. Oh yeah, he had my nose wide open.

It didn't stop there. We sexed each other down for the better part of the day and now while he was still napping, I fixed him a dinner fit for a king. Tonight it was strictly steak, with mashed potatoes, gravy and corn. It was one of his favorite dishes.

"What's gotten into you, Roxy?" Mark sopped up his gravy with a homemade biscuit.

"You. Is everything to your liking?"

"Everything is perfect," he said, sliding his hand under the table and running his fingers up and down my thigh.

"You better stop before you start something."

“Maybe that’s my objective.” He grabbed my hand and placed it in his lap. “He misses you. Would you like to kiss it?”

I knew exactly what he meant by kissing it, so I took up residency under the table and began my oral descent. It didn’t take long for Mark to join me under the table and commence knocking the boots. We were under there so long that by the time we came up for air, his food was ice cold, and the candles were down to wicks floating in bowls of wax. When we finally made it to bed all we could muster was a rushed good night before we both were out for the count.

When I awoke, it occurred to me that an entire twenty-four hours had gone by and I still hadn’t spoken to Ayana. For some reason I was too afraid to call her. I feared the worse. I felt it. I just wasn’t ready for the confirmation. I slipped out of bed and walked into the kitchen wearing nothing but a pair of black thongs. I used to be shy to walk around like that, because when I wore a thong, all you could see was the small triangle of material over my center. All other strings were lost within my folds. Then Mark came along and let me know that all this body was not meant to be covered. He persuaded me to embrace my size, because to him, I was one sensual beast. So I did. I put on a pot of coffee and popped a bagel in the toaster just as the phone rang. I picked it up and held it to my ear, too afraid to speak.

“Hello,” I heard the voice on the other end say.

“Hello,” I managed to croak out.

“May I please speak to Roxanne?”

“Who’s calling?”

“Tell her I’m a friend of Rhonda’s, another old friend of hers.” I could tell he was smiling from the sound of his voice.

“Royal, why are you calling me at nine o’clock in the morning?”

"Because I know your husband leaves at eight thirty."

"Very funny. Why are you calling me? I thought I made it clear that I never want to see you again."

"And you haven't seen me. Is it a crime to talk to me, too?"

"About what, Royal? We don't have anything to talk about."

"Yes we do. You can't just pretend like the other night didn't happen. We were both there, and things can't be left like that. We need to discuss it and plan our next step."

"Our next step? There is no next step. What happened was a mistake. One that I will have to learn to live with, and I suggest you do the same. It's done, Royal, and so are we."

"How can you say that when you may be pregnant with my child?"

I pressed end and crouched in the corner. His words cut through me like a knife, and I suddenly felt sick to my stomach. I jumped up and ran into the bathroom. I got as far as the sink when my insides exploded, and my stomach emptied into the basin. Choking back tears and wiping saliva from my chin with the back of my hand, I crawled into bed and pulled the covers tightly over my head. The phone rang again and I did my best impression of a rock, as I lay still and solid. Unmoving. Unfeeling. Unhearing. The ringing finally stopped. I quickly reached over and put the phone on silent mode. I couldn't chance talking to him again. I was too afraid to face him, and I couldn't understand why. I hadn't been this scared when I broke down and confessed to Mark, but for some obscene reason my confronting Royal was too much for me to handle. My business line now rung and I let the machine pick up.

"Roxy, I know you're home," the voice screeched. "Bitch, pick up the phone."

"Yana," I said into the receiver.

"Yeah, it's me. May I ask why you're screening your calls?"

"Bill collectors just won't give me a break. What's up with you?"

"What isn't? Girl, I'm beginning to love my job."

"Oh really? And why is that?" I frowned.

"Why you got to say it like that?"

"Like what? I'm merely asking you a question. Why are you being so defensive? Do you have something to hide?"

"Roxy, what the hell are you talking about? I call to say what's up, and find that you've gone Double-O-Seven on a bitch, and now I'm being hit with this shit. What the fuck is going on in your world, girl? Do you need a fucking valium?"

"Do you? Or has Royal cured that for you, too?"

"Listen girl. I don't know where your head is today, but I already explained that situation to you. If you can't handle it, tell me now and I'll pull back. I'm doing this for you. Remember that, because I really don't need this shit in my life."

"Yana, I'm sorry."

"Yeah, you sure are."

With that she hung up the phone. I started to call her back, but I couldn't. I didn't want to. What the fuck was I supposed to do? Apologize a second time? And exactly what the hell was I apologizing for anyway? I sent her there to find out some information for me, not to start up a relationship with Royal. Then at that, why the hell was I stressing it? I had Mark. We were engaged. We were getting married. Mark loved me, and I loved Mark. Fuck Royal. Period.

ROYAL

The moment I saw the two of them together, I knew I could kiss my lovely evening good-bye. Mocha was noticeably enchanted by Imani, and vice versa, and I was growing tired of the same scenario. See the girl. Hook the girl. Then watch the girl give the goods away to the next man, or woman. What was up with that shit anyway? Was Imani straight, gay, or bisexual? Most likely the latter. Although the thought of making it with two women at the same time was making my dick as hard as a board, the thought of sharing Imani with someone else quickly deflated it.

I rolled off the bed and jumped in the shower. The bar was closed tonight, but I still had shit to do. I had an appointment for a manicure at noon, and a lunch date with a dancer at two. She was supposed to be something special. That's the same thing I was told about Mocha and she turned out to be more trouble than she was worth.

#

About two years ago, Lyle Cunningham, one of my very prestigious customers, was interested in increasing his drug purchases. He was also looking to branch out into the escort business, and wondered if it would be a field I'd be interested in pursuing. I told him it wasn't, but I would consider being somewhat of a liaison between his employees and his clientele. I figured I'd not only collect a nice fee for doing practically nothing, but I'd also have my choice of some A-one females to pass the time whenever the need arose. And my need arose more often than necessary. YouknowwhatImean?

In as little as three months, our escort business was booming, and my proceeds increased tremendously. I had earned enough money to back some very serious investments, as well as plunk down a nice chunk of change on a beachfront in Cancun. That's where I met Christine Cordeaux AKA Baby Girl. Lyle went out with a couple of his buddies one night and came back raving about this one chocolate sister. I knew Lyle was no stranger to black women. As a matter of fact, he preferred them. I also knew he was more inclined to those of the I-can-pass-for-Caucasian persuasion. So, to hear him speak so highly of a Hershey's Kiss, as he called them, I knew she was someone worth seeing. We went back to the club on Saturday to see her perform.

A little after midnight, the lights went dim and a single, pink spotlight shone on a barstool in the middle of the stage. Out walks Baby Girl in a pink cheerleader outfit, carrying pink and white pom-poms that matched the pasties dangling from her over-sized breasts. She began gyrating to the music and simulating sex with the stool. I had to admit, she was something worth watching. According to the bulge in my pants, she was definitely worth fucking, too.

Right before the end of her set, I slipped the bouncer $300, and was personally escorted to her dressing room. I was seated on one of the plush sofas facing the door when she entered, stark naked and saturated with sweat. I thought my presence would catch her off guard, but by the nonchalant way she walked over to the dressing table and lit a cigarette, I realized I wasn't the first to brave this feat.

"I guess you slipped Sammy something extra," she sighed. "How much did you give him?"

"Three hundred." I looked her up and down, and loved what I saw.

"He would've let you in for fifty." She walked over to a closet and pulled out a green robe. She put it on, and returned to the dressing table. "So, Mr. Three Hundred Dollar Man, do you have a name?"

"It's Royal."

"I see." She took a seat atop the table. "And just what do you think you're going to get from me for the entry fee you shelled out, Royal?"

"Anything you're offering." I tried to sound as casual as she did, but I wasn't so sure I was succeeding.

"Well, fifty gets you a nice blow job. I don't know what you want for three hundred."

"How about I throw in an extra five, and you spend the night at my place."

"How about you make it ten, and you have a deal," she countered.

I must admit, it was the best $1300 I'd spent in a while. Baby Girl was able to manipulate her vagina like a trained veteran. She knew exactly when to tense and release, take more or retract, suck me or fuck me. Best of all, she did it with no strings attached. The next morning, she collected her fee off the end table and hit the road. It then became my job to find her again, because as far as she was concerned, our night together was a thing of the past.

I finally located her three days later at a very small resort on the other end of the island. It didn't take much persuasion to get her to leave her squalid conditions and agree to return with me to the States. The promise of an escort job at triple the pay was the extra incentive she needed.

The arrangement was working out fine in the beginning. Baby Girl worked for Lyle full time, moonlighted for me part time, and did her own thing in between. She had secured a nice little studio in a high-rise not too far from the bar, and was making some good money shaking what her mama gave her in front of an audience, and behind closed doors. YouknowwhatImean? But once her appetite for cocaine took over her hunger for sex, I limited our relationship to business and scratched her name from the guest registry at the front desk of my condo.

Things went downhill from there. She became a no-show at work. On the rare occasions she did show up, she was late, unkempt, stoned, or all of the above. This went on for three months, until I finally had enough and told Lyle to fire her. He said he would, but had one last job for her to do for a special out-of-town client. The night came, the job was set, and for once, Baby Girl was on time. She wasn't exactly at her best, but I'm not quite sure what her best was anymore. She looked okay, but it was a far cry from how good she looked when she first appeared on the scene.

After giving her the 411 on how the operation was supposed to go down, I dropped her at the spot, and waited outside for her return. Two hours and ten minutes went by and still no Baby Girl. The client had only paid for two hours, so I made my way up to the room to see what the fuck was going on. I busted down the door and was amazed at what I saw. Baby Girl had a gun in her hand, cowering in a corner, and her client was sprawled out on the floor in front of her with a single gunshot wound to the head.

The story made front-page news, and Baby Girl became one of America's Most Wanted. It turns out the guy was the nephew of a Texas governor, and with the power and influence he had, no way was she going to get away with a slap on the wrist for icing him. Rape, sodomy and physical abuse, or not, she was as good as convicted, and she knew it. She also knew she needed me to help her disappear, and that was going to cost her. I guess it was true when they said the beast you know is always better than the beast you don't, because she put her life in my capable hands, and I did what she needed me to do.

After some prodding and a little physical contact, Lyle agreed to keep quiet and forget he ever knew her. Christine Cordeaux AKA Baby Girl died and Monica Evans was resurrected in her place. Her first stop towards redemption came at a rehabilitation center in Upstate New York. They kept her for six months, and when she was finally released on an outpatient basis, she was better than new, and she looked fabulous. If it weren't for the hefty debt she still owed, I would've fucked her again. But I make it a point not to mix business with pleasure. YouknowwhatImean?

I hooked her up with a two-bedroom flat on the Upper East Side, and fronted her some money for clothes. We did the whole makeover routine, and then set her up with a regular, Sunday night guest spot at my bar. I dubbed her Mocha her first night back, because she was dark and hot, and the white boys just couldn't get enough of her. That night, she managed to pull in over $3,000—of which I collected my ninety percent pay off.

#

That was three months ago, and although she was pulling in the crowds, her tab was still running strong. With over $40,000 already accounted for, I figured once she did this one last job for me, we would be even. Well, not exactly even, but I was tired of her, and I just wanted her out of my life for good. Her past was bad for business, and if she kept hanging around, I was afraid it would catch up to her—to both of us. And that was some shit I didn't need. Besides, she owed me, and this was something easy. Something I knew she couldn't fuck up, because it was what she was good at. I knew that firsthand. YouknowwhatImean?

MARK

Mocha was going to prove to be more problems than she was worth. Last night, right in the middle of me sexing Roxy, she rang the doorbell. If I didn't threaten to call the cops, I'm not sure she would have left as soon as she did. I didn't know what got into me anyway. How the hell did I think I could carry on an affair with someone who lived in the same building as Roxy? Perhaps, in some sick way I wanted to be found out. Maybe the risk of getting caught turned me on and made me continue. Or, perhaps it was just I was a stupid ass and I was thinking with the wrong head. Whatever the reason, I had to cut this shit off and get out while I still could. I decided to go see Mocha before I went home.

I eased into the elevator and stood next to an old lady, who quickly grabbed her pocketbook and pulled it close to her. I looked over and sneered at her.

"Got that social security check today, did we?" I mocked, moving closer to her.

"Wh—what?" she stammered, backing into a corner.

"How about if I have a look in that purse of yours?" I moved closer to her just as the elevator doors opened. I suddenly found myself crouching in a heap in the corner from the impact of her cane to my groin. I didn't know the old bag had it in her.

"You bastard! I hope your balls triple in size!" She exited the elevator, shaking her cane at me as the doors closed behind her.

That's just what I get for fucking with the elderly. I exited the elevator on the next floor, and made my way towards Mocha's door with new confidence. Maybe it was meant for that old lady to be on the elevator, because I was in so much pain sex was the furthest thing from my mind. I rung the doorbell and stood firmly outside her door.

"Who?" Mocha screamed from the inside.

"It's Mark," I croaked. I quickly cleared my throat as I heard the locks opening.

"Hi, Daddy." Mocha opened the door and licked her lips seductively. "Did you miss your Baby Girl?" A look of panic flashed across her face, and she quickly changed the subject. "Um, why are you... I mean, what do you... Um, would you like to come in?"

"As a matter of fact, I would." My forehead furrowed. I walked inside trying to figure out why the temptress that greeted me at the door turned into this fidgety feline, apathetic and stumbling over phrases. *She always calls herself Daddy's Little Girl. But she said Baby Girl, didn't she?*

"Would you like something to drink?" She downed a shot of Vodka.

"No thanks."

"Suit yourself." She downed another and poured herself a third.

"Listen Mocha," I began and then I noticed that she was only there with me physically. "I just wanted to tell you I have AIDS, and you should probably have yourself checked out."

"That's nice." She emptied the glass and placed it on the table. "Would you like to fuck?" she slurred.

"Didn't you hear anything I just said?" I rolled my eyes at her. It was one thing to completely ignore me, but asking for sex so callously was a complete turn off. *Stop being such a wuss Mark, and fuck this bitch. Literally.*

"Yeah, I heard you." She pulled off her robe. "Now, would you like to fuck, or not?" I stared at her for a moment, and considered my options. Fuck her, forget about calling it quits, and enjoy myself for as long as I could. Tell her to go fuck herself, storm out of there, and go home to the woman who loved me. Or fuck her and then tell her to go fuck herself once I was done.

I mixed and matched my options. I fucked her in a frenzy, then went home to the woman who loved me, leaving my fate up in the air. I couldn't help myself. Hell, if the police came to the door warning us of noise complaints from the neighbors, I wouldn't have been surprised. Instead of me doing the upstanding thing, I did the thing standing up. Lying down. Sitting up. On all fours. You name it, we tried it. Then retried it. It was close to midnight when I finally sauntered into the apartment. Roxy was fast asleep, so I quietly made my way to the shower.

Did you miss your Baby Girl? I kept hearing the words spiraling through my mind as I lie in bed trying to put myself to sleep next to Roxy's warm frame. Why was the name sticking with me anyway? Did I know Mocha from somewhere? Did we used to go to school together, or something? I didn't think so, because nothing about her seemed familiar. Nothing but that name. It was driving me crazy, and I had to find out why. *Baby Girl.*

"What the fuck did you just call me?" Roxy whispered loudly as she rolled over to face me.

"What?" I asked, taken aback. I couldn't have been speaking out loud. Or was I?

“I said what the fuck did you just call me, or better yet, who the fuck is Baby Girl?”

“Roxy, I don’t know what you’re talking about.”

“Well, you better enlighten yourself pretty damn quickly, or else all hell is going to break loose.” She threw the covers off of her and sat up in the bed. “Now, where the fuck were you all night, and what bitch has you calling her Baby Girl?” Roxy folded her arms tightly across her chest. I could feel her staring at me with death in her eyes, but I was too afraid to look up. If I did, my ass would definitely turn to stone. “I’m waiting,” she said, tapping her hand against her forearm.

“Roxy, you’re hearing things. Why don’t you just go back to sleep, and we can discuss this in the morning.”

“It is morning,” she said through gritted teeth. “Or did you forget that midnight is the commencement of a new day? Now, for the last time, who the fuck is Baby Girl?”

“Roxy, I’m tired. Can you please just turn over and go back to sleep?”

“You’re right Mark, you are tired and I’ve had just about enough of it. So, you and Baby Girl enjoy.” She climbed out of bed wearing next to nothing and stormed out of the bedroom, slamming the door behind her.

Instead of worrying about her last comment, my mind ventured into the living room. I suddenly found myself jerking off to the notion of laying her out on the sofa and fucking her like I fucked Mocha a few hours earlier. I quickly ejaculated into a Kleenex and then tried to put myself to sleep. The last thing I needed to be was awake whenever Roxy resurfaced.

AYANA

If I live to be a hundred, I doubt I would ever understand Roxy. One minute she was okay with the idea of me doing the snooping on Mark, and the other she was chewing me out for being sexually involved with Royal. Something that hadn't even happened yet. For that, I'm semi-proud of myself, and she should be, too. Don't get me wrong, it was not that I didn't want to tackle that sexy giant the first time I laid my eyes on him, but I had to stay focused and remember the true reason why he was in my life at all. I also had to make sure the attraction wasn't one-sided. Once I was confident it was not, I would go in for the kill. Royal was smarter than the average man, and he wouldn't be so easy to convince. But by me holding out for this long, I was sure he would be to that point as soon as he reached his first climax.

Roxy's tirade even made me erase Mocha's number out of my phone. Females equaled drama, and between Roxanne and Jasmine, I had enough catty shit in my world to last a lifetime. Yes, I wanted to suck and fuck the shit out of Mocha, but adding yet another woman to my sexual circle was going to bring me more problems than they were worth.

I became so horny just thinking about Royal and Mocha I began to dial up Marlon with the quickness. I knew it was going on three in the morning, but if I were going to make a booty call, it was definitely going to be a good one.

"Hello." Marlon's voice was deep and scratchy.

"Hey baby, it's Yana. What you doing?"

"Nothing."

"Would you like to do me?"

"Of course, I would baby. I'm on my way."

"Good, see you in a bit." I hung up and raced into the shower. After applying a generous amount of lotion and fragrances, I lit a few scented candles and relaxed. I wished I could be like those bitches in the movies. Always sweet smelling, always ready. Never having to freshen up. Just move and shake all day, and still be confident enough to just fling off my panties with the first kiss. But real life wasn't that nice, and a woman could never be sure if her panties were going to be flowery sweet or dead-rat funky. So a shit, shower and shampoo were always the way to go.

It was close to four when Marlon arrived, and I was halfway to dreamland. The passion built up earlier had disappeared, and I was beginning to wonder why I called him in the first place. He was between my thighs, thrusting his hips into mine, whispering the freakiest obscenities he could think of. His words were turning me on, but his movements were pissing me off. One week without me, and the man had forgotten everything I taught him. I began to smile because I realized he couldn't have been with Jasmine either, not with those tired jabs. That revelation brought out newfound energy. I hurled Marlon onto his back and mounted his lap.

"Oh God!" He dug his fingernails into my behind.

"God has nothing to do with this," I taunted, as I rocked back and forth gently. "Does it feel good, baby? Whose is it?"

"Damn good, Baby, and it's yours."

"Mine or Jasmine's?"

"It's yours Baby, nobody else's. I swear, Baby, I'm all yours."

Ten minutes later, I found myself lying in Marlon's arms, inhaling his masculine aroma.

"Yana?"

"Um-hum," I intertwined my fingers in his wooly chest hair.

"I love you, baby."

What? Here I was, fresh from one of the best fucks I had in a long time, and here he was killing me with this *How Stella Got Her Groove Back* bullshit. Was that a fucking tear in his eye? I couldn't believe it, Marlon was actually crying. "What's wrong?" I touched his cheek.

"I don't know" He pushed me up gently, and turned away.

"Marlon," I began, and then I trailed off. What was I supposed to say? I love you, too? I mean, I could, but what if it was a lie? Or worst yet, what if it was the truth? "Baby, what makes you think you love me?" I rubbed his arm.

"Just by me being here, I don't think it—I know it. Yana, you disappear on me for a week with no reason given and then call me at three in the morning, out of the blue and here I am. No questions asked. No explanations needed. It's not like I haven't had any other offers, because we both know that I have, but I didn't want to be with her. Yana, I want to be with you and only you. I don't know what it is about you baby, but I love you. I'm not talking fourth grade, can-I-touch-your-butt love. I'm talking some will-you-be-my-wife type shit. I'm not asking you to reciprocate my feelings. I'm just asking you not to dog me out. If I'm not the man you want in your life, please don't play any more games with me. My heart just can't take it." Marlon sniffled and wiped his eyes with the back of his hand.

That was the first time a brother broke it down to me that way. I mean, I was used to the tearful episodes and drama a sister could bring to the table, but most of the men I've been involved with, were more fascinated with the idea of fucking a lesbian than with acquiring feelings for a woman.

"Marlon, I'm sorry. It's just that I'm going through some things right now, and I'm trying to help out a friend. I'm not trying to dog you out. I've just been busy. As far as this love thing goes, baby, I have love for you, and I do care about you, I'm just not sure that I'm in love with you. On the same note, I can't say that I'm not. But right now, I'm clinging to the notion that it's security, because when I'm around you, I don't feel like I ever have to worry about anything. Marlon, I love being with you, and I love having you in my life. I don't ever want to lose you, but I'm not the type of bitch to force you to stay either. I'm not asking you to be on standby, Baby. I would never do that to you. I'm just hoping that once I'm through with all my bullshit, if I can't be your woman, at least you'll allow me to still be in your life, even if it's only as a friend." I clung to him as if for dear life. Secretly praying that I didn't say the wrong things, because it was truly how I felt at the time.

"Your heart is racing," he mumbled, turning to face me once again.

"I'm scared."

"Scared of what?" He stroked my hair tenderly.

"Losing you."

"Baby, you'll never lose me." He massaged my cheek. "I promise, I'm not going anywhere. If the only time I can have you is at four o'clock in the morning, I'll take it. I'll take anything, just as long as you're part of the package."

"Marlon." Tears began to fall down my cheeks.

"Yes?"

"I love you, too."

ROXANNE

I didn't know what was wrong with everyone around me. It was like the whole fucking world was going crazy. First Ayana. Then Royal. Now Mark. What the fuck was going on?

I was on my way to the cleaners to pick up my black suit for tomorrow's meeting. I had to give a presentation to twelve eligible bachelors, trying to convince them I was the woman who could sell their new calendar. It was supposed to be a Playgirl-type publication, but with a little more flavor and a lot less flesh. I got the referral from one of Mark's business partners, and he was counting on me to land the damn thing. Not only to put some money in my pocket, but also to add a $2,000 finder's fee to his purse as well.

"Roxanne, is that you?" I heard a familiar voice say behind me.

I turned and came face to face with my worst fear. It was my mother, Mrs. Evelina Marie Johnson-Linden in the flesh. My first impulse was to take off in the opposite direction, but where the fuck was I going to run to? I decided to make polite conversation instead. "Ma, what are you doing in New York? I thought you and Joseph went back to the South."

"We did, but I'm up here visiting Con' Jewel. You know she took sick, don't you?"

I couldn't believe she was being so fucking nonchalant. "No, I didn't. Is it serious?"

"Serious enough. She's been in the hospital with pneumonia for the past two weeks. They don't think she's going to pull through." My mother looked at my outfit and scrunched up her face.

"I'm sorry to hear it. Are you on your way there now?"

"No, I'm not. I was actually on my way to get something to eat. Care to join me?"

There was no way in hell I could say no in a diplomatic, yet non-offensive way. So I just accepted the invitation, and dragged my heels to the sidewalk café on the next corner. After placing her order, and mine as well, my mother turned to me with the conversation I'd been avoiding for the last three and a half years.

"Roxanne, have you heard from that sister of yours?" she asked.

"Yes."

"And how does Mark feel about that? You are still with him aren't you?"

"Yes, Mom, I am. And there's nothing for him to say. She's my sister."

"Step-sister," she whispered loudly. "And she is also your lover. He caught the two of you together for Christ's sake."

"No, she's my sister. Mark knows that, I know that, and Ayana knows that. And quite frankly, that's all that matters. Why did you ask me to have lunch with you, if you're obviously not over all of this? How long have you been in town, anyway?"

"About a week, but..."

"But what? You lost my number? You forgot

where I live? What, Ma? What stopped you from calling me, or coming by to see me, or even trying to forgive me for a mistake I made more than ten years ago?"

"The fact that I didn't know anything about it until five years ago, and I had to hear it in the streets." She took a few sips of her water.

"In the streets?" I asked louder than I wanted to. "What the hell are you talking about?"

"Why didn't you tell me, Roxanne? I thought we had the kind of relationship where you could come and talk to me about anything."

"I thought we did, too." I lowered my tone. "But once it all came out in the open, that notion flew right out the fucking window. And what about Joseph? He wasn't innocent in all of this. Why the fuck didn't he tell you?"

"Don't curse at me, Roxanne."

"Don't change the fucking subject. I'm not cursing at you. I'm talking, and a curse word is part of my conversation."

"Your yelling is not going to change the facts, and you can just leave Joseph out of this. He had nothing to do with it. He's not to blame here, and neither am I."

"No, only Ayana and I are. Right, Mommy? It's a fucking shame. After all these years, you would still do anything to save face, not to mention a fucked up marriage."

"Roxanne, you're making a scene. Lower your voice." She fidgeted with the collar of her blouse and smiled apologetically at the customers at the surrounding tables.

"Can I help you?" I yelled at no one in particular. Especially since our conversation had now caught the attention of everyone on the promenade, as well as a few people walking by.

“Roxanne, why don’t you simmer down, and let everyone enjoy what’s left of their meals?” She placed her hand on my arm.

“You are always so fucking worried about everybody else.” I yanked my arm away. “Everybody else is not your daughter. I am. I don’t give a fat rat’s ass what these people think about me. I don’t know them from Adam!”

“Well, I don’t know them either, but I didn’t come here to be made a spectacle of!”

“And neither did I, but we can’t always choose what the fuck happens to us, can we?”

“I guess we can’t, because if we could, I sure as hell wouldn’t have asked to have a lesbian for a daughter.”

That comment jarred me, not because of the validity behind it, but because now everyone was staring at me and some even had the audacity to gasp and shit. Although it didn’t bother me a minute ago, I now felt naked, and I couldn’t take being ass-out in front of all these people. I kindly stood up and stormed away. I stopped on the corner against the green light, leaned my shoulder on the light post and closed my eyes.

#

Evelina Johnson and Joseph Linden were married twenty years ago in Charleston, South Carolina. My ten-year-old cousin, Jesse, was the ring bearer, and my eldest aunt, Eve, who was also his mother, served as the maid of honor. Mommy would joke that Eve was always a bridesmaid and never a bride, but Eve never seemed to mind. She would tell me it wasn't due to a shortage of prospective suitors, but to a lack of suitable prospects. She earned the name Con' Jewel from the lavish display of gems she wore on a daily basis. Namely those given to her by men hoping to break her down and fool her into marriage. It never happened. Now at well over sixty, Con' Jewel was still single, and lived alone in a beautiful, six-bedroom condo here in New York. She was also the one who instilled in me her credo for falling in love. She conveyed that a man couldn't make or break me—only I had that power. She also stressed I should never make the term “single” synonymous with incomplete, because I came into the world alone and whole, and I would venture out of it pretty much the same way. Whomever I chose to be with between those times should only be considered an accessory, and not a necessity. Because, as she often said, "Only one Man holds the key to eternity, and He should be the only Man to receive your undying love and devotion. For His love is more than a need; it's a requirement." Amen.

I was the flower girl, along with Ayana. She was Joseph's daughter from a previous relationship. We were both six years old, and became fast friends at the reception. We didn't even seem to mind when she was forced to live with us three months later and Mommy crammed the two of us into my way-too-small-for-one-person bedroom. Her mother, who became strung out on drugs and alcohol, could no longer afford to support a child and a crack habit. So she showed up on our doorstep one night, incoherent and wired, telling Daddy he could have Ayana for twenty dollars. She didn't get the money, but we got Ayana anyway. I not only got a new live-in sister, but she also became my best friend. That first night we stayed up until the wee hours of the morning talking and getting to know each other. As we lay next to each other in the moonlight, she promised me we could share her daddy since mine had been MIA ever since my mother was eight weeks pregnant. I told her we could share my mommy since hers was now a bonafide crackhead. We became inseparable and were soon dubbed "The Twins" because you would never see one without the other.

After sharing the same room for so long, one would think we would have grown tired of each other, but we never did. We spent countless hours in that room, busying ourselves with girl talk, homework and gossip. We enjoyed the gossip the most. Besides, the myriad scandals of the south are what made the dull afternoons in the Linden household bearable.

It was one of those same boring afternoons that changed my life forever. As I remember it, Mommy was downstairs in the kitchen, blasting Shirley Caesar on her portable radio. Singing along to the church music that became an all too familiar Sunday tradition, while she created tasty meals, which always contained macaroni and cheese, collard greens, candied yams, either poultry, pork or beef, peas and rice and some type of sweet pie or cake for dessert. Daddy was laid out on the sofa, remote in one hand, a beer can extending from the other, looking at old western movies starring some of America's greatest white actors. I never could understand why he loved those old films so much, and always wondered if he secretly wished he could live the free and uninhibited life of a cowboy, instead of taking care of a wife and two daughters—one of his flesh, and the other of a flesh he had grown to love and know as well as his own.

There we were, my stepsister and I. Ten years older, lying across my bed like we'd done countless times before. This day was different. The room appeared to be smaller than usual. The air seemed tight, almost constricting. I watched Ayana as if for the first time. I observed how her honey-colored lips rose into an upside down rainbow, as her smile filled the room with sunshine. I watched as her jet-black eyelashes curved sweetly over her dazzling brown eyes as she blinked back tears of joy at her newfound revelation. Although a little overweight and very unpopular, I had finally tasted of

Adam's forbidden nectar, and as mommy so callously put it, was now spoiled.

"So, how did it feel?" she asked, trying unsuccessfully to hide her excitement, especially since she had been ruined by a visiting senior two months prior to my defilement.

"I don't know. Funny, I guess," I replied, hoping I sounded mature, because sex had now made me a woman. I'm glad I found that lie out before it was too late.

"What do you mean by funny?"

"I don't know. It just wasn't what I expected." I hoped she'd either change the subject, or positions, because if I wasn't mistaken, that was a nipple escaping from the massive cleavage falling over the top of her loose fitting v-neck T-shirt.

"What exactly did you expect?" she asked. As if she had read my thoughts, she lifted slightly on her elbow, displaying the most radiant nipple I had ever seen.

I didn't answer. I was much too busy wondering if her other nipple was just as perfect.

Oblivious to my thoughts, she continued, "Well? What did you want? A brilliant display of fireworks, or for the walls to come crashing down on you as the devil led you into temptation?"

I stared at her as her tongue rolled back and forth seductively against her pearly whites, which to me favored a picket fence. Her tongue was now an open gate, inviting me to enter her realm. Begging me to come inside and make myself comfortable.

"No." I tried to sound casual, although I could feel beads of moisture between my thighs and a desire rising up in me... *Wait a minute, she's a woman damn it! And I'm not a lesbian.* Well if that were true, why couldn't I keep my eyes from wandering down to the hollow between her caramel-colored breasts? "I thought there was more to it," I continued. "The way Mommy's always ranting and warning about it, I just thought there would be more."

"I know what you mean. When I did it with what's his name I was like, that's it? That's what everyone is getting all excited for? Man, I could have had a V-8."

We laughed and joked about our unfortunate mishaps for what seemed like hours, but when I glanced over at the clock, only twenty minutes had passed. Then it happened. This gorgeous, sexy, curvaceous creature that I'd come to adore and admire asked me the unthinkable.

"Roxy, have you ever thought about making love to another woman?"

"What?" I asked, choking on air. I felt my throat go completely dry, as I wondered if she saw the way I was inconspicuously glancing at her breasts, or if she could smell the aromatic liquid flowing from my vagina. Or, if she knew about the nights I lay in bed familiarizing myself with my own body as I stared at hers. Well actually, on those nights, I was only concerned with that tempestuous cavity that peeked at me from under the covers as she slept a few feet away, spread-eagle and partially nude. I thanked God she hated the restraints of underclothes. It's funny. At first, I couldn't fathom why anyone would hate to wear panties, or for that matter—with breasts as full and immense as hers—a bra. But after watching the curves of her body and the way any material she wore seemed to dance against her nakedness, I didn't give a damn why. I was just happy she didn't.

"Well," she said, breaking into my smutty thoughts, "have you?"

"Where the hell did that come from?" I secretly wished the T-shirt she wore was just a little shorter.

"I don't know. I was just wondering, and you still didn't answer me."

I couldn't. I remained speechless as I watched her rise

to lock the door. Furious with myself for being stimulated by the way her ass cheeks dangled just above the hem. Not showing, but wanting to. Teasing me—wanting me to want them to. My inner voice grew thunderous. *She's your sister for Christ's sake! My step-sister*, I rationalized. All the while forgetting what was most important. She was also a woman, and any such thoughts were an abomination. Well, tell that to my loins.

She stood before me now. Not close enough for me to touch, but near enough to see my reaction as she slipped that skimpy T-shirt over her head. She threw it on the bed beside me and moved closer. I found myself staring at her unclothed body in amazement. I was half-smiling, half-frowning, puzzled and yet enlightened at the same time. And for the life of me, I couldn't understand why the emotions building up inside me at that moment surpassed the sensation I felt when I was alone with Lamont for the first time. I looked away quickly. I was ashamed. How could I want another woman when I was a woman myself?

Ayana Vonet Linden answered that question for me in no time.

#

A light tap on my shoulder stirred me from my reverie. I turned around wearing a scowl. "What?"

"I'm sorry, sister," a nice-looking young man said behind me. "You left this on the table when you walked away. I thought you might need it."

It was my purse. "Thank you." I smiled.

"No problem. And, um, I don't mean to be all up in your business, but you should learn to respect your mother, you only have one."

I didn't know what came over me. One minute I was smiling at a handsome young man, the next, I was hitting the nosy son-of-a-bitch in the groin with my purse. "Next time, you should learn how to protect your dick. You only have one!" I slammed my pocketbook underneath my arm and jetted across the street.

ROYAL

I looked down at my watch for the third time. It was going on two thirty and the Fantabulous Fanta was a no-show. If it weren't for the free drinks the obese waitress with the missing tooth kept sitting in front of me, I would have been long gone.

"Waiting on someone?" she asked, as she sat yet another Metropolitan down on the table.

"As a matter of fact, I am." I hoped it would discourage her from any further conversation. It didn't.

"Your wife?"

"No."

"A girlfriend?"

"No," I said in a clipped tone.

A boyfriend?" She raised her eyebrow.

Now the bitch went too far. "As a matter of fact, I'm waiting on a dentist who does weight training in her spare time. Would you care to wait with me? I think the two of you would have a lot to discuss. YouknowwhatImean?"

"I guess I do." She scribbled something down on her order pad. "You can take care of this right through those doors." She huffed, replaced my Metropolitan with a bill, and waddled away.

I looked down at the table in disgust. The bitch had charged me double what I ordered, plus added on a twenty percent gratuity. As I reached out for the bill, another hand snatched it away from me.

"It's on me," a sexy voice said. I looked up and came face to face with dividends. Ka-ching. Fanta's face wasn't fabulous, but what she lacked in looks, she more than made up for in body. "My name is Fanta, and you must be Royal." Her voice was sweet and husky.

"You're late." I tried to hide my enthusiasm. "I'm just on my way out. I have another appointment in twenty minutes."

"That other appointment can wait." She sat down across from me. "Royal, I'm not going to waste your time, and I hope you don't waste mine. If I'm not what you're looking for let me know, and I can save us both the trouble of an awkward rejection. We both know you're not the only game in town."

"Then why are you here?" I leaned back and placed my folded hands in my lap.

"Because we also know you are the best, and I'm only interested in top-notch establishments. You can keep the five and dime shit for the chickenheads. There ain't no squawking from these lips, unless that's what I'm getting paid to do. So, I'll cut to the chase. I'm not into women, so my fee is double when they make up more than sixty percent of the audience. I'm not an escort, call girl or prostitute. Any sexual favors, or fantasies, are at my discretion, and my disposal. I usually work for a flat salary of $750 a night. That doesn't include tips, but it does comprise two hour-long sets, and a half-hour recap. I don't allow touching of any kind, and I work a nine to five shift, you select the time slot. Any questions?" she asked matter-of-factly.

I must admit, I liked her forwardness, but I wasn't much of an order taker. "I'll tell you what, Fanta" I began, "I like your style, so I'll start you at $500 a night, plus tips. That will include three hour-long sets, with costume and makeup change. There will be no extra fee for an all woman audience, because I don't make up the guest list. I'm only here to satisfy my patrons. As far as the sexual favors, I'm no one's pimp. What you choose to do with those customers once you leave my establishment is completely up to you. It's not my business, unless it happens within my business, and then if it must become my business, you'd better make it your business to disappear. YouknowwhatImean? Now, do *you* have any questions?"

"Just one. When do I start?"

"Friday at midnight, and I expect you to be on time." I stood.

"I will, and I won't disappoint you." She stood and held out her hand.

"I know you won't." I shook her hand and started mentally calculating my future profits.

MARK

Another day, another penny, I thought as I dragged my ass into the office. It was a hot, sticky Wednesday, and the only thing I had to look forward to on hump day was a fucking visit from the Grim Reaper himself. I took a seat behind my desk and automatically pressed the flashing red message button on my phone.

"You have twenty-six messages," the nasal operator exclaimed. I passed over the first dozen or so, until I came to a familiar voice.

"Hey Mark-O, I'll be in around three to get that. I would have someone else pick it up for me, but you know I just love the pleasure of your company. Besides, I got something else for you, and I think this one may really be worth your while. YouknowwhatImean?"

I knew exactly what the son of a bitch meant, and I wanted no parts of it. I just wanted to pay off the last of the money I owed, and get out all in one piece. Fuck the side ventures, and the tradeoffs. I could just imagine how he'd package his latest endeavor, sugarcoating the danger, and making it all seem too good to be true. Hell, Mama taught me well. I sure as hell wasn't going to fall into another pitfall of Royal T. Roaman's. No sirree. Not I said the cat.

Royal's visit came and went. Too bad I can't say the same for his proposal. Royal asked me to swing by his bar on Friday, because he had something to show me. I told him I wasn't interested, but by the time Friday rolled around, I was still on Roxanne's shit list. She had already made other plans, so there was nothing stopping me from taking him up on his offer. They say curiosity killed the cat. I guess that made me one pussy ready to die, because I was on my way to Royalty's Bar & Grill to find out just what Royal had in store for me this time.

I found a cozy spot in the back. Not too close to the spotlight, but not all that far from the action, either. My eyes kept venturing over to the cocoa-colored sister serving the patrons at the bar. Something about her was vaguely familiar, but I couldn't put my finger on where I had seen her before. Maybe it was just my imagination, but it seemed like she was deliberately avoiding eye contact. She wouldn't even look in my general direction at first. When she did, she took quick, furtive glances, sure to turn away just as my gaze would have met hers. Two Long Island Ice Teas later, she had vanished, and another good-looking lady had taken her place. I couldn't imagine where she went, but I never forgot a face. It would only be a matter of time before I remembered where I knew her from.

Soon I had forgotten all about the mysterious bartender, and was now admiring the cream-colored sister sitting across from me in a black leather jumpsuit that looked like it was painted on. *Now that's what I call a masterpiece*, I thought, as she stood, and her ass took on the form of a whole other person. She sashayed over to my table. Well, half-sashayed, half-stumbled, and took a seat across from me.

"Buy a sister a drink," she slurred, showing off a

gold tooth as she smiled seductively.

"Looks like you had one too many already." She looked good, but she reeked of alcohol, and the stench was seeping through her pores. "Maybe you should call it a night."

"Who you s'posed to be, my daddy?"

"Not at all. I was just..."

"You was just losing your fucking mind," she slurred. "Don't nobody tell me when I've had enough to drink. I know my limit, and I damn sure haven't reached it yet. All your monkey ass had to say is that you were too cheap to buy a sister a drink. That's all. Don't sit there in your old tired suit and try to tell me when I've had enough. Shit, my mama can't even tell me when I've had enough. So you can just go fuck yourself, because you ain't that cute anyway." She left me in a huff, and made herself cozy at the next man's table.

I lingered on for another hour and still nothing much was happening. I couldn't understand why Royal asked me to come there if all I'd be exposed to were high-maintenance bitches who would rather fuck for Gucci loafers instead of working a nine to five to earn them. Every female in the joint was done up in the best Macy's had to offer. Nothing too off-the-wall, and nothing non-returnable. I peeped about twelve price tags peeking out of sleeves and necklines, and watched as the women made their rounds from table to table looking for a sucker, or a sugar daddy, whichever came first. This one chick at the next table was making nice with an overweight, balding executive who definitely had too much to drink. She was half an inch away from sitting in his lap, and one compliment away from emptying his bank account. If it weren't for the large hoops dangling from her ear, she may have fooled me, too. But Mama always told me no respectable woman would wear earrings large enough to fit on her wrist, and if she did, it only meant one thing, trouble. This old geezer was about to find himself in a whole mess of it.

After five Long Island Ice Teas, I was plastered and wondering if it were safe for me to drive myself home. When I rose and felt the bar shake, I knew it wouldn't be.

"I'm glad to see you could make it." I heard Royal's voice boom behind me. The sound was emanating from my right lobe, but I felt a strong presence to my left. I turned around unsteadily. "I see you're enjoying yourself, Mark-O. Care for another round?"

"Why not?" The liquor had now taken over my brain, and I felt like I had nothing to lose. The night so far was a total waste, and I figured it could only get better. "Is this shit the great surprise?" I asked, gesturing toward the half-empty room of drunken customers. "Or did I miss something?"

"Seems like you've missed a lot my friend, but the night is still young. Relax, the show's about to start in thirty minutes. You'll understand as soon as you see it."

"I sure as hell hope so."

"Just believe, my friend, just believe. YouknowwhatImean?" With that, he walked away, making nice with the patrons at each table as he passed by.

I scanned the scene again, and tried my best to believe in whatever it was Royal wanted me to. As far as I was concerned, whatever it was had to be better than what I had already experienced. So, I made myself comfortable at my booth and wrapped my lips around the glass of liquor the shapely waitress sat in front of me. Who knows, the way I was feeling, Royal's offer may just be the thing I needed to get the fuck from up under the rut I'd been in.

AYANA

Where the fuck did Mark appear from out of nowhere? I wouldn't have recognized his ass if it weren't for the throngs of pictures Roxy showed me recently. Why the hell was he taking up residence at table six in Royal's musty bar? All kinds of questions rushed through my head as I watched Mark order drink after drink, and I tried to think of an excuse to get my ass from behind the bar before his memory triggered and I found myself up shit's creek. I motioned for Misty to come over and once she did, I explained I wasn't feeling good—that time of the month. She went on and on about how she understood, so I kindly cut her ass off and made my way towards Royal's office. If Mark was there, it had to be for a reason and Royal's domain was the only place I could watch him, without him having the advantage of watching me.

Misty was a new sister Royal hired last week to replace another girl he had to fire for fucking around on the clock. He told me how he stumbled upon Lisa giving blowjobs to paying patrons in booth three, which was located in the far back. Directly below his window, and completely out of his sight. Her fee was seventy-five a pop, and she popped for about $600 a night. I think Royal was more pissed at the idea of her getting paid without him getting his cut, more than he was pissed at the fact that she was hoeing on company time. I knocked gently on the door and felt it open as soon as I knocked.

"I was just on my way out. Something wrong?"

"Yes and no. I'm feeling a little crampy and wondered if I could lay on your couch for a little while. You know, if it was okay with you." Royal looked past me, huffed an okay, and practically ran down the stairs. I stepped into his office, walked over to the window and watched as Royal made his way through the scarce crowd and headed straight towards Mark.

I pulled out my cell phone and quickly called Roxanne. There was no answer. I called back a second time, figuring I must have made a mistake because Roxy always picked up, but I got the same result. After the voicemail came on, I faced reality and pressed end. I looked back out the window in time enough to see Royal leave Mark's table and move towards the bar. I was taken aback by the way Misty was allowing Royal to whisper in her ear, and move his hands back and forth across her backside. *Was he this friendly with everyone?* I tried to remember if I had ever seen him touching on anyone before. I didn't believe he did, but who knew.

Half an hour went by, and Royal never returned to Mark's table. Instead he kept close to Misty, pawing at her every chance he got and that bitch was steady guffawing like Arsenio Hall when Eddie Murphy graced him with his presence on his show. I don't know why it made me so jealous, but it did. I mean, I did find Royal attractive, and I was prepared to sleep with him when the time was right. But, was I lying to myself about how I really felt for him? Maybe Roxy was right to be suspicious. Here I was supposed to be looking out for my sister's soon-to-be husband, and instead I was lusting after her lover.

ROXANNE

I didn't have any concrete plans, but no way in hell was I going to sit around Mark's smug ass and play nice. My mother was in town breaking my balls every chance she got, and the last thing I needed was to have to kiss up to him and pretend to be interested in sex. Tonight she wanted me to meet her at her hotel, because she had something she wanted to discuss with me. I didn't know what it was, but I had a feeling it damn sure wasn't anything I wanted to hear. However, I had to go. It was the only way for me to get some closure on an already out-of-hand situation. I got dressed in a black slip dress, some funky strap sandals and sprayed on a little Gucci Bamboo. I admired myself in the mirror, and made my way out of the house before Mark could start in on his irritating, where-you-going, what-time-will-you-be-back monologue.

"Well, don't you look nice," my mother said, as she stared at my outfit disapprovingly.

She led me into the suite's sitting area and we sat on the couch side by side. She was dressed for bed, and I was dressed to kill. Being the kind of woman she was, she just had to find something derogatory to say, or it just wouldn't be the same.

"Are you going to a disco once you leave here?" she asked true to form, knowing full well I had no other plans, other than coming to see her old, decrepit ass.

"I'm not sure yet." I figured two can play her fucking game. "Care to join me if I decide that's what I'm going to do?"

"Of course, not," she giggled shyly. "I haven't been on the club scene for years. I'd probably just embarrass myself."

No, you'd probably just embarrass me. "Well, don't say I didn't offer." I wanted to get past the small talk and down to the nitty-gritty. "Now, what was so important and private, that it couldn't be discussed over the phone?"

"Roxanne, I'm leaving Joseph," she deadpanned.

"Why?" I didn't really give a fuck, but I felt like faking interest was the decent thing to do.

"There comes a time in every woman's life when she has to ask herself if she plans to be a doormat for the rest of her life, or would she sooner be alone. I'm at that point, and I think I'd be better off alone."

"But, why now after all these years together?" I knew full well it must have been something special to make her finally decide to leave him alone. Mainly because she chose him over me all those years ago. "Can't the two of you work it out?"

"We probably could, but working it out is not something I wish to do. I've had all I can take of that man, and I just want to be left alone."

"You've been together for over twenty-five years," I reminded her.

"And that's over twenty-five years longer than necessary. Roxanne, I didn't want to have to tell you like this, but there's just no other way. I just can't bear to be with your father any longer. And since we haven't slept together for a while now, I don't see any reason why I shouldn't just leave all together. It's not like the old fart would miss me."

"Wait, I don't get it. I thought you and Joseph were happy."

"We were, but things just haven't been the same since..." She trailed off and looked at me with reprehension.

"Don't tell me that you're going to blame your failing marriage on me." I sucked my teeth and rolled my eyes.

"I'm not. I'm merely saying your relationship with your sister brought more tension to an already tense situation between your father and I. Don't think that was the first time he..." She trailed off again, and I could see tears forming in her eyes.

I didn't exactly want to hug and comfort her, because after she found out I was bisexual, she disowned me and had absolutely nothing to do with me. Now, after all this time, here she was crying like a baby, and my heart was supposed to go out to her? I don't think so. "Are you okay?" I opted for conversation rather than physical contact.

"I'm sorry." She dabbed her eyes with the edge of her robe. "I told myself I wouldn't break down in front of you."

"Well, we aren't always able to control our emotions." I felt very uncomfortable. I wasn't used to seeing my mother like this. She was a beautiful, strong woman who would never let her defenses down in front of anyone but Joseph. But here she was, looking dull and boring, wiping her eyes with a beat-up housecoat that had definitely seen better days. "You mind telling me what this is all about?" I tried to figure out what it was she expected me to do with this new information. "I mean, why are you telling me all this? It's not like

Joseph and I are on speaking terms, or anything."

"I know, and I feel awful about that, too. Roxanne, I was so hurt when I found out about you and Ayana. But what was more painful, was seeing Joseph..."

#

My thoughts left her at that moment and ventured back to the old house. Ayana and I were in our room sneaking in a quickie before dinnertime. We were at an age where our parents were trying to respect our privacy. They always knocked and asked permission before entering our room, so we never made a big deal out of locking the door anymore. Their trust gave us enough time to collect ourselves and fake normalcy whenever they did enter, and it wasn't often. This particular night, Mommy had asked Joseph to come upstairs and collect us for dinner like he always did. They were going to surprise us with the news of our moving to a bigger house, and Ayana and I finally having our own rooms and our own space. Joseph was so excited with the news that he rushed into our room, without knocking, and caught us in the act. At least that was the story he told.

Ayana and I were so busy into each other, that we hadn't even heard the door open. It wasn't until we heard my mother's blood-curdling shriek that we realized something was amiss. When we caught sight of Joseph with his dick in his hand leaning against the door frame and the horrified look on my mother's face, our nakedness and the fact that each of our face's had taken residency in the other's crotch was the least of our worries. Let's just say, the shit hit the fan. In the end, Joseph confessed that wasn't the first time he had witnessed us in the midst of indiscretion. That was one of the reasons he insisted on coming to get us for dinner. It gave him an excuse and allowed him to get his rocks off looking at us throwing a few stones of our own.

#

The memory was so vivid I forgot I was now sitting in a hotel room across from my mother, trying to calm her down after the revelation that she and Joseph were headed for splitsville.

"So, what happened? After that whole fiasco, I figured you two could endure anything. Especially, since you put me and Ayana out on the street, but allowed him to stay."

"Roxanne, I did not put you out on the street."

"No, then what would you call it?" I rolled my neck and folded my arms across my chest. "You told us to pack our bags, because if we were old enough to fuck like grown people, then we were old enough to pay bills like them, too. The next day, I moved in with Mark, and Ayana moved in with that nightmare of a man named Craig that you and Joseph adored. Did you know he used to beat on her?"

Evelina lowered her eyes and looked away.

"Just as I thought." I scowled at her. "You didn't give a fuck back then, and you sure as hell don't give a fuck now. Ma, you are the reason why I have been so insecure about my weight all my life and why Ayana continuously allows herself to be abused. Your so-called love has the two of us so fucked up that we wouldn't know real love if it came and bit us in the ass. I don't know what your motive is, because we will never have the mother-daughter relationship we once shared. We both know that. So, why the confession after all this time?"

"I'm trying to move on with a clear conscience. Perhaps, you should do the same."

"Perhaps, you have a suggestion. That is why you

called me over here, isn't it?"

"Well, yes. I've been thinking Roxanne, that you should confront your father. He's gotten off easy this entire time, and I think he needs to hear from you. He should not be able to walk away from this situation scot-free…"

"Ma, I am not doing your dirty work for you! If you've decided to leave that voyeuristic bastard, then do it. Don't think that shedding a few tears is going to turn me into a sympathetic moron, ready to take on your responsibilities and let the son of a bitch have it. This is your battle, and I am not going to fight it for you. If you're ready to leave, then go. Do like you told me. If you find yourself in any trouble, forget you know my number." With that, I stood and sashayed out the room.

Just who the fuck did she think she was? Was I supposed to feel sympathetic and try to fix something that was way beyond repair? I had my own problems, and I sure as hell wasn't going to add hers to my list. She hadn't done it for Ayana or me all those years ago when the shoe was on the other foot. I admit, I had no business going down on my step-sister, but my father had no right getting his masturbation thing on while he was taking it all in. I mean, doesn't that fall under the category of incest, or some shit like that? And what did my mother do? Yell, curse, scream, cry, and then she considered their relationship salvageable and ours null and void. So, fuck her! Whatever happens, happens. I have my own shit to straighten out, and my own prayers to say.

MARK

I was just about to leave when the lights suddenly went low and I caught a glimpse of a thick sister in the spotlight. She was wearing a very revealing outfit with nothing much left to the imagination. She wouldn't fall under the category of pretty or cute. Let's face it, she was butt-ugly, but her body was banging, so I made the exception. I settled back down in my seat and waited to see what Chocolate City had to offer. While she feigned intercourse with a bottle of Belvedere, Royal's voice boomed over the sound system introducing her as the Fantabulous Fanta. I must admit, she was definitely fantabulous, and I was impressed.

It was twenty minutes into her routine when my bladder just couldn't take anymore. I stood up and began making my way through the bar, which was now packed with tables of horny men looking to score. I was suddenly thrust into the spotlight. Fanta instinctively grabbed my arm and pulled me in close to her. She sat me down on the stool and mounted me like a jockey. If I had been sober I would probably have been upset at the fact that her musk oil and body paint was now staining the front of my silk slacks. Not to mention, the way she was thrusting her crotch against mine, my urine had gone to another place, and the blood was rushing to my dick making a very noticeable bulge grow in the outlines of the discoloration. She must have been impressed, because she began gyrating like I was the best thing since yellow grits, and the crowd began to go wild. Then suddenly I had two of the most perfect breasts dangling in my face, and one of the ripest nipples I've ever seen pouring from my mouth.

"Do you want more?" she yelled at the crowd, as she stood in front of me, taking me all in.

All you heard were drunken "yeses", and slurred "hell yeahs," as many of the patrons in the back were making their way closer to the spotlight to ensure that they didn't miss anything.

Next thing I knew, Fanta was in a handstand with her legs dangling over my shoulders and her crotch spread-eagle in my face. She smelled of stale musk and strawberries. Somehow, she maneuvered herself upwards, sprayed whipped cream between her legs, and brought my face to rest within its frothiness. I was lost in my own utopia as all eyes were on me, and I was performing to the best of my ability. The only thing that mattered anymore was my bringing satisfaction to the writhing body in front me. Nothing else was important—not until I was blinded by a large flash of light. I realized Royal now stood three feet in front of me, holding a digital camera and my destiny between his fingertips.

ROYAL

The setup was much easier than I thought it would be. All along Mark tried to play hardball, acting like there was nothing in this world that could break him. But every man has a price, and every man has a weakness. Too bad, the weakness for all men seemed to lie between their thighs. And Mark's dick was surely going to be his demise. Not only had I set some other things in motion, I now had a photo of Mark's face in the place, and the place definitely wasn't that of Roxanne's. But I was still faced with a dilemma. How was I going to get all the proof I was collecting to Roxanne without her knowing I was behind it all? Then faced with all the evidence, who was to say she would leave Mark and come running into my awaiting arms?

Women kill me. They always know how to talk that *if that was me* bullshit when it's their friend filling them in on her latest misadventure. Knowing full well that if it *were* them, the shit would still go down the exact same way, if not worse. It was easy to tell someone to jump out the window of a burning building, when it wasn't their ass dangling from the sill head first. YouknowwhatImean? Any woman on any given day can have the evidence laid out for her in plain sight. However, if she was under the impression she was in love, a brother could get off scot-free just by uttering that Eddie Murphy catch-phrase, "It wasn't me." Hell, I didn't care if she walked in and found him buck-naked right in mid stroke with the other woman. If she was in love, she would be blinder than Stevie Wonder in dark shades in a pitch-black room. And I had a feeling Roxanne sure as hell didn't have 20/20 vision.

I stared at the picture on the LCD display and made my way back up to my office. Imani stood next to the window with her arms crossed. She scowled at me, and it caught me a little off guard.

"What's wrong with you?" I placed my hands around her hips and pulled her close. "You look like I just ate your last apple and you planned on baking a pie."

"Royal, don't." She pulled away from me.

"Don't what?"

"Don't touch me. Not after you were pouring over that buck-toothed heifer behind the bar. Maybe she enjoys being pawed at, but that's not my thing. So, just don't."

"Is that what's bothering you?" I laughed.

"I don't see anything funny." Her hands were on her hips and her neck rolled like she was going for the hula hoop championship. "If you think I'm going to be just another one of your fucking conquests then you can just forget it, because I'm not anybody's knickknack."

"I didn't say you were."

"And furthermore, let me get one thing straight. It's not like I care about your old raggedy ass. I just don't want you to think that you can play me like you play the other bitches that work here. Mine ain't no cheap thrill. I don't get off by fucking a bankroll. It takes a lot more than money to keep me interested. When I see the canine coming into form, that's when I take the high road and pull the fuck back. So, whatever it was that started between the two of us. Consider it finished."

With that, she rushed out of my office, down the stairs and out of the bar. Although I should have been pissed off—insulted even—I was turned the fuck on. That Imani was some kind of woman. Fiery. The only type of woman who knew how to keep my ass in line. If the shit didn't go down with Roxanne the way I hoped it did, she might just get that chance. Let's face it, there was nothing wrong with having a Plan B. The harm was in not having one. YouknowwhatImean?

AYANA

When Royal finally made his way from behind the bar, he had a camera in his hand and a devious look on his face. I didn't know what was up, until I saw him moving towards Mark, who was on his way to the bathroom. In a matter of seconds, Royal had thrust a drunken Mark into the spotlight, with his new freak of the month. She was bucking like a horse, and grabbing at Mark's crotch like the rock in his pants was a solid gold bar. Knowing how anal Mark was, I was waiting for him to pull himself together and throw the freak off of him. But instead, he seemed to enjoy the spotlight. He happily became part of the show. It must have been the liquor talking, because now he had the girl bent over the barstool, ripping away her g-string, and pounding his crotch against her naked backside.

Somehow the tables turned, and he found himself face-to-face with her nappy dugout. The lure of whipped cream must have been too much to resist, because he buried his face in her cherry pie. I lost sight of Royal the entire time, but just as Mark was about to come up for air, there he was with his camera. I didn't know why he was snapping pictures, and I guess Mark didn't either. Mark looked like a deer caught in headlights, and Royal was wearing the smile of a happy hunter who had just laid his eyes on dinner.

I didn't hear Royal come in. Being caught off guard, I had to give him a little attitude so he wouldn't question me about why I was standing at the mirror when I was supposed to be laying down tending to my cramps. My eyes went immediately to the camera in his hand, but I wasn't a fool, I knew I couldn't question him about it. Not yet. Instead, I threw a fake tantrum about his rubbing all over Misty and then got the fuck up out of there.

Once on the sidewalk, I blew out air and tried to figure out my next step. I leaned against the wall and called Roxanne. She picked up before the phone even rang.

"Where the fuck are you?"

"On the corner outside the bar. What's wrong with you?" I thought she was still pissed at how I hung up the phone on her during our last conversation.

"Who the fuck is this?"

"It's Ayana. Roxy, what's up?"

She exhaled loudly. "Girl, I'm so glad to hear from you. You wouldn't believe my night."

"And you wouldn't believe..." I stopped myself. She wasn't upset with me at all and I didn't know how to tell her about what I had just witnessed. It might be nothing, and I didn't want to make a big deal out of nothing. But what if it were something?

"Guess where I was for the most part of the night?" she asked with little enthusiasm.

"I have no idea," I knew both Mark and Royal were in the bar all night so that pretty much used up all of my guesses.

"I went to see my mother. It seems she and Joseph are calling it quits."

"You've got to be kidding me. Why are they

deciding to go their separate ways after all this time?"

"Irreconcilable differences, among other things. I don't even think Joseph knows. She said she's leaving him, there was no mention of his plans." She sighed.

"I see. Are you okay?"

"I don't know, Yana. It's not like I really give a fuck, but they are our parents, and that should count for something. But after all the shit I've been through. Hell, the shit we've been through, I just don't know how I feel. Really, I don't feel anything, and that's fucked up."

"Not necessarily, Roxy. You can't beat yourself up if that's how you feel. They turned their backs on us at our most vulnerable time and that's hard to forgive. She shouldn't expect you to welcome her with open arms and comfort her through this. Where the fuck was our support back then?" I started to feel the heat of the conversation tightening up in the nape of my neck. I kicked one of the gold columns. If it weren't for the bouncer racing outside and giving me the *you okay* look, who knows what my next statement would've been. I just knew it wouldn't have been nice. So I smiled and nodded at him and decided to change the subject. "Where's Mark?"

"You're taking a break?" She ignored my question.

"Something like that. How about the husband, where's his lanky ass?" I wasn't about to let her off the hook that easy. "What did he have to say about all this?"

"He doesn't know." That's all she said. Nothing more, nothing less.

"So, you're in for the night?" I decided to drop it. If she didn't want to admit that Mark wasn't home, there was no need in pressing her. I guess she had her reasons, and in time she might let me know what they were. But tonight, I was just going to leave it alone.

"Is that an invitation?"

"Yes. So what do you say, Roxy?"

"Where do you want to meet?"

"My place in half an hour."

"Ayana, I already told you..."

"Bitch, get your mind out the gutter. I have on my uniform right now, which consists of a flaming red spandex catsuit with fur around the fucking collar, and I'm not about to let anyone see me looking this tore down. I'm going to take a shower, change clothes and then we can be on our way. I just figured before we got to where we were going, we could talk over a bottle of wine I have chilling in the fridge. I have some info for you about Mark and Royal."

"Is it juicy?" she asked, half interested, half wounded.

"I can't call it. You be the judge. So, are we on?" I crossed my fingers and said a silent prayer.

"Sure. I'll see you in about forty-five. I have to freshen up a little my damn self."

"Great. See you when I see you." I hung up and stepped off the curb to catch a cab.

I had just finished rubbing lotion into my damp skin when the intercom rang. I pressed the buzzer and quickly pulled on my red, strapless dress. I stepped into my red and black snakeskin mules and sprayed Dior on the spots Mama said were important. I admired myself in the full-length mirror then rushed to the door when the bell rung. I flung it open, smiling radiantly. My smile deflated faster than a jock's dick in a room full of hermaphrodites. "What the fuck are you doing here?" I asked, as Jasmine rushed past me and entered the apartment.

"What's going on with you, Ayana?" She made herself comfortable on the sofa. "You're never home. You're never at work. You don't return any of my calls, but you can find time to spend a night with Marlon. What did you tell him Ayana, because now he seems to be missing in action, too?"

With that I smiled. I had almost forgotten about the magical night Marlon and I had spent together. It was the first time I told a man I loved him, and meant it. Now that she confirmed he wasn't the type to take it lightly, I knew that there was no way in hell I'd be able to spread my legs or tongue for her ever again. "I didn't tell him anything. I didn't have to. Now, I'm sorry to spoil your surprise, but I'm expecting company, so you have to go. As you can see, I'm on my way out."

"Are you?" Her jaw dropped when she finally noticed it was almost two in the morning and I definitely wasn't dressed for bed.

"Yes I am." I took her up on the challenge. If this bitch left the comfort of her husband's bed and drove twenty minutes for a confrontation, then a confrontation was exactly what the fuck she was going to get. "I'm sorry Jasmine, but you have to leave."

"So, it's like that now, Ayana?" She stood. "After everything, you just think you can walk away from me like I'm nothing?"

"Jasmine, you're married. What kind of future is there for us anyway? Are you really going to leave your rich husband for a woman who's comfortable, but not seeing a quarter of the wealth you're accustomed to? I don't think so." I placed a little distance between the two of us, remembering she didn't live by Dr. King's credo of peace and non-violence. "Let's face it, the fantasy was nice while it lasted, but we're not going anywhere, and I'm tired of wasting my time and energy in dead end relationships."

"Dead end? So, I guess you think a relationship with Marlon has promise?"

"I certainly do, and so does he."

"And that's who you're all dressed up for?" She placed her hand on her hip.

"No. I'm dressed up for myself." I walked over to the door and opened it. "My sister's on her way over, and we're..."

"The same sister you used to fuck while your parents were asleep in the next room," she asked, sarcastically. She moved closer to me, and grinned. "Or the sister your crackhead mother had taken away from her because she was born addicted? Oh no, it couldn't have been her, because that bitch only lasted three days in the incubator. Guess it was her time to go."

That did it. I lunged at Jasmine, and punched that bitch in her face. I snatched her by the hair before her head had a chance to hit the floor with the rest of her body. I dragged her kicking, screaming ass out the door and into the hallway. "Don't bring your ass back over here again," I yelled, as I used my foot to move her bulk the rest of the way out of my doorway. "And lose my fucking number!" I slammed the door and fell against it with tears welling up in my eyes.

I hadn't thought about Hope in years. It was like I just shut that miserable memory out, and never allowed it to resurface. Not until that fucking nut job waved it in my face like it was nothing. Like she was nothing. Like she didn't even matter.

No one knew about Hope except me, my mother, Roxanne, the doctors at the hospital, and the nuns at the church who made sure she had a proper burial. I had woken up from a nightmare one night and confessed the entire ordeal to Jasmine. I was in a blue funk for a week when I relived the nightmare, and she helped me through it. I never thought she would turn and bite me in the ass with it one day.

#

My mother had been shooting up and smoking crack during the entire pregnancy. Hope was born premature, weighing a measly two pounds, nine ounces. All of her major organs were severely underdeveloped. She was a crack baby, and there was nothing the doctors could do to save her. She wasn't supposed to last through the night, but she hung in there. On the second day, I named her Hope, because I was secretly praying she would make it. She tried to. She really did. But on the third day, she was gone. I watched as they turned off the machines and unhooked all the cords and wires from my baby sister's body.

Two days later I watched as her body was given back to the earth and I was placed in the custody of my grandmother. I lived with her for six months until she died from diabetes. The city then placed me back with my mother, because she was now working and receiving treatment for her addiction. We lived the good life for all of two months until the streets started calling her again. The bills started piling up, there was never anything to eat and I was practically raising myself at the ripe old age of six.

One night, she came in my room and dressed me in my last year's Easter outfit. She pulled my hair into ponytails, tying big, awkward bows on the end. She made me put on my shiny black shoes and rubbed lotion on my knees and elbows. We took a cab ride across town, jumped out without paying the fare, and ended up on my father's doorstep. I don't know what went down between the two of them, but from that night on, I lived with Joseph and my mother was never heard from again.

So, I buried her memory along with Hope's and put my all into my new family. At six, I thought that was what I was supposed to do. Now that I'm older, I've come to realize you can't bury your ghosts, because they always have a way of resurfacing. They always come back to haunt you.

ROXANNE

I heard shouting coming from down the hall as I stepped off the elevator. It sounded like the Million Woman March, and I was afraid to turn the corner. I moved cautiously and witnessed Ayana kicking someone out of her apartment. And I mean that literally. The woman jumped to her feet as the door slammed and it looked like she was about to bust the door down. She stopped when she caught sight of me moving towards her. She hurriedly fixed her clothing and rushed past me. I fiddled inside my pocketbook, pretending to be looking for keys as I faced the apartment door adjacent to Ayana's. The woman finally stepped onto the elevator when I retrieved my keys and placed them inside one of the locks. When she was gone, I quickly dropped my keys back into my purse and knocked on Ayana's door. I was happy her next door neighbors were either out or fast asleep.

"Yana, it's Roxanne. Open up!" I heard the lock click and the door open slightly. Ayana peeked out at me. The chain lock cut across her eyelids.

"Are you alone?"

"I should hope so, or someone stiffed me on carfare."

We laughed as she opened the door. Her eyes were slightly puffy and I could tell she had been crying.

"Are you okay?" I touched her arm.

"I'll live."

"I guess that was Jasmine," I tried to make light of the situation as I stepped inside.

"In the flesh." She closed the door behind me.

"You still up to going out?" I gave her the once-over. She looked exhausted, like she just ran a marathon.

"Not really," she huffed. "But if you are, I don't want to ruin your evening."

"Ayana, this evening was ruined three hours ago. Staying in is probably the wisest thing to do considering all the shit we've been dealing with. Do you have anything in here to eat?" I led her into the kitchen.

"But, of course." She placed a plate of fried chicken on the table. She then passed me the ingredients for a Caesar salad. "A salad bowl should be in the top of the cabinet behind you." She buried her head in the refrigerator and came up with more goodies wrapped in foil and Tupperware.

We were halfway through the wine, and were still picking at the mounds of food we had piled on the plates in front of us.

"So, you never get the urge anymore?" she asked.

"It's not that I don't. It's just that I choose not to act on them. Mark is everything I can ask for, and then some," I lied. "I mean, we have our problems. Who doesn't? But all in all we're surviving. As far as women go, it's more like an infatuation. I don't need to be with a woman, I just enjoy the sameness of our makeup. I like making love to a man just as much, if not more."

"I feel you on that, but don't you ever find yourself missing that lifestyle?"

"I don't know. I mean, being gay seems to be the thing these days, but it's just not the thing for me. I want to have kids one day. I want to get married. I want to live my life the way it's supposed to be lived."

"And who says you can't do all that with another

woman?"

"I do. And what about you? What's up with Jasmine?"

"She's married, and she's not really future material. She's too possessive, too physical and too damn unpredictable. I can't live the rest of my life covering up black and blues. I just don't see the use in it. Besides, I'm not in love with her. I don't even think I like her. Jasmine's the type of woman who would try anything once, and that turned me on. But after you've tried everything, and you figure out that sex was the basis of the relationship, sometimes it's just not enough. It's the same thing with men. They think new ass is the best ass, but after a month or so, the new ass is old ass because everything you wanted to try has been tried. Then there's nothing left except really getting to know one another. And if you're not compatible, be it a man or a woman, it's just not going to work."

I thought about Ayana's analogy for a minute and reflected on my relationship with Mark. The sex was good and I did love him, I just wasn't sure I liked him. Don't get me wrong, we were very compatible, but were we forcing ourselves to be, or was it fate? "Do you think it's possible to be more in love with the idea of being in love than it is to actually be in love with a person?"

"Sure, it is. I've known plenty of women who act like they can't live without a man in their life, and they'll put up with just about anything to hold on to him."

"And I'm one of them," I whispered.

"What?"

"Nothing, I was just wondering about Mark and what our future holds."

Ayana exhaled loudly and slouched back. She looked like she had the weight of the world on her shoulders and she was about to crack under the pressure.

"I have to tell you something about Mark, and I'm

not sure how you're going to take it."

"Is it bad?"

"Bad enough, but it's not horrible."

"Well, whatever it is, I want to know. So lay it on me."

"Okay." She sighed loudly. "I saw Mark tonight at the bar, and let's just say he wasn't on his best behavior."

"Wait a minute." I raised my right hand. "You saw my Mark at Royal's bar tonight, and you didn't call me? What kind of shit is that?"

"First of all, I did call you, but you weren't home, Mrs. I-forgot-to-tell-you-my-mother-is-in-town. Why the hell do you think you're here now? I did say I had info for you, didn't I?"

"And I have yet to hear it, or is the big news that Mark was at the bar?"

"No…" She made sure to pronounce each word very carefully. "The big news is he was at the bar getting his nasty on with some freak Royal hired for entertainment purposes."

"He what?"

"And," she added, "Royal has the pictures to prove it." She half-smiled, half-smirked as I read victory in her face. She looked like she was the fucking Queen of Sheba and she had just dropped my ass down to peasant status.

I felt like a fool. I didn't know what to say, and it sure as hell wouldn't pay to hit her with a snappy comeback. Not since she saw my man cheating—rather getting his nasty on—firsthand. First of all, I couldn't believe his tight ass would even know what to do under the circumstances, but then it made me wonder. Perhaps he's been getting his nasty on all along. That would explain his lack of interest in me lately. Maybe he was putting up with my ass as much as I felt like I was putting up with his. All this time I was acting like I was alone in my disdain for what we had become. Not realizing Mark may be feeling the exact same way. Except that son of a bitch was out there doing something about it, while my dumb ass just stayed silent and pretended. Well, not necessarily. I mean, I did fuck Royal, but that was beside the point. At the time, I was weak and that was a mistake. His getting his nasty on was spiteful, and I was hurt.

Instead of playing into Ayana, and giving her the satisfaction of seeing me sweat, I decided to play against her complacent ass and do exactly the opposite of what she expected. I had a feeling she knew much more than she was telling me. The dumber I appeared, the more open she'd become.

"I can't believe that son of a bitch." I watched as she displayed what I felt was a practiced look of empathy. "I had a feeling he was fucking around on me, but I just didn't have any proof. Not until now." I hoped that last sentence had given my sister enough rope to hang herself with. Lord knows she just loved to throw shit in your face whenever possible.

"Roxy, it's not that serious. Mark was drunk, and he got caught up in the moment. He's not fucking around on you. He just needs to learn how to hold his liquor."

I was shocked. The years had made me bitter and Ayana wiser, and I couldn't believe she hadn't taken this *I told you so* opportunity and run with it. I began to feel guilty for my negative thoughts, and decided to come clean and tell her how I really felt.

"Well, he's doing something, because shit just ain't been right between the two of us lately, and I don't know if the problem is him, or me." The liquor started talking then because I could hear the ghetto coming out as my speech became laden with Ebonics.

"The problem is probably all in your mind. You

always did have serious trust issues, especially when it came to men. I'm not surprised you haven't sunken so low as to spying on his ass," she said with a timid smile.

"I've sunken even lower." I sulked. "I got you to do the shit for me." We looked at each other and doubled over laughing.

It felt good to let out some of the anxiety and tension that had me so balled up inside, and I was happy that I was doing it with Ayana. Although she was a royal pain in the ass at times, I loved her with all my heart and I couldn't risk losing her again. We spent the rest of the night sprawled out on her bed, pouring out our hearts about what scared us most in our relationships, and what we felt were our shortcomings in life. To say we hadn't been around each other for years, tonight made it seem like we were never separated. For the first time in a long time, I felt those old feelings creeping back as I watched Ayana stand, pull off her dress and slip into her nightgown. I guess old habits do die hard because Ayana still wasn't keen on underclothes, and I was beginning to feel a familiar moisture seeping onto my satin panties. I caught her eyeing my bosom, and I began to wonder if she was feeling the same way.

AYANA

I was drunk as hell and uncomfortable, so I quickly changed out of my confining dress and slipped into a non-restricting teddy. When I realized what I had done, and the fact I did it right in front of Roxy, it was too late. She could have easily assumed I was trying to seduce her, and flipped the script. But she didn't. I quickly looked at her face to read her expression. Everything but displeasure was in her eyes.

"I see you still don't like underclothes," she slurred, as she poured herself yet another drink. "Gravity's been good to you."

"Yeah, so far. But I've put a lot of work into this body. Shit, I owe half of it to Fabio."

"Fabio," she mocked. "You better get with the brothers and get that Shaun T thing going. Fabio doesn't know how to shape a sister."

"Look bitch, firm is firm. I don't care who the fuck helps me achieve it. Fat don't know no color," I slurred. *Double negatives? Shit, I had to be drunk*, I thought with a smile.

"What are you smiling about?" She moved closer to me.

"Us." I inched towards her direction. Moments later we were in a heated embrace, playing tag with our tongues and discovery with our hands and fingers.

“We got to stop. We can’t do this.” She pulled away.

“Why not?” I desperately hoped she was just trying to play hard to get.

“Because it’s not right.” She stood and adjusted her clothes.

“Roxy, don’t.” I pulled her back down on the bed beside me. “I need this. We both need this.” I began to kiss her neck, then her face and lips. “Please, let me make love to you.”

“I want you to so badly, Yana, but it’s not right. None of this is right, and I can’t keep fucking away my problems. It’s deeper than that.”

“Don’t you think I know that?” I tried to remove her dress.

“Stop it, Yana.” She pulled away again. “I have to go. I have to figure out what it is I really want out of this life of mine. I’m running in fucking circles and I can’t take it anymore. If I allow us to make love again, I know there won’t be any turning back. Yana, I’ve never loved anyone the way I love you, and I doubt I ever will. That’s why I have to go. So, please let me go.”

Roxy’s eyes told me she wanted me to talk her into staying more than anything else, but her heart told me she was confused. Making love to me would only make matters worse for her. I decided to follow her heart, and send her on her way with my blessings. I figured if we were truly meant to be, then it wouldn’t have to take convincing either her, or me. I walked her to the door, kissed her gently on the lips and watched her walk onto the elevator. I returned to my room, emotionally drained and sexually aroused. I dialed Marlon’s number.

“Hello.” I could tell he was awoken from a sound sleep.

“Marlon, I need you. Can I come over?” I knew I sounded desperate, but I didn’t care. Marlon was the only one who wanted to be with me for me. I needed to be with someone who could help me relieve the pain and devastation of rejection.

"Ayana, it's almost six in the morning. What's wrong, you can't sleep?"

"No," I lied. "Can I come over?"

"You know you can, Baby. The doorman has a set of keys. Don't be afraid to wake me in your own special way." He laughed deeply. "I can't wait to see you, Baby."

He hung up, and I began to get dressed.

MARK

It was damn near six in the morning when I finally staggered into the apartment, and I was waiting for Roxanne to start in on me. This time, I wouldn't even argue back. I deserved everything she threw at me, and for once, I was prepared to take the abuse like a man. I used the wall as my crutch as I slowly made my way down the hall and into our bedroom. I entered quietly and tiptoed towards the bed. I stopped short as I noticed the bed was still made up, and Roxanne was nowhere to be found. My mind started racing, and I thought of every possible scenario. Then I started retracing my own tracks.

I had left the bar over three hours ago, but instead of going straight home and coming clean to Roxanne, I spent the time walking the streets of New York. I strolled down the new Times Square, where only a few XXX-rated spots lingered, and sauntered into one of them. Once inside, I picked a corner booth and paid a painted-up, stoned teenager a dollar a pop to do all the filthy things I told her to do before the window closed between us, and the machine begged for more change.

"What can I do for you, Daddy?" she asked, as the slit opened and the light came on inside her booth. We had been going at it for almost thirty minutes, and my right arm was getting tired. Those had been the first words she'd uttered, and as soon as she called me Daddy, she awakened something in me. My mind drifted back to my first time with Mocha and my movements became swifter, my breathing heavier. This time, I decided to keep it going even though the window had closed and the neon money slot was blinking erratically inside the dark booth. I finally bought myself to satisfaction, adding some of my own secretions to the already stained walls. I cleaned myself off the best I could with the mini towelettes the dark-haired lady at the front door supplied me with, and exited the booth.

I decided to delay my fate even further, and took a stroll along Central Park West. When I finally reached my block, I said a silent prayer and made my way to the building. I kept my fingers crossed for the elevator ride, and begged for mercy as I turned my key in the lock. All my praying paid off, because I had made it inside our bedroom without a hitch. The only problem with that was I was alone. *Where the fuck could she be?*

Just then I saw the flash of light pass before my eyes, and all my questions had been answered. While I was jerking off in a seedy booth downtown, Royal had made his way to my place and showed Roxanne the pictures. She, in turn, fell into his compassionate arms and he packed her up and moved her out with promises of a better life without me. I ran to the closet and yanked open the doors. Her clothes were still lined up neatly, as they had been earlier that evening. I jumped over the bed and opened her dresser drawers. Everything was still in tact. I slammed the drawer closed and sat on the edge of the bed. Defeated and drained, I placed my head in my hands and began to cry. Roxanne had finally broken down and given into my every desire, and I was acting like a fucking kid in grade school. Stir crazy because I had finally gotten my first taste of sideline pussy, and relentless because I couldn't get enough of it. The house phone rang. I sprang to my feet and grabbed it off the nightstand.

"Roxanne," I screeched desperately into the phone receiver.

"You mean to tell me she's not home, Mark-O," the male voice said with a snicker. "I wonder where she could..."

I slammed the phone down on the nightstand and started cursing at the walls. Royal had a way of getting under my skin, and right now I could feel the fungus growing. It quickly dawned on me Royal had to know Roxanne wasn't home. Why else would he call? The only way he could know was if she was with him. Royal was fucking with me again, but this time I wasn't going to let him get away with it. I called his ass back and gave him an earful. If he wanted to treat me like a bitch, a bitch I would be.

"Why the fuck did you call my house, man?" I yelled into the phone.

"Is it against the law to check up on a friend?" His relaxed tone was getting me more pissed, and I'm quite sure he knew it. That's why he kept it up. "You were a little drunk when you left my place, and I just wanted to make sure you got home all right."

"And if I didn't?" I started pacing back and forth on the side of the bed.

"Then I wanted to make sure I made myself available to Roxanne in your absence. You know, to console her in her time of need."

"Is that what you're doing now?"

"What's that, Mark-O?"

"Is that what it's called nowadays? Well, you can tell that bitch I hope she enjoys the ghetto, because you ain't nothing but a lowlife piece of shit, and if I ever catch you in the street..."

"What the fuck did you just say?" He cut me off and made me realize exactly who I was threatening. Fear took hold of my heart and I quickly ended the call, slamming the phone down again.

I glanced at the clock. It was now six forty-five and I was livid. I had already showered and changed and Roxanne was still not home. I was about to reach for the phone again when I heard Roxy's key turn in the lock. I sprinted into the living room and sprung the door open before she even had a chance to.

"Where the fuck have you been all night?" I yelled loud enough to wake the entire building.

"Out."

That's all she said. Quietly and calmly. Then she pushed past me and headed towards the bedroom like it was nothing. Leaving me standing at the door staring into an empty hallway. *Oh no that bitch didn't.* I slammed the door and took off after her. By the time I reached the bedroom, Roxanne had already peeled her clothes off and was now in the shower. *Getting rid of all the evidence, yet again, my boy.* Paranoia took control of me. I snatched Roxanne out of the shower and pulled her into the bedroom. She was dripping wet, but I didn't give a damn. I pushed her back on the bed and jumped on top of her.

"Let me smell your pussy." I clawed at her crotch while she tried to fight me off.

"What the fuck are you doing? Get the hell off of me!"

"I said, let me smell your pussy!" I threw her back on the bed once more and tried to place my face between her massive thighs.

"Mark, what the fuck has gotten into you?" She pushed me away, and stood up.

"No, the right question is who the fuck has gotten into you." At this point, I was standing and so was my

Johnson. Roxy was dripping wet and naked and I had to tear my eyes away from her bush and focus on her face. Unbeknownst to her, she was looking into the eyes of a hungry lion. I guess she didn't realize she was the main course. "Now, are you going to tell me where the fuck you were all night, or am I going to have to..."

"What, Mark? What the fuck are you going to do?" she prodded. Her hands were on her hips and her breasts rose and fell along with her heightened breathing. "It's amazing how you want to know so fucking much about me, when your ass wasn't home either. You mind telling me where the fuck you were last night?"

That question caught me off guard, and brought my ass back to reality with the quickness. There was no way in hell I could tell Roxanne all that had transpired within the last ten hours, and even if I did, I didn't have the energy to discuss it. So, I took the easy route and took the onus off of myself. "This is not about me, Roxy. I'm asking you a simple question. Where the fuck were you last night, and who the fuck were you with?"

"Well, I don't hear you offering any information about your whereabouts, Mark. So, why the fuck should I be forthcoming? If you want to know where I was last night, simply tell me all that you got into. Since you're so righteous, and into smelling pussies and all that good shit, why not tell me where your dick has been. Or better yet, your tongue."

She stormed back into the bathroom, and I was wise enough to leave it alone. At least for the moment. If she could come at me like that, then she had to know what was up. In my absence, Royal had gotten to Roxanne and filled her in on my antics. It was just a matter of time before the bomb exploded.

As I sat on the edge of the bed counting down the minutes to the end of her shower, I felt like Bruce Willis in *Armageddon*. I was bracing myself for the explosion. I figured if I was going to go out anyway, I might as well be like him and go out like a hero.

ROYAL

Instead of my usual seduction of Imani, this morning I found myself closing down the bar with a way-too-eager Misty. Misty was new meat. Not yet broken in. Well, at least not by me. You could tell she was the kind of chick that had been around the block, the boulevard, and the freeway. Wild and worldly, not afraid to try anything, or anyone, once. She was now looking at me with bedroom eyes, and a smile that showed an overbite that would've made Dracula jealous. Mental note to self, blowjobs are definitely out with this one.

"So, you going straight home?" She licked her lips seductively.

"Yeah, it's been a long night," I answered in a clipped tone. I didn't want to give Misty the wrong impression. It wasn't like I was a boy scout, or anything, but at the moment I just wasn't in the mood for anything sexual. My mind was on more important things. "Do you need me to drop you off somewhere?"

"I would say your place," she began, but when she saw the *please don't go there* look in my eyes, she quickly changed her tune. "But honestly, I'm just as beat as you are, so I guess we'll just have to do that another time."

"Yeah," I said with little interest.

"Well, I live up in Harlem on 149th and Lenox." She dropped her head to the side and licked her lips.

"Okay." I was pissed with myself for offering, because there was no way in hell I was driving all the way up to Harlem at five in the morning on a Saturday. I was just about to fill her in on my decision when a brother who frequented the bar came by and started kicking it to her. Moments later he informed me he would make the trek. The two of them walked off nuzzling each other's necks and grabbing at each other's flesh.

After blowing Misty off, I went home to ponder my next move with Roxanne. Once I got up enough courage to dial her number, Roxanne sent my calls straight to voice mail. When I decided to call the home phone, Mark picked up in a panic. After exchanging a few pleasantries, he hung up on me, dialed back and then proceeded to insult me. I found it amusing at first, but I couldn't let the punk get the best of me. I put the fear of God in him and made him bow down. He hung up in the same panic he picked up in. He probably pissed his pants—the little wuss, but it served him right. Who the hell was he to think he could tell me something about myself? YouknowwhatImean?

I awoke about an hour later in a cold sweat. I had dreamed I was making love to Roxanne, and just as I was about to hit my mark she turned into the bluish-hued Rachel I had stumbled upon in my bathroom—cold, dead and gone from my life forever. I quickly walked to the bathroom and splashed my face with cold water. It was just a dream, I kept reminding myself. I noticed I was shaking. I grabbed myself tightly around the shoulders. "Stop it!" I screamed, trying to gain control. I splashed my face a few more times. When I realized water wasn't helping any, I turned to an alternative liquid and swallowed down a scotch on the rocks. The vision appeared again and finally disappeared a few drinks later.

I was nursing a well-deserved hangover when Imani walked into the bar looking dazzling. I really didn't think she was coming back after the way she stormed out last night, but like all the others, I knew she couldn't stay away either. I watched as she worked her way through the crowd with an incandescence I hadn't seen since a regular named Delicious got her attention. Maybe it was just my imagination, but she looked like she just got fucked but good. The only problem with that is I had nothing to do with it, and I wanted to get to the bottom of this shit before it got out of hand, and she got away. I finished filling the register and walked to the back.

"Well good night to you, too." I barged into the dressing room hoping to catch a glimpse of her semi-nude body. No such luck—she had on her uniform under her trench coat.

"Royal, didn't I tell you to knock before you enter?"

"And didn't I tell you this is my place, and I'll pretty much do whatever the fuck I want to do. If you don't like it, grab your shit and bounce."

Imani fixed her mouth to say something, but smiled instead and opted to say nothing. She was a smart one and I loved her style.

"I'm docking you for leaving early last night." I handed her a half empty envelope filled with cash.

She took the envelope from my hands, stuffed it into her purse and left out. She made sure to brush past me just enough to throw me off balance, but not enough to knock me completely over. If she were a man I would have kicked her ass, but I wasn't about to go back to jail for no bitch. No matter how fucking fine and fiery she was. Instead, I grabbed her back into the dressing room and let my dick do the talking. I slammed her against the wall, and pushed my body tightly against hers.

"What's gotten into you lately?" I thrust my hips into hers. There was no mistaking the bulge in my pants, and the heat and moisture I felt seeping through the fabric of her jumpsuit. That along with the fact she didn't push me off of her only confirmed what I already knew. She wanted me just as much as I wanted her. "You don't like it here anymore?" I grabbed her waist with both hands.

"Royal, what do you want? Why are you fucking with me?"

"Believe me, Imani, if I were fucking with you, you'd know it. YouknowwhatImean?"

Again, she did that body thrust shit, and this time I found myself flat on my ass as I watched her walk out of the dressing room. If it weren't for the fact I wanted to fuck the shit out of her, she would definitely have found herself out of a job. When I made my way from the back, Imani had already taken up space behind the bar and was mixing drinks for two men seated in front of her. One was short, dark and unattractive. The other was more of the same, only a little taller. "I see you got a light crowd tonight," he was saying, as she passed him his drink. *Shit, anything is light to your dark chocolate ass*, I thought, as I moved closer to hear her response.

"So far," she said. "Together or separate?"

"Me and you," the short one replied with a chuckle. "Or me and him?"

"I was talking about the two of you. Will you be paying together or separate?" Imani smiled at the man, but I didn't miss her eyes rolling up.

"Oh," the short one continued with a sigh. "I was about to say, I'm not a fag or nothing, if that was what you were implying." Damn, brother was ugly and ignorant. By the look in Imani's eyes, I could tell she was thinking the exact same thing.

"Not at all. I could never think such a thing about you two fine, chocolate brothers. That'll be sixteen dollars, handsome."

"No problem." He handed her a twenty. "Keep the change."

"Thanks." She stroked his cheek lightly. He blushed as she walked over to the register to retrieve her cut. I looked at homeboy—all smiles and chitchat—and all I could think was boy, Imani sure knew how to work a nigger. My dumb ass included. As she was placing bills in her bust line, I walked over and whispered in her ear.

"Are you all right, Imani?"

"Couldn't be better." She walked away.

I was just about to go after her and put her in her place, when Misty appeared at the bar asking for refills. Imani took the glasses from her tray and smiled. Misty smiled back, and when she caught sight of me, started glowing.

"Royal, I'm sorry I couldn't kick it with you last night as planned." Misty grinned and leaned her elbow on the bar. Imani looked up at me through the mirror with a face that could crack glass. "But you know how it is when something more intriguing comes along."

Misty not only had Imani's undivided attention, but I could see the men at the bar whispering and joking amongst themselves as well. "Misty, don't flatter yourself," I was far from embarrassed, but in the backyard of a place called pissed off. "The only thing we had going on last night was a drop home, and little did your ghetto ass know once I heard Harlem, you were on your own. So, be thankful Rufus found his way to you, or you would have been on the same subway that brought your ass in here today." I marched towards her and stood in front of her on the opposite side of the bar. "For future reference, never pretend that it's more than it really is, because games only get your ass fired around here." I walked away, noticing a smirk rising on Imani's face. I wasn't sure if she was smiling because I put Misty in her place, or because now she knew I wasn't interested in her. Really, I was too agitated to care. I stepped from behind the bar and made my way to my office.

ROXANNE

I took my time in the shower, trying hard to calculate my next move. I wasn't really mad at Mark, because Ayana took up for him and I knew she wouldn't lie to me. I couldn't let him think his indiscretion would go unpunished either. I bided my time and reminisced about my encounter with Ayana. I smiled at our openness and longing for each other after all these years. I was proud of myself for stopping and leaving before we went too far, but the desire was still there. I opened my legs wider and thrust my groin towards the steady spray of water hoping it would cleanse away the moisture that was starting to make its way down my thighs. No such luck. The strong pulse of the water against my naked flesh soon had me writhing, probing and moaning a sinful tune, as my body exploded from the inside out and my inner juices mixed with the whirlpool winding down the drain.

I stepped out the shower and took my time getting dressed. I casually brushed my teeth, and finally made my way into the bedroom. I wasn't quite sure what type of mood I was supposed to be in, but the look on Mark's face said he was prepared to do battle. Since, I'm never one to go with the flow, I decided to play the nice role and catch his ass slipping.

"What are you planning to do with your Saturday?" I asked sweetly.

"What?" He wasn't able to hide his surprise. I smiled as tiny beads of sweat started forming on his upper lip. "I did...didn't make any yet. I..."

"Good. I have a surprise for you. I hope you enjoy it. Now, get some sleep." I kissed him softly on the lips and quickly eased myself under the covers. I made sure to turn my back to him, so he couldn't see my eyes and he couldn't read my expression.

"What kind of surprise?" I could feel the worry lines forming on his forehead, even if I couldn't see them.

"It wouldn't be a surprise if I told you, would it? Now get some sleep. We have a big day ahead of us."

Mark finally drifted off to sleep after tossing, turning, fidgeting and fretting. I slept off and on, and when I finally felt the bed stop moving, I made my way into the living room. I turned on my Jill Scott CD and pulled on my Capri cigarette while I took a long walk with her around the park. I sipped my first vodka tonic as she told me how much he loves me. Polished off my second as she told me that one was the magic number. When the CD changed, I found myself smoking cigarettes with Tweet, and smiling as she sang "Oops," and I remembered my own session this morning in the shower. As she started crooning about being drunk, I started feeling the effects of my fourth drink. I was in the midst of rocking the boat with Aaliyah when Mark walked into the room and my ass sobered up with the quickness.

"How long have you been up?" He scratched his ass with one hand and adjusted his balls with the other.

"Not long," I tried not to slur my words. "I couldn't sleep, so I came in here to relax."

"I see." He lifted my legs, took a seat beside me on the couch, and placed them back in his lap. He massaged my feet gently. "So, what's this big surprise you have for me?" He squeezed the balls of my feet, and it turned me on instantly.

"I guess you'll just have to wait and see." I felt the liquor take effect, and my body gave into his kneading. I stroked his head with my palm, and formed small circles with my fingertips. I used my nails to scratch at his scalp, something I knew he could not resist.

"You want to carry this party back into the bedroom?" He moved his hands slowly up my thighs.

"In due time, Sweetie." I jumped up and turned off the CD as Aaliyah was telling him to read between the lines. If he wasn't catching my drift, he damn sure wasn't going to catch hers. "Let's go get dressed." I made my way down the hall.

Mark and I stepped out of the taxi in front of the W Hotel in Union Square shining. The passersby on the street, as well as the guides who opened the taxi door for us and held open the hotel doors admired us. They ushered us into the lobby. We made a quick right and walked into their Living Room Lounge for a drink.

"Very impressive." Mark looked around, admiring the scenery. From the drapes, to the carpeting, to the various tables, chairs and couches, I could see he didn't expect me to bring him to a place like this. Really, I never would have. If it weren't for the old lady who held the key to my happiness sulking away upstairs in a $400 a night room, our black asses would have made due with The Watering Hole, a bar on Nineteenth between Park Avenue South and Irving Place. The bar was not the usual NYC upscale atmosphere, nor a place for fashion statements. But they could sure mix one hell of a drink and everyone from the owners to the staff made a person feel welcome.

"What would you like to drink?" the uptight matron asked from behind the bar.

"A cosmopolitan for me, and a Hennessy on the rocks for the gentleman." I watched her as she gave Mark the once over, and slipped him a sly *I would love to get to know you better* smile. Mark blushed, put his arm around my waist and began to nuzzle my neck. She huffed her disapproval and turned to fix our drinks. She got exactly what she deserved. Just because a brother walked in looking like money, smelling like high-priced cologne, and acting like he was somebody, didn't mean he was going to fall for the first white woman who batted her fucking eyelashes at him. I mean, Mark and I have our differences, but we would never outright disrespect each other—not intentionally, anyway. I kissed the side of his face and smoothed down his collar as she sat the drinks on the bar in front of us.

"Twenty-eight dollars." All of a sudden she was very rude and impatient. Mark flipped off two twenties and flung them on the bar.

"You may want to stick around," Mark told the bartender when she returned with his change. "We'll be needing refreshers soon."

"I'll do that." She knew full well our black asses would dry up before she rushed over to fix us another drink.

"So, this is the surprise?" Mark smiled at me with nothing but love in his eyes. I stared back at him and tried to fathom why he wasn't enough to keep me happy. I mean, let's face it, my baby is P-H-I-N-E. Fine. Finer than any other brother I ever let get close to me. He had a bachelor's degree in marketing, a master's degree in business, owned his own company, and loved the shit out of my trifling, confused ass. Mark was the kind of person who always saw the sun through the rain. He was also the only one who could put up with my many moods, and not complain. Truth be told, Mark was damn near perfect, and I was just looking for reasons to dislike him.

"Not exactly." I didn't want to give away too much. If he knew I brought him downtown with the intentions of confronting Evelina, all that good shit I just said about him would fly right out the fucking window.

I coerced him into three more drinks, and when he finally mellowed I led him upstairs to the fourth floor. We stopped in front of the door and I turned to him. "Mark, do you love me?"

"You know I do, Roxy." He gathered me up in his arms and kissed me gently.

"Would you do anything for me?" Tears started to form in my eyes.

"You know I would, Baby." He kissed my tears away. "Are you okay?"

"I'm fine. Just a little nervous, that's all."

"Well, it's not like it's our first time, or anything." He had no idea his ass was dripping with honey and I was about to toss him into an angry beehive.

There was no use in me trying to postpone the unavoidable. I tapped lightly on the door as Mark fixed me with an inquisitive gaze. I placed my finger on his lips, quieting him. Not allowing him to say one word. Making sure he couldn't ask any questions I wasn't prepared to answer. He just shook his head from side to side and smiled. Like every man, he must have thought I had another woman on the other side of the door waiting to fulfill his every fantasy. His smile soon turned to anguish when Evelina opened the door. Gasoline and matches sure as hell don't mix, and if the two of them came within one more inch of each other, I'm quite sure they would've started a fire. Evelina huffed. Mark puffed. And they blew my fucking straw house down. Mark stomped away from the door just as Evelina slammed it in my face.

MARK

"What the fuck were you thinking taking me to see that, that woman?" I really wanted to call Evelina a bitch, but that would be disrespectful. Besides, anyone capable of bringing such a beautiful woman into this world didn't deserve that title. "You know how much I hate her, and you took me there anyway. What the fuck were you thinking?"

"Mark, I...," Roxanne followed me into the apartment.

"Shut the fuck up, Roxy!" I knew full well if it wasn't her turn to kiss ass, my jaw would be bright crimson, and I'd be in the emergency room trying to get the doctors to remove a size ten stiletto out of my anus. "I don't want to hear anything you have to say."

I doubled back, walked out the door and slammed it behind me. I wasn't sure where I was going. I just knew I couldn't stay in the same house with her a minute longer.

I only made it two feet when the whole episode turned into a soap opera. I cursed and carried on, marching down the hall screaming so loud, I could crack plaster. Roxanne ran out of the apartment with tears streaming down her face. She fell to her knees, pulled on my leg, and begged me not to leave her. Now don't get me wrong, Roxanne is more thick than obese, but I almost pulled a groin muscle trying to drag her big ass to the elevator. "What the fuck was on your mind?" I screamed at the top of my lungs.

"I don't know, Mark, I don't know." Tears streamed down her face. She sniffled loudly and used the back of her hand to wipe away the snot pouring from her nose. "I just want to be happy, Baby. You always say you want to make me happy..."

"And what about my happiness, Roxanne, huh? Why the fuck does it always have to be about you? Why the fuck is it always about what the fuck you want? Don't I have any fucking say in the matter?" I finally reached the elevator and pressed the down arrow.

"Mark, please don't leave me like this." She stood and tried to hold me. "Let's go inside and talk this over. Okay, Baby? Let's..."

"Roxanne!" I snatched her arms from around my neck and stared her dead in the eyes. "I've had just about enough of you and your shit. First Royal, now your mother, what the fuck is next? Is Ayana going to suddenly appear at my motherfucking doorstep, too?" There was a loud beep and the elevator doors opened slowly. "I'll tell you what, you go inside and talk this shit over with the only person who fucked it all up to begin with—yourself." I stepped on the elevator and let the doors close as I watched Roxanne shrink to the floor, wallowing in her own misery. I felt sorry for her, but I was tired of being weak. Tired of acting soft. Sick of always letting Roxy get her way, then being miserable in the end. Let her worry about me for once, I thought as I stepped outside the building. I looked from left to right, and then left again. I didn't have anywhere to go, but I was too damn selfish and proud to go back upstairs to talk it through with Roxanne.

It was that same selfish pride that took my black ass

back down to Seventeenth Street to see Evelina. I didn't know why I allowed her to get under my skin in the first place. I knew just as well as she did we had to come to some kind of terms, or else her daughter and I would never truly be happy. It was not like I was the one to drop the bomb on her about Roxanne and Ayana to start with. It was something she already knew. It was the reason Roxanne came to live with me in the first place. There was no hiding that fact now. I guess the embarrassment of not only Roxanne's improprieties, but Joseph's as well, was just too much for her to handle. I mean, it's one thing to live a lie within the safety of your own walls. When the walls come tumbling down and all your skeletons are exposed, that was a whole other ball game. Strike one was Joseph. Strike two was Ayana. Strike three was Roxanne. No matter how much I tried to argue my point with Evelina, I knew I would still be out. Game over. I lost. But it was worth a try.

"What are you doing back here?" Those words accompanied a brutal stare as Evelina opened the hotel door to my morose expression.

"I came to talk to you. Can I come in?"

She moved aside without a word and gestured for me to enter. I walked into the sitting area of the suite and took a seat on one of the plush chairs in the corner. She sat across from me on the silken chaise. She laid back, crossed her arms over her chest, looked right through me and uttered one word, "Talk." And that was barely audible.

"Evelina…" I didn't recognize my own unsteady voice. I cleared my throat loudly. "I know you blame me for exposing Roxanne and Ayana's relationship, and breaking up your family, but..."

"But what, Mark?" she said in a whisper. "We

should try to get past that. We should pretend like nothing ever happened, just so you and Roxanne can live happily ever after?"

"Yes. I mean, no. I mean..." I didn't know what I meant, and I was beginning to wonder why I was there my damn self. I sat silently and tried to think of something intelligent to say. Nothing came to mind.

"Would you like a drink?" Evelina finally asked, cutting through four minutes of silence.

I nodded and she walked over to the bar and fixed us apple martinis, straight up—the same way Roxanne liked hers. She handed one to me, and downed hers in one gulp.

"Care for another?" she asked, not realizing I hadn't even tasted the first one yet. I quickly swigged my drink, and passed her the empty glass. She returned to the bar, poured new drinks and handed one to me. She sipped hers slowly and sat back down on the lounger, finally looking in my direction.

"Mark, understand something. I don't have anything against you as a person. Any woman would be proud to have such a handsome, successful and loving man in their daughter's life. You are a mother-in-law's dream. However, I cannot respect a man who can't stand up for himself."

"What are you talking about, Evelina? I..."

"Mark," she continued as if I never even began. "You will never be happy with Roxanne, because you let her call all the shots. She makes the rules in your relationship. Always has, always will. When are you going to stand up and be a man?"

"I am a man." I sat up a little and puffed out my chest.

"Then act like one and make my daughter respect you. Stop trying to make her happy, and think of your own happiness for once. Do you really care if I ever speak to you again in life?"

"Well honestly, no, I..."

"I didn't think so and if you never said another word to me, it wouldn't kill me either. But that's not going to work. Roxanne has manipulated me all of her life, and now I see she's doing the same thing to you. She used her father's leaving as leverage for me. What is she holding over your head, Mark?"

"What? I don't think I understand your question."

"Well, let me spell it out for you then. All of her life, Roxanne got her way by playing the *my father left me because of you* card. Is she using that same card with you? This time, using you as the excuse for why she doesn't consider us mother and daughter of the year anymore?"

"I believe so..."

"I thought so," she said matter-of-factly. "Now what are you going to do about it?"

"I thought my being here was doing something about it." I hated myself for letting her put words into my mouth. Although all of it was true, she didn't have to put me on the spot the way she was doing. I finished off the last of my drink and sat my glass on the table in front of me. "Evelina, I came here to speak to you…"

"Because it's what Roxanne wants. What do you want, Mark?"

I couldn't answer, because I didn't know my damn self. Evelina polished off the remainder of her martini then sat up on the edge of the lounger. She placed her glass next to mine on the table, stared at me and smiled. I smiled back. I didn't know what else to do. She walked over and stood in front of me.

"Mark, do us both a favor and take the advice Roxanne gave to me not too long ago. Go back home and let her come over here to do her own dirty work. My issues aren't with you, and your issues aren't with me. I love you, Mark, and I love the idea of you and Roxanne sharing the rest of your lives together. I don't blame you for breaking up my family. My family was broken up long before you learned the truth. We both know that. I blame you for allowing Roxanne to make your life miserable just as I've allowed Joseph to make mine miserable ever since the truth came out. Nothing that happened is either one of our faults, but we've been treated like it since day one and I for one am tired of it. And you should be, too."

"I am, that's why I came here. Evelina, I don't know what to do anymore. I love Roxanne. I love her with everything I am, and I want to spend the rest of my life with her. It's just so hard, and I don't know what will make it better. I figured if I came and made peace with you..."

"Don't you see what a waste of time that is Mark? We've always been at peace. I don't have anything against you. Is there something that you're holding against me?"

I thought for a moment, and came to realize that once again, she was right. I didn't hate Evelina either. I didn't even have any real beef with her. I hated her because Roxanne made me think I was the reason the two of them no longer got along. It made sense back then, but listening to Evelina now made me realize it had nothing to do with me. I was just Roxanne's scapegoat, and Evelina had been Joseph's. But all that was going to end. Tonight.

"Evelina, you're right and I love you, too. Always have. I respect you for being honest with me. I know you're in a lot of pain, we both are, but I can't fix something that's not broken. Only Roxanne can repair her relationship with you. I see that now, and I thank you for making it clear to me." I reached out my hand, and she placed it between her own.

"Go home, Mark, and be the man we both know you are. The man you used to be. Regain the respect you lost, and start living your life for you. Roxanne's a big girl now, and it's time she started behaving like one. Only you have the power to make her realize that. That's the only way the two of you will ever truly be happy." She touched my face gently and I stood. I followed her to the door, where we embraced. "Take care of yourself, Mark, and don't be a stranger."

"I won't. And thank you again, Evelina. I still love you, Mom."

"I know." She dabbed at her watery eyes. "I still love you, too, Son."

She opened the door and I walked out, just as the tears fell from my eyes too.

AYANA

I got to Marlon's in record time. I tipped the doorman ten dollars, grabbed the door keys and made my way upstairs. I walked into the room and stared at him while he was sleeping. Looking angelic. Not a care in the world. Oblivious to everything going on around him. I leaned down and kissed him gently on the temple. He didn't even budge. I got undressed and spooned with his warm body underneath the covers. He placed his arms around my waist and kissed me on the nape of the neck.

"Hey there, beautiful," he whispered.

"Hey there, sexy. Did you miss me?"

"You know I did." He began to caress my already erect nipples. I turned to face him and kissed him deeply on the lips. He ran his hands down my body.

"I love the way you touch me," I cooed.

"I love the way you feel. I've never been with a woman with skin so soft and smooth, and you always smell so damn good. I just want to eat you up."

"So what's stopping you? Ain't nothing here but space and opportunity." I pushed the covers off of me and lay back wide-legged and expectant.

Marlon didn't disappoint me.

"Damn baby, you even taste good."

My inner juices dripped from his bottom lip as he stared up in my eyes with so much affection. I started to cum just looking at him. He licked up every drop, and I returned the favor. I sucked his dick like I was the star in one of those corny-ass porno flicks. Moaning and groaning. Making all kinds of unnecessary noises, and loving every grunt as it escaped his lips. I didn't want to disappoint him either, so I sopped up every drop as he ejaculated in my mouth, and lined my throat with his milky discharge.

I soon found myself imitating an Uncle Luke lyric... *Face down. Ass up. That's the way I like to fuck*, or rather be fucked. But I wasn't into that anal shit. At least not yet. It was something Marlon wanted to experience with me, but understood my trepidation. I mean, pissing and shitting were two separate things, and though my vagina stretched to receive him, I just wasn't comfortable with the stretch-factor if he tried to stick that thick shit in my ass. Cause didn't I tell you? Honey was truly blessed and I was a fucking chicken when it came right down to it.

"How does it feel, baby?" he half whispered, half grunted.

"It feels good," I replied, thrusting my ass against his thighs, loving the way he felt pulsating inside me.

"Is this my shit, baby?"

"Yes," I moaned, not wanting to fuck up the moment. Because truth be told, it was definitely his unless Roxy came to her senses. "It feels good to you, baby?" I tried to concentrate on the moment, which was becoming increasingly harder now that Roxanne had invaded my psyche.

"You know it does. Turn over," he instructed. He flipped me over gently, and began to suck on my breasts while he reinserted himself deep inside me.

I quickly pushed Roxy out of my mind and moved

my body along with his. It was amazing how good Marlon had become, considering how awful he was the first time we were together. I dug my nails into his ass, and started bucking like a horse. He was hitting my fucking spot, and nothing could stop my flow once you got it started. I felt my juices coming out in spurts as Marlon began breathing heavier and thrusting harder inside me. Within moments, we were laying in each other's arms, kissing gently on various parts of the other's body.

"When am I going to see you again?" he whispered into my hair.

"I don't know. You know my work schedule has become very demanding lately."

"Yeah, I know. It's just that I miss you so much. I mean, I finally find the perfect woman for me, and I can't even be with you the way I want to. It's just not fair."

"Life's not fair."

"I know that, too, but baby I want to be with you more than once or twice every other week. I want to be with you every single day. Can you understand that?"

"Yes, Marlon, but this is just a bad time for me. Don't get me wrong, I want to be with you, too. Only I can't right now. Not how you'd like. So if you can't handle these drive-by encounters, I understand."

"What? You expect me to give up the one good woman for me just because she's got other priorities right now? Never. Ayana, I love you. I don't know why I feel so strongly about you, but I do. Like I've told you a thousand times, if this is all you're able to give me, I'll take it. Because I know one day, you'll be able to give me your all. That's what I'm holding out for."

"What am I going to do with you?" I asked, kissing his lips gently. Tears flowing silently down my face.

"Why are you crying?"

"Just because." I didn't want to spoil the moment. I was in turmoil, and I didn't need him to know that although I loved him, I also loved Roxanne. Though I couldn't quite figure it out yet, I was even beginning to feel a strange longing for Royal's no good ass. Before I could commit to him, I had to make sure I was ready, because the last thing I ever wanted to do was bring Marlon pain.

ROXANNE

I had never felt as alone as I did right then. I had no idea where Mark was. Ayana was probably laid up with Marlon and my trifling ass was here applying ice to my puffy eyes, hoping the swelling would go down. That was what the fuck I got for crying. No. That was what the fuck I got for trying to manipulate the situation again. But I just couldn't help myself. I didn't know what the fuck was wrong with me. Here I was, sitting on top of the fucking world, and you would think my life was miserable the way I was acting. I had my own company, a great man, good friends, my health, money in the bank, all the clothes and shoes a woman could want, and it was still not enough. Not for Roxanne. No, Roxanne needed a whole hell of a lot more. Bullshit.

I laid back on the bed staring at the ceiling, trying to figure out just when everything began heading downhill. I didn't know if it was Royal, or Ayana, or even the combination of both, but I could honestly say I had been spreading myself too thin lately. Maybe a drink would help even me out. Might even calm my hyperventilating ass down a little. I walked into the living room and poured myself a Jack and Coke. I might as well get good and fucked up, because there was no telling what was going to happen when Mark got home. That was if he came home at all. If he didn't, I couldn't even blame him. It was bad enough about Royal, and then Evelina, but what if he found out about Ayana? When he mentioned her name in the hallway earlier I almost shit on myself. Just to have him pull her name out of the air like that was hitting just a little too close to home. Especially, since I almost fucked her again, and that wasn't even a full twenty-four hours ago. I poured myself another drink and stepped out onto the patio. Just as I was enjoying the skyline, the home phone rang. I sobered up quickly and ran inside to answer it.

"Hello." I tried to sound sluggish just in case it was anyone else besides Mark.

"Hey there sleepyhead. What are you doing in bed so early?"

It was Royal. I didn't know what to say, so I didn't say anything. I should have hung up, but my body wouldn't allow it. Just the sound of his voice was sending chills down my spine. I looked at the glass in my hand, and slammed it down on the counter. It was alcohol that had me infatuated with his ass in the first place. I shook my head for clarity, and placed the receiver closer to my ear. I breathed deeply.

"Roxanne, I know you're there. I can hear you breathing. Where's the husband?"

I still couldn't say anything. Everything in my head said to hang up the fucking phone, but my heart kept the son of a bitch glued to my right ear.

"I guess he's out, or you would've spoken by now. Would you like some company?"

Silence.

"Good, I'll be there in say twenty..."

"No, Royal. I don't think that's such a good idea. If you don't mind, I'll be hanging up now."

"Why are you trying to get rid of me so quickly? Do

I scare you, Roxanne?"

"No." I was lying through my teeth and I was quite sure he knew it.

"Tell you what. Since I can't come to you, why don't you come to me? I'll stick around here for another hour. If you show, you show. If you don't... Well, let's just say I hope you do."

"I don't think so, Royal."

"Think about it, Roxanne. You might have a change of heart. The clock's ticking. Like Cinderella, my coach turns into a pumpkin at midnight." And just like that he was gone.

I replaced the receiver on the hook and downed the remainder of my drink. I looked up at the clock. It was five after eleven. My nightly rituals were already taken care of. All I had to do was slip into something... *Stop it!* It was that same thinking that got my ass in this fucked up predicament to start with. I walked over to the bar and fixed myself another drink. I heard Mark's key turning in the door just as I was enjoying my first sip. He opened and shut the door, and walked into the back without even acknowledging my presence. I let him be. I sank back into the sofa and reacquainted myself with Jack Daniels and his partner, Coca Cola. Just as I started to feel a buzz, Mark fucked it all up for me.

"What were you thinking, Roxanne?" He looked down at me, with one hand on his hip and one swinging at his side. He looked more bitch than butch, but I wasn't about to burst his bubble.

"That's the problem. I wasn't thinking, Mark." I figured if I shouldered the blame and went along with everything he said, he'd shut the fuck up and leave me alone.

"You're damn right, you weren't. I don't know what the fuck has gotten into you lately, but things are going to change around here. First off, all this sneaking around is going to stop."

"Okay." I gave all my attention to my drink.

"And that shit you pulled with Evelina, never again. If things are not right between you two, fix it. It has absolutely nothing to do with me. Understand?"

It was kind of cute how Mark was trying to take charge, but it was the wrong time. All I wanted to do was get good and fucked up then fall into my own inebriated dreamland. But looking at Mark, in his *let me set this bitch straight* mode, I knew it was a far-off fantasy.

"What can I say? You're absolutely right, Mark." I tried to shut his ass up for good.

"You're damn right, I'm right. From now on, I'm going to be calling the shots. No more of your bullshit, Roxanne. Do you understand me?"

"Yes Mark, I do. You're a man, and you should be treated like one. I'll make sure I keep that in mind." I wobbled over to the bar, and poured yet another drink.

"And all this drinking. You have to cut that shit out, too. No decent, self-respecting woman would..."

That did it. I downed my last drink in one gulp and threw the glass across the room in his direction. It caught him on the hand that was clinging to his hip.

"Let me tell you one motherfucking thing, Mark, you are not my father, and..."

"You're damn right I'm not Joseph. I don't get my jollies off watching you make it with another wom…"

I crossed the room in record time and punched Mark in the jaw. Well at least that was what I wanted to do, but my aim and balance were off. I did manage to scratch his cheek though. When he rushed in the bathroom to tend to the blood seeping from the gash, I made my way back to the bedroom. I slipped into my black thongs, a yellow sundress and my black mules and headed out the door. I checked my watch. It was only eleven thirty.

If I hurried, I could still catch Royal.

ROYAL

I handed the keys to Imani and told her to lock up, because I was calling it an early night. She eyed me suspiciously, but when she saw no women were lingering near the door, and all the waitresses were still on duty, she lightened up a bit.

"Do I need to get here a little earlier tomorrow night to open up?"

"No, it's okay. I have a spare set back at my place. I'll see you regular time tomorrow night. But, do be careful. I'm leaving my baby in your hands." I gestured towards the bar and its surroundings.

"I know, Royal. I won't disappoint you."

"I know you won't, Imani. I know that for damn sure." I fixed her with an *I can't wait to fuck you* gaze. She returned the look and smiled sheepishly.

"Good night, Royal."

"Good night, Imani."

I walked out into the crisp New York air, and looked down at my watch. It was five to midnight. I moved away from the open doorway, and leaned against the front side of the building. I checked my watch again. A minute had passed. I was hoping Roxanne wouldn't disappoint me either. She didn't. At one minute to twelve, a taxi pulled up in front and the back door swung open.

"Get in." She arched her pointer finger back and forth in a come-hither type of way. I sauntered over to the taxi and jumped in.

"Where to?" the driver asked, before I could even close the door.

"His place." Roxanne leaned into my body with one hand on my crotch and the other massaging her love box.

We could hardly contain ourselves. We were half-naked by the time we stepped off the elevator, and we didn't even make it through the door before we began ravishing each other.

"Royal, I want you to take me," Roxanne moaned.

"I will, baby."

"No, I don't mean have sex with me. I want you to take me. No niceties. Just throw me back and take this shit. Fuck me like you've never fucked anyone before. No mercy. Okay?"

"Okay." I couldn't believe my ears. I wanted to take Roxanne since the first moment I saw her, and here she was dangling that shit right in front of my face. So I did what any man in my predicament would do. I threw her ass across the arm of the couch, and stuck my dick deep inside her. To my surprise, she was already nice and wet.

"Harder, Royal. Fuck me harder."

And I did. I must have come six times before I gave up. I couldn't take it. Roxanne wore me the fuck out. I didn't even know when I fell asleep. All I knew was I did. I awoke to an empty house, and was grateful. I didn't think I could have handled anymore of that shit. Roxanne was a handful. Literally. YouknowwhatImean?

AYANA

Royal called it an early night, and I was thrilled. After my evening with Marlon, I was too tired to act upbeat. With his ass gone, I damn sure didn't have to. I turned around and scanned the bar. Everything was fine until I spotted Misty sitting at a table with a bunch of older men. She had a glass of liquor in one hand, a Newport dangling from the other, and was holding everyone's attention with her size 44DDs trying to squeeze into a 34B push-up bra. This heifer must have lost her mind. If she thought she was going to sit back and relax while I stood behind that bar and slaved, she had another think coming. I called one of the other girls over to watch the bar for a moment, and marched over to the table.

"Misty, I don't think it's break time yet," I said casually.

"Girl, please." She brushed me off and continued her conversation as if I never interrupted. "As I was saying," she began.

"Misty," I said, a little louder. "It's not break time, so I advise you to get back to work."

She turned around, glared at me, and pulled deeply on her cigarette. She then blew the smoke in my face.

"Who died and made you boss?" The men at the

table began to move closer to each other, and away from the two of us as if they knew a storm was brewing.

"Misty, you have all of ten seconds to put out that damn cigarette, and get your ass back to work, or..."

"Or what, Imani?" She was now standing directly in front of me. "This ain't your place, and you ain't got no fucking authority over me. Now get the fuck out my face, bitch."

Mind you, I wasn't a physical person. But when this buck-toothed heifer breathed all her halitosis in my face, and then had the nerve to call me out my name, that's when shit got real.

"What did you call me?"

"I called you a bitch." Her hands were all up in my face. "Now what the fuck are you going to do about it?"

I stood there completely still, because I was in shock.

"Yeah, that's what the fuck I thought." She pushed into me, causing me to stumble backward. I quickly regained my balance.

We now had the full attention of the bar, but I didn't give a damn. Just as Misty was about to squat her fat ass back on the seat, I pulled it out from under her. Before she knew what hit her, she was flat out on the floor and I was rocking in the chair on her neck asking her if she wanted to rethink her outlook on things. She tried desperately to free herself, but to no avail.

"Now," I was still sitting in the chair on her neck. "Are you going to get back to work, or do I have to throw your ass out of here?"

As blue-black as she was, I didn't think it was possible for her to turn red. But her face looked like a big, juicy tomato ready to burst. She struggled against my weight on the chair, and finally found a little wind. "Get the fuck off of me!"

I stood up, removed the chair and stood firm. She squirmed on the floor for a few moments and tried to catch her breath. "Bitch, you must be crazy." She coughed loudly.

"So I've been told."

She jumped up and tried to lunge at me. I stood my ground, but she was cut off by Chris, one of the burly bouncers Royal kept around just in case shit got out of hand.

"You okay, Imani?" He held Misty back with one hand and rubbed my shoulder with the other.

"I'm fine, Chris."

"That bitch attacked me, and you're asking if she's all right?" Misty suddenly grabbed for him. "Nig..."

Misty found herself out on the concrete before she could even get the word out.

"Now carry your trifling ass back to the projects where you belong," Chris said as he flung her out onto the pavement. Misty stood up and started cursing and carrying on. Chris just pulled the door closed, and walked back inside as if nothing happened.

It took a few minutes for everyone to get over the excitement, but things quickly went back to normal. By the end of the night, I was exhausted. I waited until everyone left, and locked up the cash register and the liquor cabinets. I then made my way towards the door. I was being overly cautious, because I had the days receipts pinned inside my bra. One could never be too sure, and maybe this was a test. I shut down the lights and stepped outside. After locking the door and pocketing the key, a pair of strong hands grabbing my shoulders startled me. I spun around quickly.

"Chris, you scared the shit out of me." I was glad it was someone friendly, and not Misty's deranged ass coming back for revenge.

"I'm sorry. I just wanted to make sure you got home okay. You can never be too safe, you know." He caressed my cheek.

"Well, thank you, but I'm okay."

"You sure?" His hand moved up and down my arm.

"I'm sure." I moved back a little because he was being a little too touchy-feely for my taste.

"Do you need a lift home?"

"No, I have a ride. Thank you." I was lying, but he didn't need to know that. I leaned back against the front of the building and checked my watch. I looked up and down the block pretending to be looking for someone. "I guess he's running late."

"I guess so." He leaned next to me on the wall.

The sun was coming up, and I began to relax. Although there was no one around for miles, I still felt safer in the morning light. "There's no need for you to wait with me, Chris. I'll be all right." I hoped he'd take the hint and get to stepping. No such luck.

"It's okay. I'll wait it out with you. I wouldn't want anything to happen to you standing out here by your lonesome. I'd never forgive myself." He smiled. I smiled back.

We waited there in silence for a good ten minutes. My ride never showed up.

"Looks like you've been stood up."

"Yeah, it certainly looks that way, doesn't it? I guess he had to work a double after all."

"And I guess you'll be needing that lift. Come on." He yanked gingerly on my arm.

I lifted off the wall reluctantly just as a cab pulled up to the curb. I was too happy to see Roxanne spilling out of the backseat. She looked a fucking mess, but I could have cared less. Chris eyed her suspiciously. I guess he thought she was a derelict, or something. Hell, if it weren't for the expensive jewelry she donned, she sure as hell could've passed for one. Her hair was disheveled, her clothes were wrinkled, and she had that *I didn't go home last night* look.

"Giiirrrrllll," she slurred, "I'm so glad you're still here."

"You almost missed me." I winked at her and nodded inconspicuously towards Chris. "I guess Marlon sent you to pick me up."

"Yeah, that's right," she said quickly. "I see I made it just in the nick of time." She giggled, caught herself and tried to look casual.

"Well Chris…" I turned towards him, and pouted. "I guess I'll just have to take you up on your offer another time. Okay?"

"You do that." He kissed me on the cheek and sauntered away slowly. He turned back quickly. "You ladies get home safe."

"Thank you," Roxanne yelled out. "We will."

Chris turned back around and walked away.

"Who was that?" She asked as soon as he was out of earshot.

"I'll tell you all about it later." I grabbed her arm and we started down the block in the opposite direction.

MARK

When I went into the bathroom to survey the damage of Roxy's latest tirade, I was amazed to see all the blood was spilling from a tiny cut above my right eyelid. I grabbed some peroxide and a cotton ball, and cleaned it out. I then placed a mini bandage across the gash and made my way back into the living room. I was about to clean up the small pool of blood in the middle of the floor as well as the droplets that led into the bathroom, but I didn't. Fuck it. Roxanne wanted to be boss, so let her clean that shit up. I went back into the bathroom and jumped into the shower. Since Roxanne wanted to be the man of the house, she damn sure didn't need me hanging around fucking up her flow. I pulled on my Sean John sweat suit with my spanking new Jordans, and bounced.

"Who is it?" Mocha asked groggily through her closed door.

"A secret admirer," I said, in my best baritone.

Mocha opened the door. She was stark naked. "To what do I owe this pleasant surprise?"

"This..." I moved inside and closed the door behind me. I pushed my erection against her nakedness and led her back into the bedroom.

"I didn't think you'd be coming back here anytime soon, Daddy."

"Well, you know me. Daddy misses his Little Girl."

"Why don't you show me just how much?" Mocha lay back on the bed and began fingering herself. She stared into my eyes as she licked her fingers and then placed them back inside of her.

I quickly relieved myself of my sweat suit, and kneeled down in front of her, burying my face where her fingers were playing mercilessly.

"Goddamn, I miss you, Daddy," she moaned. "Nobody eats this shit like you do."

I knew she was just talking shit, but I let her. For once I wanted to feel like the king of the jungle, and this bitch was the only one who would let me. I licked and sucked, until her clitoris was a bright red, brick hard, pulsating button. I then slipped my fingers deep inside of her, rubbing around in her moisture. I found her g-spot it in a matter of seconds. While she called me every lewd name in the book, I caressed her into her first full-fledged climax.

Scene two found me as vulnerable as she was, as she had me down on all fours with her tongue buried deep inside my anus. One hand was massaging my ass cheek, the other was jerking me off. The double sensation was too much for me to handle, and my toes began to curl up like fists. I could feel the blood rushing to my middle. My dick soon spewed hot lava all over her satin sheets.

"Damn Daddy, either you're happy to see me, too, or you haven't been getting much action lately." She giggled.

I looked down at the white mounds on her bed and laughed a little, too.

"I guess it's a combination of both. Now come over here, and help Daddy get it back up."

What I loved about Mocha, is you never had to ask her anything twice. She was down on her knees, dick to jaw in a matter of seconds. As soon as she felt the slightest erection, she jumped up, and guided me into her anal canal. The tightness of her opening almost drove me over the edge before I could even begin, but I held on. I tried every mental maneuver I could think of, not wanting the sensation of her pounding away at my lap to end. She had my dick in a vice grip, and it felt too fucking good.

"Does it feel good to you, Daddy?" She bounced up and down on my erection.

"Yeah, baby," I groaned.

"I want you to come all up in me, Daddy." She rocked back and forth, sliding my dick in and out of her anus. The friction made my toes curl once again.

"Not yet, baby." I tried to hold out. But I couldn't. It was damn near impossible.

"Yes Daddy, now." She gave me all the ass one man could handle, and then some.

I squirted for a good two minutes, as she eased up on the speed, but doubled up on her gyrations. Each rotation of her hip, sucked more sperm from my semi-limp penis.

"Are you thirsty, Daddy?" Mocha asked, as she nibbled gently on my earlobe.

"Yeah, I could use a drink."

"Name your poison," she said, sexily.

"You." I gave her ass a quick squeeze. She purred throatily.

"Will a rum and coke suffice, Daddy? I'm parched."

"No you're not." I placed my fingers deep inside her moisture.

"Yes, I am." She removed my fingers and did a summersault off the bed. She landed in a perfect split, bounced up and switched out of the room.

I peeled back the top layer of wet sheets, and was about to lie down on the dry ones when something hard hit my knee. I looked down, and saw a tiny transistor. It was black with two buttons on the face. I pushed the top one, nothing happened. I pushed the bottom one, and a panel opened up on Mocha's wall. The panel was always hidden by a huge self-portrait, so I never noticed it. Not until tonight. Not until now. Inside was a flat panel screen, featuring an X-rated flick. I was enjoying the view of a woman's ass, bent over sucking off some guy. You could see her pussy lips and pubic hair peeking out from between her legs. The sight was something else, and it was turning me on. I started to rub myself, when all of a sudden the woman turned around, and smiled at the camera. It was Mocha. I knew she was into some freaky shit, but porn was something new to me. I was just about to scream out to her, and comment on her video library, when I came into full focus on the screen. Grunting and moaning behind a smiling Mocha, as she hopped up and down on my lap.

Mocha entered carrying two drinks. Her eyes went from my jaw-dropped expression to the TV screen, and she didn't even bat an eyelash. She placed my drink on the end table and then walked over to the screen.

"So what do you think?"

"What the fuck is that?" I pointed to the screen and gathered the covers around myself. I stood up.

Mocha looked from me to the screen then back to me. "What do you mean?" she asked, all sugary and shit. "That's us, Daddy." She walked over to me and tried to put her arms around my shoulders. I backed away.

"How many of those do you have?"

"Just the one, Daddy." I knew she was lying. "Why, you want to add to the collection?" She advanced towards me.

I moved out of her grasp. I couldn't believe this bitch

had been taping us all along. She didn't seem like the type to do it for leisure, because women weren't into that type of shit. She was doing it for a reason, and I needed to know what that reason was. I had to find out just what the fuck was going on, because I had a future with Roxy to protect. It was now or never, and if I didn't get ahead of it now, there would definitely be no way out of it later.

The moment Mocha made that glitch with her namesake, I should have known something was up. I did a little research on the Internet and came up with a story that happened a couple of years back about a Texan governor's nephew being shot by some trick who called herself Baby Girl. There were other details given and they never showed a picture of her, but the description fit Mocha to a tee. I knew I was grabbing at straws when I read it, and I knew it was too far-fetched to be the same person, but it was the only thing I could find. I trusted my gut and used it as leverage. Mocha wouldn't admit it at first, but after some physical provocation she confirmed my suspicions and let it be known she had been taping us ever since the first time we were together. A little more prodding revealed our whole meeting, and her moving into my building was not fate, it was formula. When I threw her past into the mix, she tried to deny it as well, but I pretended to know more than I really did about the whole episode, and she broke like a pregnant woman's water.

She went on and on about how Royal helped her, saved her, and then fucked her in the end. Royal had her paying him back outrageous amounts for her silence, even though we both knew he'd be in just as much hot water as she was if the truth ever came out. But that was neither here nor there. He had my punk ass doing the exact same thing, and I felt a little sorry for her, but I couldn't let that sidetrack me.

"If you want to walk away from all this, you have to do something for me, too," I said, to a puffy-eyed Mocha.

"What is it, Mark? I'll do anything."

"I need you to help me beat Royal at his own game. Since it's apparent you have an effect on men, I don't think it'll be too hard to turn him on, either."

"You're crazy, Mark. Royal can't stand me. Simply put, he hates me. If he finds out I double-crossed him, that's the end for me. For the both of us."

"But he won't find out, and if he does, I'll take care of it. You won't be in any danger. I promise."

"How can you be so sure?"

"Because I know what he wants, and if you can get him into a compromising position, I'll make sure he gets it."

"Mark, you aren't making any sense."

"I don't have to make sense. I know what I'm talking about, and that's all that matters. Look, call him. Tell him I have the tapes. Listen to what he says, and I'll take it from there."

"You must be out of your mind if..."

"Look either you call Royal, or I call the police. It's up to you."

Reluctantly, Mocha called Royal. I saw panic flash in her eyes when she told him what she had to tell him, but I had to stay focused. If I started feeling sorry for this bitch, I'd never get Roxanne back. She hung up slowly.

"What did he say?"

"He wants me to come over."

"Good. All you have to do is seduce his ass, and we're both on easy street."

"How do you figure?"

"Just trust me, Mocha. But there's something else you have to do."

"What's that?"

"Make one more phone call."

It was a little embarrassing to admit my fiancée was stepping out on me with Royal, but what could I do? Besides, who was she to judge, when I was stepping out on my fiancée with her? Even though it was all a set up, it was still cheating, and something told me Roxanne was not as forgiving as I was. It was one thing for me to face her like a man and tell her the truth, but it was another to hear it from her fuck buddy. Especially when that fuck buddy not only had a witness, but photos and videos to back up his accusations. In a nutshell, I had to let Roxanne see Royal for who he really was before she fell too deeply in love with him, and my ass was out the door. I also had to break it off with Mocha before I lost the one woman I truly loved. Last but not least, I had to stand up to Royal and get him the fuck out of my life once and for all. I just hoped everything went as planned.

ROYAL

He has the tapes.

That's all I heard. That's all I needed to hear. Mocha was mumbling about something else, but all that other shit was irrelevant. I wanted answers. "What the fuck do you mean, he has the tapes? How the fuck did he get the tapes?"

"He just took them," she said with trepidation.

"How the fuck did he find out about them? I thought you said they were in a safe place."

"Royal, I swear they were, but he found them, and..."

"Fuck the excuses. Bring your ass over here."

"But, Royal..."

"No buts, bitch. Get your ass over here right now!" I hurled the phone across the room.

Here I was, fresh off the best pussy a man could ever dream of, and here was this bitch spoiling it by telling me that my last taste may be just that—my last taste. If I hadn't witnessed it myself, I would never believe one man could secrete so much in one evening. Roxanne had my ass weak, drained, sore and satisfied. That is, until the call. How the hell could Mocha fuck this up? All she had to do was fuck this man, make a few tapes, and that's that. It didn't take fucking brain surgery. Just press record and perform. What the fuck was so hard about that? I mean, in an entire two-bedroom, two-bath condominium with walk in closets in every room and enough extra space to house three Mexican families, she couldn't find a good hiding space for a few fucking tapes? This shit was unbelievable.

I poured myself a shot of Jack Daniels and sat back in the recliner with a full bottle in tow. By the time Mocha made her way across town, I had to be good and fucked up. Or then she would have to face that fate. YouknowwhatImean?

Mocha arrived forty-five minutes later, disheveled and smelling of stale musk oil and sweat. It was a womanly funk, but it was a funk nonetheless, and the shit was turning my stomach. I watched her walk gingerly across the room, looking around furtively, and moving as if she may step on a land mine at any moment. I followed her scent into the living room and couldn't take it anymore.

"Why the fuck didn't you shower before you brought your funky ass over here?"

"You said right now, so I got dressed and caught the first thing moving. Look Royal…"

"No, you look. You are stinking up my place and fucking with my nose hairs. Go in the bathroom, wash your funky ass and then come back and talk to me. I can't take the sight of you right now, let alone the smell."

"Okay, Royal." She moved towards the rear of the apartment. "Do you have something for me to put on?"

"There's a terry robe behind the bathroom door. Put that on for now. I'll look for something else after we've had our little talk."

I heard the bathroom door close just as I emptied the last of the Jack into my shot glass. I leaned back in the recliner once more, closed my eyes and reminisced about my night with Roxanne. I suddenly felt her hand run across my face.

"Royal," she said sweetly.

"Yeah, baby."

"Royal." Mocha called my name a little louder.

I opened my eyes and tried to regroup. I must have dozed off without knowing it. It wasn't Roxanne standing in front of me. It was Mocha. I sized her up quickly and wasn't disappointed by what I saw. She had on my white terry robe. It was a little oversized, but the way she had the belt tied tightly around her small waist, it accentuated her flawless figure. Her hair was wet and stringy, and the frightened look on her face made her even sexier than I remembered her to be. My thoughts of Roxanne and the sight of Mocha's half naked body, coupled with the fact that I downed half a bottle of Jack was too much to handle. I could feel myself growing in my silk pajama bottoms, and it was taking all the restraint in the world not to fuck the shit out of her.

"You okay?" She asked in a husky tone.

"I'm fine." I adjusted myself in the recliner so my hard-on wasn't so noticeable.

"Mind if I pour myself a drink before we get down to business?" More huskiness. More sexiness. More dick juice running down my inner thigh.

"Not at all."

"Would you like one?" She made herself comfortable behind my stainless steel bar.

"Nah, I'm good." I tried to sound casual even though my hormones were racing and I wanted to fuck her, but good.

Mocha filled a tumbler with Malibu Caribbean Rum, downed it in one gulp and then refilled it. This time she added a little Coca Cola. She drank that down half the way, refilled the tumbler, and then placed the bottles back underneath the bar. She came around to where I was sitting, and squatted on the edge of the marble tabletop in front of my recliner.

"Let's cut to the chase, Royal." She sat directly in front of me. The robe was closed to the waist, but was opened slightly below it, showing a hint of her Brazilian wax. It was turning me the fuck on, but I tried to concentrate on what she was saying. "I know I fucked up, and I need to know from you what I can do to make it right. I know I don't have the tapes, but I can always make more. This isn't over between me and Mark. He knows it. I know it. I just need you to know it."

"How can you be so sure?"

"Because, who can say no to all of this?" She downed the rest of her drink and stood up. She untied the belt on the robe and let it drop to the floor. She then walked towards me and straddled me on the recliner. "How about if I fuck you so good I spoil you for every other bitch out there, and then we talk about this over breakfast?"

"You think you can just waltz your ass in here, offer me some pussy, and everything's going to be okay?" I hoped I sounded more powerful than I felt, because at the moment all I wanted to do was enter her warmth.

"No. I'm hoping I can get some of the best dick on earth one last time, because if anything were to happen to me, at least I'd go out happy. Please don't tell me you're going to deny me that pleasure. Royal, only you know how to please a woman the way she needs to be pleased." She ran her tongue up and down my neck.

I knew she was just trying to distract me from the task at hand, but I didn't care. I was drunk, horny and excited, and she was available. Plus, from what I could remember, she was one of the best fucks I ever had my damn self. So what the hell? YouknowwhatImean?

ROXANNE

Ayana had to be crazy if she thought I was going to stop seeing Royal. I told her about my evening, and she had the nerve to get pissed off. I didn't send her to the bar to fall in love with Royal. I sent her there to get me information—something she still hadn't done yet, mind you. Now she wanted to curse me out, because he and I couldn't seem to get enough of each other? Well tough shit. I knew I had Mark, but I wanted Royal, too. If I had it my way, I would've thrown her ass in the mix for good measure. But a bitch can eat but so much cake, before that shit took a toll on her. After getting an earful and then some, I told her to forget I ever asked for her fucking help, and let her know she could stuff our friendship up her ass. I didn't even wait to hear the rest of her mess. I just collected myself and got the fuck out of dodge. That was two hours ago, and the bitch still hadn't called to apologize. Oh well, fuck her.

I turned on the television and channel surfed for about fifteen minutes. There were three good movies on, but my mood wouldn't allow me to focus on any of them. I shut off the TV and walked into the living room for yet another drink. Mark wasn't home, and I didn't even give a fuck. I could tell he left as soon as I did, because the blood stains from last night's bout were dried up and discolored in the middle of the floor. I put the drink on pause and went to get the sponge and cleanser from the bathroom. After wiping up every drop of dry blood, I retired on the sofa with a novel and a fifth of Hennessy.

I was completely engrossed in the erotica when the phone rang. I snatched it up. “Hello.”

“Hello,” a woman’s voice whispered on the other end. “Is this Roxanne?”

“Who’s this?” I put the book down, but held strong to my drink.

“Just a friend. I have some information for you.”

“What information?”

“Not now. Meet me in one hour at Royal’s place. You do know where that is, don’t you?”

“Is this some kind of joke? Who is this?”

“Don’t be upset, Roxanne. I need to show you the kind of man you’ve been forking over that free pussy to. Meet me in one hour. It’ll change your life.”

With that she hung up. The phone slid from my hands as I polished off the last of my drink. I started pacing across the wood floors, not knowing what to do next. I picked up the phone and began to dial Ayana. I hung up quickly. I wasn’t about to involve that bitch in anything else that concerned Royal. If she couldn’t take me fucking him, she damn sure wouldn’t be able to handle this new revelation.

Wait a minute. That was probably her ass on the phone. She was probably on her way to Royal’s right now, half-dressed and begging to be fucked. That bitch. I took one long swig from the bottle then ran into the room to get dressed. If that bitch wanted to play with fire, this time she damn sure was going to get burned.

I arrived at Royal’s fifteen minutes later than instructed, but I was there and I was prepared to do battle. I was just about to ring the doorbell when I heard a woman's moans and Royal's telltale throaty yelps coming from the other side of the door. I twisted the doorknob and entered. It was no surprise it was unlocked. The real shock was in the fact that the bitch riding his chocolate stallion was unknown to me, but the body pulsating underneath her was none other than the man who invaded my sugar walls all of five hours ago.

"Hope I'm not interrupting anything," I said casually, catching Royal's smug ass off guard. I could tell whoever the woman was, she was expecting me. She didn't have to say anything, or do anything. I could just tell. She reacted the way she was supposed to. Grabbing her shit, covering herself, screaming at Royal about this and that, but I ignored her. She was nobody—and nobody didn't count. I needed to hear from him.

"Having fun, baby?" I asked.

Royal was standing in front of his recliner, stark naked. Pajamas rolled down around his ankles. His dick was as hard as a rock, with a slippery, slimy condom still plastered to the edge of it.

"Roxanne, what the fuck are you doing here?"

"I was invited. What the fuck is she doing here? Was she invited, too?"

"Roxanne, listen..."

"No Royal, you listen. I'm not mad. I'm not upset. I really don't care. We are all adults here. Whatever the two of you were doing, you can continue. Sorry to interrupt," I turned to leave and he grabbed my arm.

"Where do you think you're going? She doesn't mean anything to me." He pointed to the woman in the corner who had now pulled a tight black dress over her nakedness.

"Well, I wish she did. At least the fuck would have been worth it. Good-bye, Royal. And this time, I mean it." I walked over to the door and let myself out. I was just about to walk off, when I remembered I was letting that hoe off too easy. No one sets up Roxanne Emile Linden, and I mean no one. I opened the door once again to find Royal pulling his pants up, and the woman trying to make her way to the door. She moved back as I entered.

"By the way, girlfriend thanks for the tip." I moved towards her.

"What are you talking about?" She continued to back up as Royal eyed the two of us suspiciously.

"Don't play shy now. I'm talking about the phone call. If you hadn't called and forewarned me, that may have been my free pussy sprawled on top of that recliner instead of yours. So, thanks for the heads up." With that I punched her dead in the throat and watched as she fell backwards, holding onto her neck and gasping for air. "I hope the dick was worth it."

I saw unadulterated hatred in Royal's eyes, and pure shock and terror in hers, but I didn't give a fuck. I smiled a smile of victory and let the door slam behind me. Fuck him and fuck her, too. Like I said, if a bitch wanted to play with fire, she damn sure was going to get burned. Mo'Nique was right; skinny bitches were evil.

AYANA

Roxanne was losing her fucking mind. Not only was she obsessed with Royal's ass, she wanted my fucking stamp of approval on the shit. After my evening with Marlon, and all the mixed emotions over my love for him versus my love for other women, sorting through her sordid life was the last thing on my mind. It was not that I didn't want to see her with Royal because I wanted him for myself. I didn't want to see her with Royal, because I didn't trust him. Yes, he was charming. Yes, he was attractive. Yes, he was rich. Yes, he made you want to drop your drawers and get down on all fours, but that wasn't enough. I told her there had to be more to life than physical attraction. I mean, I understood the man was well endowed, and his dick spoke an exotic language to her body, but maybe she needed to take all that energy she put into cheating and teach her real man's dick how to speak in tongues. You would think I told her to go fuck Joseph, because she cursed me out, hurled a few insults in my direction and stormed out my apartment. That was two hours ago, and the bitch still hadn't called to apologize. Oh well, fuck her.

I was putting the finishing touches on breakfast when the doorbell rung.

"Who is it?" I peered through the peephole.

"Ayana, it's me." It was Jasmine. With all the other shit going on in my life, I totally forgot about her. It wasn't that I hadn't heard from her lately, because she left me three to four daily voicemails, which were none too pleasant. It was just that by now, I thought she'd get the hint. "Ayana, open the door. I know you're in there."

"What do you want, Jasmine?" I slid the chain quietly in place.

"I need to talk to you Ayana. Please open the door."

"Jasmine, this isn't a good time for me. I'm in the middle of something, and..."

"Well, if you won't open the door for me, maybe you'll open it for him."

I heard a loud crash against the apartment door, and heard Marlon let out a low grunt. I snatched the chain off and sprung the door open. Jasmine led a bloodied Marlon into my apartment. His hands were tied behind him with a silk scarf. She pushed him towards me, then closed and locked the door behind herself. I was about to rush her and get ghetto when I noticed she had a gun pointing towards us and was holding onto a large, black duffel bag. I looked at her then down at Marlon, who was kneeling beside me. She kicked him in the side of the head, and he fell to the ground. Lifeless. At that very moment, I realized that I truly was in love with him.

"What's this all about, Jasmine?" I was scared shitless. I was just too fucking upset to show it. Who the fuck did this bitch think she was?

"What do you think it's about, Ayana? You think you can just throw away what we have and you and this piece of shit would live happily ever after?" She kicked Marlon in the side for good measure. "I already told you, it's not over until I say it's over."

"Jasmine, why are you doing this? You're married to a very handsome, very wealthy man, who worships the ground you walk on. You get everything your little heart desires. You don't want for anything. So, what could you possibly want with me?"

"Don't you get it, Ayana? You said it yourself. I get everything my little heart desires—everything except you. I don't take too kindly to rejection. Now, I want you to move this bastard to the back bedroom, and then we can get down to business."

"How the fuck am I supposed to move him?"

"Push him, pull him or drag him. I don't give a fuck. Get him back there, lock the fucking door and don't question me again, you got it?" She pointed the gun at my head, and gestured for me to get a move on.

She didn't have to ask me twice. I half-pulled, half-dragged Marlon to the back and locked the bedroom door from the outside. "Now what?"

"Get in the room." She opened the master bedroom door with the hand that held the duffel bag. She kept the gun pointed at my head with the other.

I squeezed past her and walked slowly inside.

"Get on the bed, and take your clothes off."

I did what she said. She undressed as well, never taking the gun off of me.

"Now Ayana, I want you to eat me like your life depended on it." She climbed on the bed and stood over my seated frame, running the gun across my lips. "Because baby, in case you haven't noticed, it does."

Oral sex was one of the most pleasurable acts for giver and receiver when both were willing participants. Being forced into the shit had to be the fucking worst. I was usually more than happy to canvas another woman's crotch. That was when it was something I wanted to do. Having to do the shit when my heart wasn't in it? Now that's another ballgame altogether. I tried unsuccessfully to talk myself into it, but to no avail. It was hard to pretend with the barrel of a gun pressed against my temple.

"What's wrong, Ayana? You don't like the taste of pussy anymore?" She rose up on her tip toes, grinding her hips against my lips and pushing my face deeper into her middle. "You better eat this shit like you used to, or else."

I tried again, but I couldn't make it happen. Jasmine, still holding the gun, jumped off the bed, pulled me up by the back of my hair and smashed me across the mouth with the back of her hand. I flew halfway across the room and cowered in the corner.

"I tried to be nice to you, Ayana. But you don't want nice." She was digging through the duffel bag, never letting the gun waver from my direction. "I guess, if it's dick you want, it's dick you're going to get."

Jasmine pulled a harness-type contraption from the bag. There was a long, black, rubber penis dangling from the middle. She strapped it on and motioned for me to come back over to the bed. I didn't know what to do. I sure as hell didn't want her using that shit on me, but I knew I couldn't run. She had double bolted the door and placed the chain lock on. It would take me years to get through all of that. It would only take her a few seconds to pump my ass full of bullets. So the decision was easy. I crawled up on the bed and looked her in the eyes.

"Jasmine, why are you doing this to me? The only reason I'm trying to break it off, is because I know I can never really have you. Not the way I want to, so..."

"Cut the bullshit, Ayana. No more lies, okay? Since you find it so hard to eat my pussy, perhaps you won't have a problem sucking my dick."

She grabbed me by the back of my head and pulled me down to the rubber penis. She forced it into my mouth and between my teeth, as she began moving her hips back and forth. The size of the penis was unreal, and with every stroke, I gagged. She had the damn thing hitting the back of my throat, and I couldn't take it. Last night's dinner found its way onto her lap. She smashed me across the mouth once again.

"Go get a rag and clean this shit off, before I make you eat it off."

I went into the bathroom and retrieved a rag. I was trying to find something to use as a weapon, but I didn't think a toilet brush would do any real damage against a gun. I went back in the room with a basin full of soapy water and cleaned up the mess. I wiped down the sheets, Jasmine's crotch, the fake dick and the floor. Jasmine never took her eyes off of me, but I did have a chance to inconspicuously slip the lock on the other bedroom door on my way back. I figured if Marlon ever came to, and found a way out of that scarf, he'd come to my rescue. It was a long shot, but it was the only shot I had.

"What now?" I looked at the weird getup around Jasmine's midsection.

"What do you think, baby? I want to fuck you one last time. Now, come over here and lay down beside me."

I walked slowly to the bed and did as I was told.

"Get it wet." Jasmine stroked my upper thigh with the gun.

I tried everything, but nothing worked. Jasmine handed me a tube of lubricant out the nightstand drawer. I applied it, and she went to work. She climbed on top of me and began kissing my face. She licked my ears, sucked on my neck, and massaged my breasts. All the while, she rubbed the phony penis between my thighs. I closed my eyes as tight as I could, and began to imagine I was anywhere but there. The pressure of the penis began to invade me, and I felt my dry walls tear as the thick shaft rammed its way into my opening. I screamed out in pain.

"That's right baby, I want to make sure you will

never want a man's dick inside you ever again." She continued to rip and tear me as she rocked her hips ferociously against mine. I felt myself slipping into oblivion. My inner walls were ripping with every thrust of her hips, and I could feel the blood dripping freely down my legs. The pain was too much to bear. I had to leave my body there and let my mind drift elsewhere. The agony soon disappeared and my world went completely dark.

ROYAL

If Mocha's scandalous ass wasn't giving me the eye, I would have chased Roxanne to hell and back to explain my side. But I had a rep to protect, and I damn sure wasn't going to let no one see me sweat. I adjusted my pants, never taking my eyes off of her. I wasn't sure what my next move would be, but she didn't have to know that. I could tell she was scared shitless, and that was good enough for me. I had to know everything Roxanne knew before I polished her off anyway, so I switched tactics and became complacent.

"Boy, oh boy, what a night." I fell back into the recliner. "First the tapes, then Roxanne. What's going to happen next?"

The doorbell rang catching us off guard. We both jumped and stared at each other.

"Expecting more company, are you?" I asked sarcastically. I walked over and opened the door. Mark was standing on my doorstep like he was fucking king of the world. I didn't know what his visit was all about, so I played it cool. "Mark-O, Mark-O, Mark-O, to what do I owe this pleasant surprise?"

"Royal, old buddy, I just saw my fiancée scampering out of here like her drawers were on fire, so I decided to stop in and see what's up. I mean, do you plan to continue fucking Roxanne, or is it pretty much over now that she caught you with your pants down?"

"It's not the first time I've been caught with my pants down, and it won't be the last. Either she comes back, or she doesn't. It's not going to make me shed any tears either way. YouknowwhatImean?"

"I guess I do. Aren't you going to invite me in?" He didn't even wait for an answer. He just pushed his way in and stopped dead in his tracks at the sight of Mocha. "You still here?" he asked.

Mocha just nodded, trying to find her voice again.

"I thought I told you to leave with Roxanne."

"I didn't have much choice in the matter," she choked out, looking at me nervously.

I didn't know what the fuck was going on, and I damn sure didn't know what to think. Here was Mark, all up in my spot, calling shots as if I wasn't even standing there and this bitch, over here answering him as if I didn't even exist. I had a right mind to light both their asses on fire, but I played it cool.

"Okay Mark-O, you and this bitch did a number on me with Roxanne. Not a big thing. Ain't no love lost. I just have to go to Plan B. That's for Roxanne only. As for you two..."

"Royal, he…he knows all about Ba-baby Girl," Mocha sputtered.

I could have slapped the bitch clear into next week. The problem with women was they were so fucking naïve. Mark probably had no clue about Baby Girl. He probably said something obscure, and her dumb ass told on herself. I had to get to the bottom of all this, but at my own pace.

"Who the fuck is Baby Girl?" I shrugged my shoulders.

"Cut the bullshit, Royal. I know. She knows I know, and you know I know, and now that we all know I know, there's a few things I need you to do for me." Mark finally found his balls, and he was using them to his full advantage.

"You come into my home, and think you can order me around?" I tried to scare him. The shit wasn't working though.

"You're damn right, Royal. I wouldn't have it any other way. You see, I've been paying all kinds of money for something that wasn't even my fault, and rumor has it you've been extorting Mocha for about the same. The way we see it is, if we go down, you'll go deeper. So, why don't we just call it even? You let us walk away, our debt at zero, and we forget all the lowdown shit we know about you."

"Is that a threat, Mark?"

"Nah. I'm not the type to threaten anybody. We both know that." He said this with all the confidence in the world. "I'm just tired of your shit, and I want you out of my life once and for all. Mocha told me this was her last job with you, so I'm figuring she wants the same thing. Let's call it a truce. Let's let bygones be bygones, and call it a fucking day. What do you say?"

"I say you must be out of your motherfucking mind. Do you know what I can do to you?"

"No, the question is, do you know what I can do to you?" Mark scowled and pointed at me. "Since you're into videotaping and all, let's just say I have a video confession from good old Mocha here, and I wouldn't be too afraid to get that to the proper authorities. Just in case you're thinking of getting me before I get to them. I made three tapes—one for you, one for Roxanne and one that's sitting in the mailbox of the New York Times' editor. I have a friend who works in the mailroom, and if he doesn't hear from me within an hour, you'll be watching yourself on the Weekend Edition."

I sat back in the recliner and let all Mark's bullshit sink in. He had me between a rock and a hard place, and the only thing I could do was agree. But it had to be on my terms, or the shit would just have to get ugly.

"I'll tell you what, Mark-O. You and this bitch are free to go. All debts are paid. As for Roxanne..."

"Let it go, Royal. Let it go. Once I show her a copy of that tape and she sees the kind of man you are, then..."

"And what if I tell her about our past together? She wouldn't be none too happy to hear that you're paying off the debt of some dead bitch, who..."

I didn't see it coming. I don't think he did either, but Mark caught me square in the jaw. I found myself flat on my back, arms flailing on top of an upturned recliner with the taste of blood in my mouth.

"If I ever hear you refer to Rachel as a bitch ever again, I'll try my best to kill you. Do you understand me?"

I had enough. I stood upright, and caught Mark by the collar. I lifted his weak ass into the air, and gave him as good as he gave me. I used his head as a punching bag and pummeled him until Mocha pulled on my arm, screaming to let him go. I backslapped that bitch and sent her flying into the wall. She cowered in the corner and I turned my attention back to Mark, who I still had pinned to the wall.

"Listen you little punk. Coming in here playing game on me is one thing. Okay, you got me. Fine. You and this bitch get the fuck on. I don't need your little table scraps no how. But if you ever put your hands on me again, I don't give a fuck about no videotape. They'd never be able to find your body. Do I make myself clear?"

Mark didn't answer. He just nodded. I let him go, and he stumbled backwards against the wall. He wiped the blood from his mouth with the back of his hand.

"Royal, I don't want to go back and forth on this. Roxanne is just as much off limits as I am." He made sure to back as far away from me as possible. He moved closer to Mocha and continued. "Whatever your plans, forget about them. I think it's time Roxanne does find out about us, but it will be from me. As soon as I get home. If shit doesn't work out, then and only then will I let her go. Up until then, consider her taboo."

He grabbed Mocha by the hand, and they left. Just like that. No good-bye. No take care. Just fucked me raw and hit the door. If it weren't for Imani, I would've shown them a thing or two; but if he wanted Roxanne, he could have her. The bitch wasn't worth all the trouble anyway. Ain't no pussy worth serving time for. YouknowwhatImean?

ROXANNE

Royal definitely did a number on my ass, and I damn sure owed Ayana an apology. I owed Mark much more than that. Once he walked through the door, I planned to pay in full. No more lies. No more deceptions. No more binge drinking. No more cheating. No more blaming him for my own faults. No more pretending I didn't love him, because I knew I did. I also knew it was not him I was afraid of. It was me. I always felt because I was overweight, no one could possibly love me—at least not for me. There had to be some sort of ulterior motive. With Mark being so successful, and any woman's wet dream, he couldn't possibly find true happiness with me, let alone true love. I was so fucked up in the head and convinced myself he deserved so much better, that I kept trying to push him away. Maybe there was something he saw in me I couldn't see in myself that made him stick around. Maybe he knew my heart. Maybe he saw promise. Maybe it was time I started being optimistic, too. I heard his key turn in the lock, and my stomach began doing back flips. He walked in nursing a busted lip and a black eye.

"Baby, what happened?" I rushed over to him.

"Nothing. I'm okay."

"You sure?"

"Not really. Roxanne, we need to talk. Right now. I have some things that I need to get off my chest."

"Me too, Mark."

"Would you like a drink?" He walked towards the bar, but I pulled him back and led him to the sofa.

"Let's do this one sober. I need to know you plan to make this work because you want it to. Okay?"

He nodded.

Three hours later, we found ourselves in the throes of passion. I told him all about Ayana, Evelina and Royal, and he didn't even flinch. He understood when I explained Ayana was going to be a part of my life for the rest of my life, and even told me he looked forward to getting to know her. As far as Evelina, we came to the conclusion she was one nut I had to crack, and I promised him I would mend that relationship as soon as I could. He told me it wouldn't happen overnight, but he'd be there for me for as long as it took to get us back on track.

As for Royal, I let him know he was just something I needed at the time. I felt myself getting too close to him, and I had always been afraid of closeness. That was why I turned to Royal in the first place, but no more. Royal was old news. I agreed that Mark was the only man for me, and for once, I believed in us.

Mark let his skeletons out of the closet, too. He told me a bunch of stuff. Things I suspected, but never believed to be true. In the end, we couldn't find fault. I mean, how could either of us be upset, when we were both doing wrong? We made a few promises I was sure we were both going to keep. We also set a date for the wedding. It would be a small ceremony—just the two of us the following Saturday in Jamaica.

AYANA

When I finally came to, I found myself lying in a hospital bed. I was hooked up to several different monitors, with various tubes and wires attached to my body. Marlon was sitting on the edge of the bed, looking at me with tears in his eyes.

"You had me scared there for a minute, Baby." He rubbed my cheek softly.

"What... what happened?"

"Do you remember anything?"

"I remember everything. I must have passed out from the pain."

"It wasn't the pain that did it. You were shot in the abdomen."

"What?" I tried to sit up and flinched as a sharp pain tore through my stomach. He pushed me back down gently.

"Easy now. You lost a lot of blood, but don't worry, you're going to be all right. It was a clean shot—in and out. Nothing major was hit. You're going to be just fine."

"What about Jasmine?"

"She was arrested at the scene. I was awakened by your screams. I broke out of the scarves and when I saw what was going on in the bedroom, I lost my mind. I jumped on Jasmine and grabbed her. I didn't realize she still had the gun. While we were struggling, it went off. When I saw your eyes close, I lost it. I threw her to the floor and restrained her as best I could. When that didn't work, I knocked her ass out and tied her up. I then called 911, but several neighbors had already called when they heard the gunshot. By the time I hung up, the fire department and the police were at the door. And, well, here we are. You sure you're okay?"

"Just a little stiff and a lot embarrassed."

"Embarrassed for what? This isn't your fault?"

"Yes it is. I knew Jasmine was dangerous from the start. I should have put an end to it then, and I didn't. All of this could have been avoided. If only I didn't accept the abuse."

"Look baby, it's really not your fault.'

"But it is, Marlon. It is. I've been abused in every single relationship I've been in, outside of one that was all wrong anyway, but I accepted it. I made myself believe it was okay, that I deserved it…"

"But you didn't deserve it. You don't deserve it."

"I know that now. I also know I need help to break the cycle and get past all this. I can't continue to live my life thinking it's okay to be someone's punching bag, and then have something like this happen again."

"Ayana, if it wasn't you, it would have been someone else. Jasmine has mental and emotional issues that have nothing to do with you. I just hope her crazy ass gets what she deserves—psychological help included. As for you, I will never let anything happen to you. If you feel you need counseling, I will go with you. Baby, we are going to get through this together. My main concern is getting you all better and making sure you are okay from this point forward."

"Thank you, Marlon. That means a lot to me."

Marlon suddenly fell silent. Worry lines indented his forehead.

"Are you okay?" I asked.

"I am now." He looked at me and smiled. "What now?"

"What do you mean?"

"I mean, what now? What are you going to do when they let you go?"

"I don't know," I said, smiling shyly. "There's this man I've fallen completely in love with, and I can't imagine being without. So, I'm guessing I'm not going to want to return to my apartment anyway. Maybe, while I'm in here, he'd do me the honor of moving all my crap to storage, and allowing me to stay with him."

"Do you mean it?" There was a twinkle in his eye and an even bigger smile on his face.

"More than you'll ever know."

Marlon kissed me like no man, or woman, ever kissed me before, and I knew I had made the right decision.

"By the way, I have someone I would like you to meet." I pulled away slightly.

"Who's that?"

"My sister, Roxanne, and she's going to love you."

"Not as much as I love you, Ayana." He kissed me deeply.

"And not as much as I love you, Marlon."

And I meant it. I had sculpted a perfect HeShe, and my dreams had come true. Marlon was a man with all the characteristics, sentiments and compassion of a woman. One who not only knew the meaning of love, but also knew the countless ways in which to express it. And I was never going to let him go. Never.

ROYAL

I knew it was over between Roxanne and I before I even dialed the number. The four-letter-word diatribe that ensued before she ended the call reinforced it. Fuck her. I wasn't one to chase no bitch that wasn't worth chasing anyway. All this time I had been putting my efforts into the wrong woman. Imani was the true love of my life. Roxanne's fat, juicy pussy was just blocking the vision. I jumped in the shower to prepare myself for a life with my true calling.

I hated to admit it, but I didn't know Mark had it in him. I had to respect any man bold enough to step to me. He didn't do it like a bitch either. He came correct. If I wanted to, I could fuck with him, but I was going to let it slide. He wasn't worth it. Neither was that hoe-bitch, Mocha. Fuck her, too. I jumped out the shower, and generously applied lotion to every crevice of my body. I shaved, brushed my teeth and headed for the bedroom. I opened my closet, selected one of my silk pajama sets, and laid it out on the bed. I picked up the phone and licked my lips. Imani didn't know what she was in for tonight. Neither did I.

When I called Imani, the police picked up. They wanted to know who I was, why I was calling, what relationship I was to an Ayana Linden. I told them I must have dialed the wrong number because I was looking for Imani Daniels. They told me that no Imani Daniels lived there, so I quickly hung up. I was a little suspicious. I had Imani's number programmed in my phone and I knew I pressed the right button. Something was going on. I got dressed quickly and set off to Imani's. I arrived to chaos. Her block was swarming with police cars, a fire truck and an ambulance. I drove by slowly, but didn't see anything. I decided to go back home.

My heart was racing. What if something happened to her? What if they tried to pin it on me? What if she killed this Ayana chick, and involved the bar in some kind of way? All kinds of things ran through my mind. Imani was no Mocha, but what if she was? I sure as hell didn't want to go through all that again. Imani was a smart one, and she had access to every file in my office on numerous occasions. She was the type of woman who could easily blackmail me for whatever the fuck she wanted, and her scandalous ass would probably get it. I didn't want to wait around to find out anything. I packed a few suitcases, tipped the doorman an extra $500 to see that the rest of my shit was moved the next day to storage under an alias. I gave him cash to pay the debt, and knew he'd make good on it, because I had enough on his ass to make his wife not only leave him, but take him for everything he had when she did.

I went by the bar, and loaded all my personal files into the trunk. I called Chris from my cell phone. I told him something came up, and I had to leave town for a few weeks on family business. I told him to open up and operate like normal, and I'd be in touch every day to make sure everything was running smoothly. If someone came there looking for me, no one would be able to tell them anything. They wouldn't find anything, because everything was in my trunk. I covered my ass on all counts.

I figured, I would lay low for a couple of weeks, and if nothing happened, I would come back and start from scratch. A good bitch wasn't hard to find, and I always knew how to spot one. I gassed up my Cadillac, bought a pack of smokes and was on my way the hell out of dodge when I saw Her. She was as beautiful as Rachel, Roxanne and Imani put together.

"Hey beautiful, where you heading?" I sidled up next to her.

"Away from here for a little while," she said, angelically. "I need a break from the bullshit."

"I know what you mean. Which way you going?"

"Don't know yet. Haven't made up my mind."

"Would you like a little company while you're deciding?" I asked, laying on the charm.

"If it's your company, I'd love it," she said, laying on some charm of her own.

"Where to?"

"I don't know. Surprise me."

She jumped into her car and pulled up behind me. I lit a cigarette, turned on some tunes and headed straight to the nearest hotel. Like all the others, it was destiny. I didn't even know her name, but I knew that she was the one for me. And this time, I swear, I won't fuck it up. YouknowwhatImean?

MARK

After leaving Royal's, we headed back to Mocha's. She packed the things she needed and headed for the airport. She didn't tell me where she was going, and I didn't ask. It was best we split ways unattached. It was a mutual agreement that was beneficial for both of us.

I knew I had a lot to own up to, so I made my way back home to Roxanne. I told her all about Rachel and Royal, and she told me she never knew a man with so much love in their heart, but was glad I belonged to her. I also told her about Mocha and the set up, and she said she understood. She shouldered part of the blame for both of us straying outside the relationship, so she was going to step back and allow me to stake my claim as the man in the relationship. She also set a date for the wedding—next week, Saturday. I didn't know it would be so soon, but I was ready. And since we were both looking to be more risqué together, we decided to make it happen at Hedonism III. You know, set it off the right way—love and happiness for Mr. and Mrs. Mark Anthony Watkins.

THE END

A READING GROUP GUIDE

LOVE & HAPPINESS

Michelle Cuttino

About This Guide

The questions that follow are included to enhance your group's reading of this book.

1. What was your initial take on Roxanne and Mark's relationship? Was Roxanne right to feel the way she did about Mark, or were her insecurities all in her head?

2. Why do you think Ayana really resurfaced? Did she want to have a real relationship with her step-sister, or was it only for her personal gain?

3. If you were Roxanne, would you have done things differently when it came to Royal? Why or why not?

4. Discuss Mark's need to keep his past with Royal away from Roxanne. What do you think he was really protecting since his secret wasn't as bad as he made it seem?

5. Do you believe that someone can love more than one person at a time?

6. Why do you think Marlon fell in love with Ayana so hard and so fast? Do you think Ayana will be satisfied living a life solely with him?

7. How do you feel about Mark's involvement with Mocha? Was he justified, or do you believe he made the wrong choice?

8. Do you think this is the last Mark will see of Royal?

9. How do you see Mark and Roxanne's nuptials working out? Do you think their marriage will last?

Host a Book Club Talk Radio Party

Is one of Michelle's titles the book of the month for your book club? If so host a Big Body Broadcasting Talk Radio Party.

What's a Talk Radio Party?

Michelle will host your Book Club for an intimate one-on-one talk radio interview session, where the members of your club have an opportunity to call in and interact with Michelle one on one, ask questions and discuss the book in detail. The broadcast can remain private between your book club and Michelle, or it can be made public to promote amongst your members and social media followers.

Michelle provides special giveaways and upgrades your Book Club to Celeb status, which includes Big Body Publishing discounts and access to news releases before they go public.

Contact Monroe Smith at Monroe@BigBodyPublishing.com for more details. Please allow at least two to four weeks advance notice to make the proper arrangements.

Schedule your Talk Radio Party today!
www.BlogTalkRadio.com/Big-Body-Broadcasting

About The Author

www.MichelleCuttino.com

Michelle Cuttino is the "Queen of Plus-Size Fiction," and serves as a motivational speaker, freelance writer, talk radio host, and body positive advocate. She is the President of Big Body Publishing, the premiere publisher for content written by and geared towards plus-size women. She is the author of *Love & Happiness, Love Is Blind*, and *Me & Mrs. Jones*, an eBook series adaptation of her screenplay once optioned with Queen Latifah's Flavor Unit Films. She is also co-author of the erotica anthology, *Zane Presents... Cougar Cocktails*, under the Strebor/Simon & Schuster imprint.

Cuttino is a plus-size lifestyle blogger, who also blogs about publishing advice and industry events. She is a book reviewer and contributing writer for African Americans on the Move Book Club (AAMBC), and a columnist at Proud Times, Black Literature, Real Life Real Faith, and Curve Appeal Magazines. She is the owner and Executive Producer of Big Body Broadcasting and Big Body Media.

Cuttino has conducted print and radio interviews with controversial authors and literary greats such as Brenda Jackson, Reshonda Tate Billingsley, J.L. King, Kimberla Lawson Roby, Abiola Abrams, Noire, Ashley & JaQuavis, Treasure Blue, Shashicka Tyre-Hill, Joey Pinkney, Dawniel Winningham, Dawn Michelle Hardy, Winter Ramos, Tamika Newhouse, Elissa Gabrielle, N'Tyse and Erica Mena. She has provided content for many notable websites and blogs.

Cuttino was born and raised in Bronx, New York, and spent her formative years between New York and her parents' hometown of Georgetown, South Carolina. She is single and still resides in the Bronx with her son.

MICHELLE CUTTINO's Social Media Info

/MichelleCuttino
/BigBodyPublishing

@MichelleCuttino
@BigBodyPub

http://www.linkedin.com/in/michellecuttino

https://plus.google.com/+MichelleCuttinoBBW

BigBodyPub

www.BigBodysBlog.com

BigBodyPub

https://www.goodreads.com/MichelleCuttino

http://www.blogtalkradio.com/big-body-broadcasting
Facebook.com/BigBodyBroadcasting
@BigBodyMedia

ISBN: 9781310406775

Brenda Jones is a plus-size beauty with a no-nonsense attitude. After being married to John for over ten years, she yearned for something new and exciting. Her wish came true when Kevin Baker was hired by her firm. Their harmless flirting soon developed into a whirlwind affair. Though Brenda is committed to living out her sexual fantasies with Kevin, she would never allow their fling to jeopardize her financial security with John.

Kim Baker is thick, sexy, naïve and completely enamored with her husband, Kevin. While there is nothing Kim wouldn't do to keep their love alive, Kevin behaves as if their union is a sham. His long nights at the office and disparaging remarks about her weight gain, have left Kim feeling unappreciated and vulnerable. His neglect is the reason Kim welcomed John's advances when car trouble led to their blossoming friendship.

Stephanie Brown is Brenda's new assistant. When she meets Kevin, their chemistry is undeniable. Brenda is unnerved, and sets a plan in motion to thwart their attraction to the other. Since Brenda is married, Stephanie disregards her interference and actively pursues Kevin.

Fate brings them all together to teach one important lesson… In the game of love, the things you take for granted, are the things someone else is silently praying for.